T0278650

DEATH at Morning House

ALSO BY MAUREEN JOHNSON

The Stevie Bell Mysteries
Truly Devious
The Vanishing Stair
The Hand on the Wall
The Box in the Woods
Nine Liars

13 Little Blue Envelopes
The Last Little Blue Envelope
The Key to the Golden Firebird
On the Count of Three
Girl at Sea
Devilish
Let It Snow

The Shades of London series
The Suite Scarlett series

DEATH
at
Morning House

MAUREEN
JOHNSON

HARPER TEEN
An Imprint of HarperCollinsPublishers

HarperTeen is an imprint of HarperCollins Publishers.

Death at Morning House
Copyright © 2024 by Maureen Johnson
Map art by Leo Hartas
All rights reserved. Printed in the United States of America.
No part of this book may be used or reproduced in any manner
whatsoever without written permission except in the case of
brief quotations embodied in critical articles and reviews. For
information address HarperCollins Children's Books, a division of
HarperCollins Publishers, 195 Broadway, New York, NY 10007.
epicreads.com

Library of Congress Control Number: 2023944531
ISBN 978-0-06-325595-1 — ISBN 978-0-06-339916-7 (intl ed)

Typography by Jessie Gang
24 25 26 27 28 LBC 5 4 3 2 1
First Edition

To all the librarians, media specialists, and teachers fighting book banners. You're the reason they won't win.

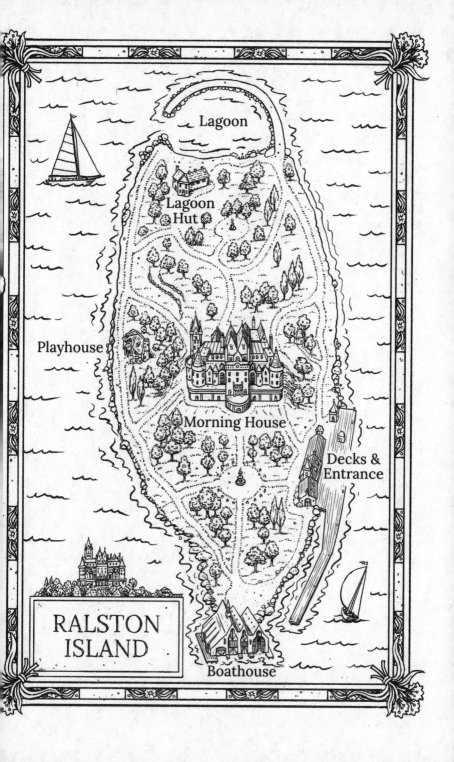

Lagoon

Lagoon
Hut

Playhouse

Morning House

Decks &
Entrance

RALSTON
ISLAND

Boathouse

DEATH at Morning House

THE ALL-AMERICAN RALSTON FAMILY AND THEIR IDEAL SUMMER HOME

Photo essay in *Life* magazine, July 1932

Dr. Phillip Ralston of New York City and his wife, theater star Faye Ralston, have certainly mastered the art of good living. And they have quite a lot of lives in their care!

The doctor adopted six of his children in 1915 while working in England during the war. They welcomed their seventh child, Max, four years ago. The doctor and his wife spend most of the year in New York City and the older children board at school. In the summer, they come together in their private paradise in the Thousand Islands region. It is called Ralston Island now, though it was formerly known as Cutter Island. Their magnificent home is called Morning House. Built at a cost of $4 million, Morning House is designed to foster good health and creativity.

"Whenever my children show a gift in a particular direction," Dr. Ralston says, "I make sure to nurture it."

For this purpose, Dr. Ralston called in architect P. Anderson Little of Los Angeles to build a two-story playhouse that would not be out of place in a story by the Brothers Grimm. It is a cheerful place, built of stone, with windows of varying sizes and a turret on the side. Most people would imagine a playhouse to be a small affair—this one is the size of a large family home. The first floor boasts a large library, an art studio, and a room for study. The second floor is high-ceilinged and features a large open space with mirrored walls and a ballet barre, as well as a piano and other musical instruments.

The family follows a precise schedule. They breakfast together at seven thirty each morning. Dr. Ralston and his family follow the natural diet prescribed by institutions such as the Battle Creek Sanitarium. There is no meat, no sugar, no coffee or tea. Instead, the family enjoys large helpings of yogurt, cooked fruits, nut cutlets, stewed peas, and custard. By eight, they are out on the lawn, practicing calisthenics in matching uniforms. The boys and the girls exercise together. After this, the group either swim laps in a walled-off lagoon that serves as an outdoor swimming pool or compete to see who can swim around the island the fastest.

"My daughter Clara is the strongest swimmer in the bunch," Dr. Ralston adds proudly. "No one can beat her time to the shore and back. We're working to get her into the next Olympics, though she would rather concentrate on her dancing."

By nine thirty, exercises are complete for the morning. The children have two hours of instruction led by Dr. Ralston. Topics include medicine, chemistry, heredity, history, politics, and geography. Lunch is served at noon—another round of nourishing natural foods. The children then have the afternoon to pursue their individual interests. There's another round of swimming at four. If the weather is inclement, they practice diving in the twelve-foot-deep pool in the lower level of the house. At dinner, the family reviews their day. They relax in the evening, sometimes with games, or perhaps with a motion picture.

It's hard to imagine a more wholesome and idyllic summer than one spent with the Ralstons at Morning House.

TWO CHILDREN DEAD IN MORNING HOUSE TRAGEDY
The New York Times, July 28, 1932

Tragedy has befallen the family of doctor and philanthropist Dr. Phillip Ralston. His youngest child, Max Ralston, aged four, was found drowned in the waters of the St. Lawrence River yesterday afternoon. It is thought the child left his room while his nurse was asleep and attempted to swim on his own. Hours later, overcome by grief, his oldest sister, Clara, aged 16, jumped four stories from the roof of the house. . . .

Petrichor. That's how this all started—from a single smell. Do you know this word? I learned it from Akilah Jones.

Akilah, Akilah, Akilah . . .

I first set eyes on her in freshman-year French. She was conjugating the absolute hell out of her first irregular verb and wearing a soft yellow sweater when I realized I was in love with her. I always knew I liked girls, but when I saw Akilah, I *knew* knew. I genuinely don't understand how you could see Akilah and *not* fall in love with her. The lift of her chin. Her ever-changing hair—braided, straight, natural, sometimes shot through with purple stripes. She played piano in our school's jazz band. She also played guitar. She smiled like she knew the joke you were about to tell and was already laughing. And her laugh? Like the bells of a cathedral.

I'd had four classes with her in total—freshman French I; biology and first-semester American history in sophomore year; and English III this last year. I usually didn't get to sit close to her, because my last name is Wexler and a lot of teachers go alphabetically, but our English teacher let us pick

4

our own seats at six tables around the room. Unfortunately, I was late on the first day and her table was full, but I snagged a pretty good seat nearby and basked in the warmth of her magnificence. I always tried to look my best before I got there, but I'm not working with what Akilah is working with.

I'm fine. I'm Marlowe Wexler and I'm fine.

My name makes it sound like I spend my time lurking around the shadowy alleyways of some big city. One of those alleyways full of old boxes, metal trash cans, and cats that knock things over and make that *yowlllll* sound. Like there's a bartender who knows my name somewhere. Like I have three ex-wives and I don't talk to two of them but there's something smoldering between me and the third one. We never got over each other. My name is more exciting than I am. Akilah was exceptional, and I was fine, and that was the problem.

I never got to spend any real time with her until that summer when we both got jobs at Guffy's, our local ice cream place. Guffy's has thirty-two homemade flavors and locally famous hot caramel sauce. Say you want your cone "hot bottom" and you'll get some of the caramel pooled into the bottom of your cone and everyone will laugh except us, because you can only hear this so many times before you think about putting your hand inside the waffle iron just to feel something again.

I had no idea Akilah would be working there too until I showed up for my second shift in a cat hair–covered T-shirt (which I could get away with by wearing the Guffy's apron) and my most awkward shorts (because people only saw me from the waist up). She was behind the counter in a baby-blue romper and a Guffy's apron, scooping out some black raspberry ripple and smiling with the wattage of a power plant. I genuinely staggered in the doorway on seeing her and realizing that we would be working together. It was the most amazing thing that had happened to me up until that point. We were coworkers; just she and I would be behind the little counter two nights a week and one full day on weekends. (At least until I manipulated the schedule so that we had all our shifts together. I made this my mission.)

This is when I got to know Akilah properly. She was easy to talk to. If she said she liked a show, I went home and streamed that show until my eyeballs dried up. If there was a song she liked, that became my soundtrack. Sometimes my brain opens a chamber and says "fill me up." I'm not saying I know what I'm doing—I'm saying I can fill up my brain like a bucket and carry the information from place to place and it generally doesn't leak. I have no idea whether this makes me smart. But it definitely helped when I wanted to have things to talk to Akilah about.

"Do you know what my favorite smell is?" she said one day when we were in a lull and waiting for a customer to come by for a hot bottom. "Petrichor."

I was about to open my mouth and say *the smell of a flying dinosaur?* But something told me to shut it and nod knowingly. (That's a *pterosaur*, which you have to admit is pretty close.)

"That smell of soil after it's been struck by rain. That's

what it's called. That ozone-y, earthy smell. It's my favorite smell in the world."

That night I spent somewhere in the vicinity of six hours reading scented candle reviews until I found the internet's favorite petrichor-scented candle. It was thirty bucks. For thirty bucks, you expect a quality product, right? I ordered the candle, paid eight dollars for expedited shipping, and made my plan.

See, I had another job. I helped take care of our family friends Juan and Carlita's lakeside cottage on Lake Oneida, about ten minutes from our house. Juan and Carlita teach at New York University, but they used to be professors at Syracuse, where my dad works. They still came up some weekends and in the summers. I took care of the place for them when they were away. I mowed their tiny lawn if it needed it. I watered the flowers if they were dry. I gave everything a light dusting and vacuuming, flushed the toilets to keep sewer gas from building up, took in the mail, and generally kept the place alive. It was an easy job. It only took me a few hours a week, and I was allowed to sit around there if I liked and study or whatever.

Or whatever.

We'd never had a specific conversation about how to use the cottage, but I never did anything weird with it. No one ever said, "You can't take a date there, Marlowe." I felt that as long as I used the place responsibly and left it better than when I arrived, everything was fine. And it was fine. Until that night with the petrichor.

My parents won a gift card to the Cheesecake Factory in a raffle, which they let me have. I'd kept it in my wallet for eight months like it was my entire inheritance, too precious to be spent right away. This was the occasion I didn't know I had been waiting for. One night, as I was emptying out the soft serve machine, I turned to Akilah.

"I have this gift certificate to the Cheesecake Factory," I said, shrugging. "I need to use it. Do you want to . . ."

I gulped down some air.

". . . go?"

She looked over her shoulder at me from where she was refilling the toppings bar.

"Sure," she replied. "Can't let a good gift card go to waste."

I had already studied the schedule and knew that we both had Thursday night off. I wandered over to it and read it like it was all new information.

"We have . . . oh, we both have Thursday off. Are you . . ."

"Not doing anything," she said. "Let's go. Sounds fun."

From that point until Thursday, I itched and twitched my way minute by minute. I dumped every item of clothing I owned onto my bed and tried to figure out what to wear. I got a peachy-colored dotted blouse for my birthday (and if you squint you realize the dots on it are tiny horses). I considered it my lucky shirt even though it had never brought me any luck up until this point. Sometimes, you just have to believe in your shirt. I did a bunch of stuff with my hair that

8

went nowhere. I have brownish-reddish hair the consistency of which I think is best described as uncertain. Is it wavy? Is it straight? Will it stay if I try to put it up? It does not know. Stop asking it. It will zig when I need it to zag. I left it down and allowed it to do what it felt like it needed to do.

I picked her up. I drive a Smart Car, which is the smallest car in the entire world. It is red, so it looks like I'm cruising along in a cartoon apple. I inherited it from my grandparents, who bought it for driving around Key West, where they live, before they decided that it was ruining their image. It was given to me because it was considered a sensible way for me to get back and forth from school and could never be used for anything even remotely dangerous. What was I going to say on my crazed Smart Car spree? *Get in, nobody, because we're going to do a sweet twenty-one miles an hour, and definitely not on the highway.*

But it was a car and therefore I loved it. It tried its best even though it was very small.

Akilah was wearing white shorts and a red top that I think was new. She'd twisted her box braids into an elegant bun, partially wrapped in a red scarf. Akilah always had good makeup, but I could see that she had made a special effort, using a combination of white liner toward her nose and a darker one winging back off her eye, with layers of yellow and orange on her lids. The overall effect was that of two sunrises blossoming on her face.

"You look nice," she said. "I like your shirt."

9

I tried not to crumple up in my seat. Was that a good thing? Or did I normally look terrible and she was just happy that I tried?

It is often embarrassing to be me, but that night, walking into the Cheesecake Factory with Akilah Jones by my side, I felt like I was stepping into human society for the first time in a full and complete way. I was the best version of myself, bursting with a confidence I had never had previously. I wasn't expecting everyone to stand up and applaud, but if they had, I would have accepted it. It would have made sense.

"My favorite things are always in the appetizers," she said as we looked at the menu. "Do you want to get a few of those and share them?"

Sharing meant that this was going well. This wasn't my food over here and hers over there. These would be *our* apps that we'd enjoy together. We filled the table with sliders, crab puffs, pot stickers, and buffalo cauliflower.

"I feel kind of stupid," she said, "but I got you something. We were talking about makeup the other day . . ."

Well, Akilah had been talking about makeup. I had been saying that I was bad at it, that I misused color palettes, that I never understood why half the colors were there, and generally bemoaning my ineptitude.

". . . and I realized there is a perfect color lipstick for you. Here . . ."

She reached into her big red purse and pulled out a gold tube. She removed the cap and indicated I should give her my hand. My hands were cold from gripping a glass and I didn't want to give her a partially wet, cold hand, but I also wanted to give her my hand in all ways. I extended one to her, and she took it. She held it, my palm touching hers (so warm, so soft) and she delicately drew a line of lipstick down the back of mine. It was a cheerful bright pink, not something I would have picked for myself, but pleasing to look at.

"Midnight Rose," she said. "I thought it would be a good color for you. Do you like it? Because you were saying you thought your lips looked thin—I don't think so, but—I think this would suit you."

My head was swimming. Akilah Jones had been looking at my mouth. She bought me a lipstick.

We were going to *kiss*.

Akilah Jones was going to kiss me and then I would ascend into the sky and keep going up and up, high-fiving the International Space Station as I made my way out into the farthest reaches of the cosmos. Nothing was real, and yet all the stories were true. This was what people meant by being struck by love. I felt the bolt go in through the top of my head and it exited, somewhat weirdly, through my right hip. I jumped a little in my booth seat.

"Is it okay?" she said. "You don't have to keep it."

"No! No. No. I love it. I . . ."

"Try it on."

Some fumbling with my phone, looking at my own ridiculous face on the screen as I applied it. She put a napkin over her finger and gently cleaned the edges of my work with her nail.

"It's a good color on you," she said. "You look amazing. I mean, even without, but . . ."

My actual, biological heart was going to actually explode. It was going to crack my ribs and flood my chest with blood. I forced myself to speak and prayed I didn't spontaneously barf from the force of emotion.

"I like it. Love it. I mean, I love the color."

She laughed, that bright noise of joy, and I was able to steady myself and make my move.

"I take care of this place on the lake," I said. "A cabin. That I can use. Do you want to maybe see it or something . . . ?"

I lived and died in the pause before her answer, but she smiled and said, "Sure. Yeah."

Check. Gift card. *Poot poot poot* to the lake in the Smart Car.

It had started to rain. The Smart Car does not love the rain because it is tiny like a spider and thinks it will be washed away. I don't know how I drove because my hands were shaking and I gripped the wheel so hard I'm amazed it didn't snap. I'd made sure the house was clean and that the floor cushions in the little living room were arranged *just so*. I made sure my phone was connected to the speakers correctly, because they had a tendency to crap out. I planned the playlist based on everything she had ever mentioned about music she liked. I placed the petrichor candle on a table by the window where the scent would blow onto us. As Akilah looked around the cozy living room, I lit the candle with a wobbly hand.

"I got this," I said as casually as I could, "because you

mentioned you like the smell of petrichor . . ."

Akilah spun around to see what I was talking about. She fixed her gaze on the little flicker of light. It coughed a bit as it took a big gulp of oxygen from the slightly open window and then took a bigger bite of wick. The scent began to bloom.

"Oh my god," she said. "Marlowe, that's . . ."

Oh no. Oh no. What. *What?*

". . . amazing. This is the best first date I've ever been on."

Date.

I had to sit down because my legs could no longer hold me up. She plopped down on the cushion next to me. There was rain and thunder—a sign!—and there was this cloud of petrichor in the room.

"I'm really glad you asked me out," Akilah said. "Because I was trying to work up the nerve to ask you myself."

Kissing is weird. If you think about the concept, it seems gross. Absolutely should not work. There should be something more elegant than smacking down on someone else's food and talking holes (I am a poet; let me know if you want me to write your Valentine's card). But once I felt that little puff of air from her nostrils as she came close, breathed in the scent of her shampoo, brushed the cool softness of her cheek, and felt her lips press to mine . . . my entire body seemed to liquify. I began my trip to the ISS. The astronauts were about to see Marlowe Wexler drift past the window. I lost all sense of time as we tangled our arms around each other and fell back against the floor cushions. The joy of looking at her was topped only by the glory of pressing closer to her, and her to me. She rolled me slightly onto my back, and Akilah was over me. Everything was bright—even through my closed lids there was a luminescent glow, like we were creating light together. And warmth. And tiny crackling noises. Some kind of big orange thing that I was distantly aware had come into the room. I welcomed it, in my state of bliss. *Sure, new bright orange thing, hang out with us. Everything is perfect, everyone, and yes, you too, orange thing. The world is warm and wonderful and . . .*

Suddenly, Akilah pulled away and screamed.

The big orange friend—this visitor—was a wall of fire that had spread itself around the little table the candle had been on and eaten the billowing curtains on its way to the ceiling.

I want to be able to tell you that I was gallant and in control, that I pushed her behind me to keep her from the flames, that I ran to the kitchen for a fire extinguisher, because Juan and Carlita are the kind of responsible people who would have a fire extinguisher and of course it would be in the kitchen, and that I ran back in and extinguished the curtains and whisked Akilah out the door, and that she cried out "Marlowe, you saved my life *and* the house!" before we kissed under the moonlight by the lake and that we would laugh about it with our grandchildren.

Not so much.

I remember running around and saying "We gotta put it out, we gotta put it out" as Akilah was pushing me out the door and calling 911.

14

I remember trying to fill a flower planter from a bird-bath, forgetting that flower planters have holes at the bottom and that birdbaths do not contain enough water to put out house fires.

I remember I considered driving to Canada at twenty-one miles an hour in my tiny car to start a new life.

I remember standing on the little patch of grass and snot-sobbing and heaving while Akilah waved the fire truck in and shouted warnings to the neighbors, who had all come out to see the fire whipping up the side of the cottage.

This was where the date portion of the evening ended.

2

I don't like to lie. No one would have believed me, anyway. That's the thing about lies—they are a temporary measure at best. The truth is always there at the bottom. The fire didn't sneak in. I brought it in the form of a candle.

There was some confusion at first as to what we two were doing in the house, as we were not Professors Juan and Carlita Manzano-Solis of NYU and were instead two weeping teenagers with Guffy's Ice Cream napkins pressed to our noses. I explained, through increasingly winded sobs, that I took care of the place for them and had taken Akilah there on a date and gotten her this special candle and I was really, really, really sorry. They got us both blankets while they called Juan and Carlita. My parents came. Her parents came. Everyone came—fire and rescue, police, EMTs, neighbors, complete strangers who just wanted to film a house burn down and post the video. It was the event of the summer. You should have been there.

The fire investigators confirmed, based on our information and what they found, that the candle exploded. This, I know from the thousand Google searches I've done since, is something candles do sometimes. Not often, but sometimes. This was why I wanted you to know that I spent thirty dollars. I expected a good product with a nice smell. And to be fair, it had a great smell until it blew up.

The fire gutted one side of the house. What was still standing had smoke and water damage. If it hadn't been raining, they said the whole thing would probably be gone. Juan and Carlita came up from New York City to survey the charred remains of their happiness. I've known them most of my life—my dad met them when I was three or four. They're sort of like an aunt and uncle to me, so they were shockingly nice about it. It was an accident, they said. We're just glad you're okay, they said. Houses can be replaced but people can't, they said.

But it wasn't that they were saying, "Great job, Marlowe! You did it! You really *burned that house down!*" Juan and Carlita were clearly sad that their house was gone. Their tone was flat. They had come to make sure I was generally all right and to let us know that the fire department said this was an accident. I assumed that meant they blamed me, but they'd had so much therapy that they ascribed all bad tidings to the whims of the universe. (Is that how therapy works?) They didn't stay long, and I didn't have the courage to lift my head and fully look at them, because we all knew that while I was *technically* allowed to be in the house, I should not have been there. It wasn't okay, what I had done. I had taken advantage of the situation, and now their house was gone.

After two days off, I turned up for my shift at Guffy's with Akilah. I wore one of my dad's old hoodies, which gave off Unabomber vibes, but at least I could hide my face. I put in earbuds and went into the back and did the jobs we always avoided, like taking inventory of the toppings bar supplies. I ran through this quickly, so I started making up new jobs for myself. I organized containers by size, wiped the shelves and walls down with bleach solution, and went berserk with the label maker. I was relatively safe in the closet of bleach, labels, and pain, coming out only when we had a line and lurking in my hoodie like a ghoul.

Akilah handled the public. I couldn't speak to her. The few times I came out from the back to help, someone would notice me and say something to the person they were with in a low voice. It was all looks and whispers, the frantic sounds of tapping on phones. Messages spread around town that the firebug was back at Guffy's. How the story had spread that soon, I have no real idea, but stories always do, don't they? At least everyone knew it was my fault, not Akilah's. I had the keys. I brought the candle.

The requests for hot bottoms were endless, usually punctuated by a muffled fart of a laugh. When I checked my phone, I noticed that random people started leaving fire emojis in the comments of my posts, or GIFs from *Firestarter*, or that one of the creepily smiling little girl with the house burning down around her.

I took my socials to private.

At the end of the shift, we silently dished up our free

18

employee scoops (we were entitled to one medium cup per shift, arguably the best perk that exists). Akilah had mint chocolate chip with malt powder and I had rocky road as a symbolic gesture, even though my favorite flavor is Moose Tracks.

"So, um . . ." she began as we closed and locked the door. "Are you . . ."

I pulled on the hoodie strings and vanished into my cave a bit.

"Okay? Okay, um . . . I . . . the other night when we were at the Cheesecake Factory I noticed that they were hiring. I applied, and they called this morning. I'm going in for an interview. The tips . . . they're more than here. And I'm saving up to buy a new keyboard. . . ."

The world seemed to be spinning into the empty depths of my cup. I understood. We'd had one date and I'd burned a house down. Why would she—the most beautiful girl I had ever seen—want to tie herself to a quasi-arsonist girlfriend?

"That's great," I said. "Good luck."

Then I got into my tiny car and drove home at twenty-one miles an hour and I stayed there.

I called in sick to work the next day, and the day after that. I went into my room, shut the door, and ghosted the world. Somewhere in there Guffy's fired me for not showing up. Guilt piled on guilt. Guilt about taking advantage of Juan and Carlita. Guilt about the fire, no matter how accidental. Guilt about not responding to messages. Guilt about not going in to Guffy's. Guilt about being a loser daughter. Guilt for having guilt. It got heavier and heavier, and yet, I seemed to summon more. I was like that guy in the witch trials who they accused of being a witch and pressed under heavy rocks to force him to confess, and the only thing that guy ever said was "More weight." Like that, but for pathetic people. I was a guilt collector.

My lifeline came from an unexpected place. Several days into my self-imposed exile, my mom extracted me from my room. We had a visitor in the form of my history teacher, Mx. Gibson. They were sitting at the kitchen table, drinking apple tea. I was friendly with Mx. Gibson—they lived a few doors down from us and let me choose some side reading for extra credit. I liked Mx. Gibson, but I had no idea why they were in our kitchen.

(I want to note here that I have friends aside from *my history teacher*. But I came here to tell you what happened at Morning House and my friends don't really factor into it. Suffice it to say they exist; they had been listening to me talk about Akilah for three entire years and now I was ghosting them too. This is the hard part about telling stories—you can't tell everything. You have to select what's relevant and shape the story around the facts, or at least around the facts as you want them to be. Now back to my history teacher, at the table with the tea.)

There was a round of "how are you doing?" which I answered in mumbles. Then they got right down to it.

"Listen," they said, "what if you could get out of here for a bit?"

Getting out of here for a bit sounded like a good start, especially if they meant sending me on an exploratory mission to Mars with a single potato and a note of farewell.

"A friend of mine is a professor of history at Syracuse and lives upstate in Clement Bay. She's working on a history of a place called Morning House. Have you heard of it?"

It sounded only vaguely familiar, so I shook my head.

"It's a mansion built on one of the Thousand Islands, a place called Ralston Island. There was a tragedy in the family that owned it, so they abandoned it back in the 1930s and it's been empty ever since. It's just been sold to some company, but Belinda managed to get them to agree to let the public in for one summer. There's a group of local teenagers that live and work there as guides. She's down one person and needed someone who can learn things quickly. I thought of you. And I thought you might like to . . ."

"Leave town?" I said.

"Spend the rest of the summer on a beautiful island giving tours of a mansion. There's a swimming lagoon; the meals are included. The pay is . . . okay. Probably what you were making at Guffy's. But it's a good opportunity, and it would be helping out a friend of mine. If you're up for it, she can use you immediately. You'd have to read and learn the materials kind of quickly, but I think you might really enjoy it."

This conflicted heavily with my new plans for the summer, which were: one, hiding in my house; two, evaporating.

But what else was I going to do? I'd lost the girl of my

dreams. I had no job. Who was going to hire me now? My parents were going to let me wallow for three more days, max, before they demanded that I get out and do something. Something far away was about the best offer I was going to get.

"Sure," I said, forcing a smile. "Sounds great."

JULY 8, 1932

Clara Ralston peeled her eyelids apart and groaned. She considered throwing up, made a few attempts at a burp, and found that her stomach was sound. This was a mid-level hangover at best. It was 7:26, according to her bedside clock. She ejected herself from bed, splashed water on her face and under her arms, then tugged on a pair of long white shorts and a white short-sleeved collared shirt with a large gold *R* embroidered on the front.

Clara was a dancer—one with a quick step and exceptional balance. She ran down the stairs at speed, taking three at a time, sliding across the slick herringbone of the great hall floor and into the breakfast room, where her family sat in front of their yogurts. She threw herself into her chair just as the clock ticked over to 7:31.

"You're late," her father said with a smile. He was firm in his routines, but this was part of the routine. Clara was always the last one to arrive. Usually she made it right before the minute hand moved. Her arrival was the sign that breakfast could begin.

Waiting for her at her place always was a dish of fresh yogurt with some kind of fruit—in this case, cooked black raspberries. The yogurt was a nonnegotiable item, served at every meal. People in the natural food movement were obsessed with digestion, and yogurt was considered necessary for life. When she was small, Clara thought she would actually die if she didn't eat it every day. She had been shocked when she went to boarding school for the first time and looked around at her classmates' plates, filled with bacon and sausage and pancakes covered in syrup. Not a yogurt in sight, except for the ones in front of her, Victory, and Unity. She realized for the first time that her family was a bit odd in its habits, and that this would not endear her to the other children. After one week, Clara switched to pancakes and sausage—tasting meat and sugar for the first time. She became a devotee of all things sweet and meaty.

Clara managed to get the yogurt down without signs of violence from her body. In fact, it seemed to have an improving effect. She was slightly more alert than she had been upon arrival. She stared at the lace curtains billowing softly in the breakfast room windows. Her head began to throb in time. She watched Faye going through her mail. She had been a singer before marrying their father, and she got correspondence every day from her friends in the city, filling her in on all the Broadway gossip. Clara always felt a pang of jealousy. She didn't get a pile of letters from actors and dancers every day and she never would if she didn't get back to the city and study dance properly. Every day she wasn't in New York was another day wasted, another opportunity gone.

"All right," her father said. "I received a telephone call from the reporter and the photographer from *Life* magazine. Their boat is leaving Clayton at eight, so we'll meet them by the dock. They want to take photographs of our morning exercises. So let's finish up here a minute or two early."

Of course. The *Life* magazine thing. She had managed to block that out.

"What do they want to know about us?" Unity asked.

Unity. All aglow in the morning. She'd never had a hangover. She believed whatever Father said. She was a good girl who liked being on the island, away from everyone else. It was easier for her. It was easier for all of them. Most of them, anyway. Not William, who sat across from Clara now, glancing at her through his long blond lashes. She gave him a half smile and made a subtle heaving gesture. He rolled his eyes and stifled a laugh.

"Our routines," Father said. "Our family structure. The benefits of healthy foods and exercise, things like that. Eat up!"

He was antsy. Father was excited to be in the magazine, apparently. Faye looked less so, but she had been in magazines before. On their covers as well. Faye had given up so much, and for what? Responsibility for six kids, pulled away from the glamour of her life to sit here on this island eating yogurt and talking about breeding and digestion all day. Clara couldn't think about this for too long or she would become furious; how *dare* Faye walk away from Broadway. Clara wouldn't, that was for sure. She would claw her nails

25

into the stage and they'd never get her off.

When the bowls were empty, Phillip gestured that they had permission to leave the table. Clara took a last, long drink of water and pushed herself up, walking out with Edward.

"I guess we're show ponies today," she said to him. "They're coming to watch us run around."

"Because we're exceptional," Unity said, coming up behind them.

"Because we're freaks," Edward countered.

Clara smirked. Thank god someone else was thinking it.

The six older Ralston children, plus Phillip and Faye, stood by the grand receiving dock that rarely received anyone. While they had the occasional guest, they didn't socialize like anyone else here in the islands, on Millionaires' Row. All day long, boats came and went from their neighbors' houses, full of people laughing, singing, playing music. You could hear orchestras playing at night on other islands. You could hear laughter.

Very few people experienced the Ralstons' guest rooms papered in silk, their fine dining room, or sunny breakfast room. They might come for tennis or to consult with their father, but generally no one stayed the night at Morning House, not like they stayed at the other great houses of the river. Everyone aside from Phillip knew why—people hated the food. Visitors might be able to go without a cocktail, and they could privately get some coffee in their rooms at breakfast, but the family meals were intolerable. Perhaps they also disliked this house of seven children and rigid schedules and its obsession with exercise. Perhaps the Ralstons were simply too . . . exceptional, as Unity thought.

Too weird. They were too weird.

But they had all the things to impress people with, even if they didn't use them for that purpose. Clara watched the two newcomers take in the stone boathouse, the lagoon with its black swans, the fountain, and the massive house that towered over them all.

"What a magnificent sight," the reporter said. It was easy to tell who was the reporter and who was the photographer, as one helpfully carried two bags of equipment and had a camera around his neck. He was fully prepared to document the Ralstons.

"Yes, it's all right, isn't it?" Phillip Ralston turned to look at Morning House like it had snuck up behind him.

"It's more than all right, I'd say."

Introductions were made as the photographer took a few shots of the house from the dock, then they went to the lawn. There he got some shots of Faye looking elegant, which meant Faye looking like Faye, then they posed in a row in their matching white exercise outfits.

"You're all similar in height," he said, "so I think father and mother in the middle. Girls on one side, boys on the other."

They were photographed doing jumping jacks and short sprints. The workout was shorter than the usual hour due to the outsiders. The staff brought out cold ginger water and apple juice for the family, plus a pot of coffee for the visitors, and they all sat together on the massive veranda that aproned the house.

"So many people are moved by the story of how you got your children," the reporter said. "Could you tell me a little about that, in your own words?"

"Well," Phillip said, looking around at his children with affection. "My medical specialty is obstetrics. I went to England during the Great War to lend my assistance, both in terms of money and in medical services. I was able to help fund some clinics. And with so many men injured or killed in battle, and so many doctors having to help the wounded, I found my services were most useful helping deliver babies. My older children were born under conditions that were all too common—fathers off at war, possibly dead, the mothers with other children at home with no money or support. I delivered all six and adopted them with their mothers' blessings. Clara here came first. Then William, Victory, Unity, Edward, and Benjamin brought up the rear just six months later."

Clara forced a smile. The bile in her throat was sliding back down.

"To be a father six times over in that short space of time, with no mother for the children . . ."

"My sister Dagmar . . ."

Aunt Dagmar had appeared, as if on cue, dressed in a black sundress patterned in yellow birds, with a matching yellow belt. Aunt Dagmar had more severe features than Father—a sharper chin, tighter lips. She wore her hair elegantly finger-curled tight against her head. Despite the fact that smoking was forbidden for the rest of the family, she screwed a cigarette into her long holder and lit it with a silver lighter.

". . . was an absolute godsend. She mothered the children until my wife, Faye, came along, and she remains a stabilizing influence."

Dagmar Ralston took a long inhale. It was unclear what she thought of being a stabilizing influence. Faye Ralston smoothed her exercise clothes self-consciously.

"That was very good of you," the reporter said.

"I love the children," Dagmar replied simply.

From inside, there was an ear-piercing scream and a patter of feet. Max Ralston came tearing out the front door riding a stick pony.

"My youngest son," Phillip said, rising. "Spirited. Excited for visitors."

So excited was Max that he continued right past the group, racing down the steps to the lawn, screaming the entire way. His nurse hurried behind him in a way that suggested she was trying not to run but really needed to.

"Toddlers," the reporter said with a smile. "It must have been a lot to handle when you had six at that age . . ." He nodded to the assembled. ". . . all at once. It must have been mayhem."

"Remarkably, no," Phillip said. "They were all very disciplined, even then. Why, they'd line up and recite their lessons and touch their toes and swim their laps."

"Still do, it appears."

"They still do." Phillip cast a quick eye in the direction of Max and his nurse. The chase had continued across the lower part of the lawn. "My daughter Clara is the strongest swimmer in the bunch. No one can beat her time. She can swim to the shore and back, through the St. Lawrence current. She's quite exceptional. We're working to get her into the next Olympics, though she would rather concentrate on her dancing. In fact, Clara, why don't you put on your suit? Or maybe a dance? Which would be better?"

"The dancing, I think," the photographer said.

"Then change for dancing. Everyone, let's go to the playhouse and show them what you can do."

Clara smiled stiffly, rose from her seat, and made it far enough before she vomited all over the ground, just out of sight of the reporter.

It was time to dance for the camera.

3

Unlike a lot of people in my area, I am not a river rat.

In this part of upper New York State, where we live, is the St. Lawrence River—a massive, deep river that separates the United States and Canada. It's a major shipping channel, and more than that, it is a way of life. People love the St. Lawrence because it's enormous and deep and clean, with luminescent water. Everything is the river, and the river is everything. People wear shirts that say how much they love the river. Everyone has a boat up there and fishes and swims and Jet Skis around. If you are one of the people who live the St. Lawrence lifestyle, you are a river rat. I don't know why they chose *rat* as their term, aside from the alliteration. Beach bum. River rat. I'm not sure what this makes me. A land locust? Anyway, it's a thing.

Even though it's about two hours from our house, we'd only been there once, and that was when I was little. My mom's an English teacher and my dad researches socioeconomics, so we go to places where everyone reads a lot, or to my grandparents' house in Florida, where we still read a lot, but do so with someone playing Jimmy Buffett in the background or while being watched by an unblinking iguana.

In this river, in a section where the two countries are within touching distance, there is an area called the Thousand Islands, even though everyone there will tell you that there are over 1,800 islands. Only a few of these islands are very big. Most are hilariously small. All you need to be classified as an island there is to be above and surrounded by water and to have one tree. It counts if you *used* to have a tree. This was the only thing I remembered from our trip: little spots of land with houses like candy sitting on them, surrounded by water like green glass.

It was a straight shot up the highway to Clement Bay, the closest town to Morning House. Clement Bay is a tourist town, with one main street right along the water full of boutiques and places to eat. I was supposed to catch my boat at Uncle Jim's River Cruises, right at the far end. It was a big enough operation, with a few multistory sightseeing boats and a dinner cruise. My parents bought my sixteen-dollar ticket and helped me wheel my two suitcases into the line with all the tourists. They offered to take the ride with me, but I thought it was best for me to get on the boat and go. It looks weird to show up at your new summer job with your parents with you. I got surprisingly emotional when the line started to move, and I began dragging my suitcases away from them, across the asphalt of the parking lot and to the dock. An older couple in matching American flag T-shirts regarded my suitcases with confusion and gave each other a look, like I had offended them by bringing so much stuff, and this is just what kids are like now, with their phones and their two suitcases on a sightseeing boat.

Because Morning House was the last stop, where people could get off and explore the island and house for an hour or two, I had to ride the entire scenic cruise to get there. The Thousand Islands really are beautiful. In some places, the water takes on a tropical glow—a pure aqua that seems to emit light. The boat drifted around Pine Island, with its slanted trees that had been bent by the wind. There was Bluff Island, the one someone won in a poker game. There was a scrappy little island called Willie Nelson Island. I heard about the five thousand or so shipwrecks that littered the bottom of the river, and the gold treasure that might be buried on Maple Island. There were stories of how this part of the river was how so much illegal liquor came into the United States from Canada during Prohibition, how bootleggers outfitted their boats and dumped booze in the water in packages that would float up to the surface to be picked up and smuggled into the country, how there were trails of bottles and beer cans marking their paths to this day.

"That's Just Enough Room Island," the guide said as we passed an island with one house stubbornly built on every inch, so that if you took too long of a step out the front door you went directly into the water.

"More like Leave Me the Fuck Alone Island," I mumbled.

The older couple in the American flag shirts looked at me disapprovingly. I rested my chin on the rail and shut up.

33

I imagined Akilah and me spending the summer here together as we passed the elegant parts of Wellesley Island, covered in houses owned by people who use *summer* as a verb. These were the houses I remembered seeing—big, storybook-looking ones, wildly colored in pastels and ginger-bread decoration. It's always weird when an old memory like that lines up pretty well with reality.

"Fire is the enemy on these islands," the guide said. "This was the site of the great Frontenac Hotel, which burned down in 1911 when a member of the band playing that night dropped a lit cigarette. It remains a serious concern. In fact, we have a fireboat here called *Last Chance*, because when it shows up . . ."

I put in earbuds for the rest of the tour.

We made our way along the river, me tuning everything out, until a mini-castle structure on a tiny island appeared in front of us, connected to the main one with a small stone bridge, maybe six feet long.

"Our last stop," the captain said. "Right in front of us here is the boathouse for Ralston Island and the famous Morning House. It's open to the public for the very first time this summer. Built between 1920 and 1922, the house was sealed up after two of the family's children died here on the same day in the summer of 1932. But it's been preserved and you can see it for the first time. . . ."

I got off last, clanging my rolling suitcases along the metal floor of the boat.

"That's a lot of stuff you've got there," the guide said as

I heaved my bags over the small platform between the boat and the dock, trying hard not to drop everything I had for the summer into the water.

"I'm very serious about sightseeing," I replied.

I'd been told to go to the ticket office when I got off the boat. It was right there at the dock, along with a tiny US border control office, which was just one bored guy staring at his phone. I went over to the window in the ticket hut.

"I don't need a ticket, I don't think?" I said. "Dr. Henson brought me here? I'm . . . going to be working?"

I spoke in questions and was answered with one from another direction.

"Are you Marlowe Wexler?"

I turned around to see a girl with pale, densely freckled skin and thick red hair that hung long and triumphant over her shoulders. She had a delicate build that was swamped in an oversized maroon Morning House polo shirt, open slightly at the neck to reveal a white-gold chain with a fragile letter *A* dangling from it. Before I replied, she removed a walkie-talkie from her hip and raised it to her mouth.

"She's here," she said into it.

"She won't make the final tour," the voice on the walkie went on, ominously, "so take her to the playhouse. Have her meet me at five in the hall."

"Okay!" She clipped the walkie back onto the pocket of her shorts and opened the wheelchair-accessible entrance. "I'm April. Welcome to Morning House! Here . . ."

She took the handle of the heavier of my bags and

gallantly began dragging it up the weaving path. I wanted to stop her since she looked like someone who could be carried off by a bird, but she moved my bags with more ease than I could manage. She was tiny but had wiry strength.

"Marlowe is such a cool name," she said over her shoulder.

It was a compliment, but I hadn't done anything to deserve it, so I was my usual smooth self and tried to laugh it off. What came out was an uneasy snickering noise, which I got away with because it blended in with the sound of the suitcase wheels on the path. I shouldn't be allowed to talk to cute girls. Whenever I see one, I should put a box over my head.

As we passed a cluster of trees, the view suddenly opened and Morning House revealed itself. I had to tilt my head back to see all of it, because it was built up on the natural high point of the island and soared above. It was made of gray stone, with a red roof that was a jumble of peaks and turrets of differing heights. Windows large and small, round and square, glinted in the sun from copper-green frames. It looked like an Ivy League school, or possibly Dracula's castle—or some combination of the two from a movie where Dracula goes to Yale.

Over the front door, there was a massive stained-glass relief of a rising sun that seemed to glow from its very own power source.

"Wait until you get inside," April said. "The place is full of stained glass. It's like a cathedral in there. But the play-house is good too."

"Playhouse?"

She didn't need to explain, because we had turned a corner and found ourselves in front of a smaller but still sizable building. If the big house was for a happy Dracula, this one had come from Hansel and Gretel. The stone blocks in the walls were of varying sizes, jumbled together solidly. There were tiny round windows and long ones, dotted around in a broken rhythm.

I had arrived at my summer home, and it appeared to be fictional.

4

We entered the cool, low-ceilinged entryway of the playhouse. The walls were a beige color, like old parchment, and timber beams marked the corners. The doors had odd shapes, with slanted lintels and one side longer than the other. There were transoms with more stained-glass sunrises. But what really got my attention was the circular staircase in the middle, which was made of wood and carved in the shape of a tree, with etchings of bark and wooded limbs that crawled along the ceiling, with painted green wooden leaves. It felt like Disney World—expensive fakery.

"This is where we stay," she said. "The playhouse."

"We live in here?" I asked. "With a fake tree?"

"I know, right? This room here . . ." She indicated a sunny room to the right, with windows facing the water. It had two sofas, beanbags, a TV, and a few video game consoles. ". . . is our lounge. It used to be their classroom. We use the rest for bedrooms. We had to move things around a little. This way . . ."

She tried the door to the left and it opened. It was lined

with shelves—floor to ceiling—that must have once been filled with books. Now it had two beds and two distinct areas. One was tidy, spare, a reasonably made bed with a plain green blanket, everything put away but a laundry bag on the floor. There was some fishing gear in the corner, tucked up against an exposed beam. The other was lively, with a black fleece blanket with silver bolts on the bed, purple sheets, a spill of bright clothes, and a row of Lego figurines on the windowsill.

"Tom and Van are in here," she said. "Tom's family is into fishing and marinas. He handles a lot of the boats. Van's with us in the house. Up here—you can leave your stuff for a second . . ."

She ushered me out and to the tree stairs. At the top, they opened on a large, sunny space that encompassed the entire second floor. One wall was covered in mirrors, and there were floor-to-ceiling windows, with trees right outside, partially shading and obscuring the view. This room also had two beds, which were placed on opposite sides of the room. There was more symmetry here in terms of neatness, though one side had a bold red bedspread and bathing suits drying on a rack. The other side had baby-blue sheets with a white bedspread, and there were several tiny stuffed animals along the sill, with framed pictures on every surface.

"Liani and I are up here," she said. "We weren't sure where you would want to stay. We thought maybe up here, but maybe you'd prefer privacy. You can choose! We can move you up here, but for now . . ."

She showed me back down the tree and took me to the

single room in the back. This room wasn't quite like the others. It ran along the back of the house and had stone walls and was as wide as the single bed, but three times as long. It had three large windows that were all pushed open, filling the room with soft breezes. It was deeply shaded by the trees. There was an old dresser on the far side of the room. The room was cool, even a little cavelike. It appealed to me. It fit my mood. I could live in this fairy-tale hut, in my stone room, away from the world.

"This was the art studio," she explained. "Originally, we were going to configure it all differently and have you upstairs with me and Liani, but we thought since you don't know us yet, you might like privacy? But you can come up if you want! Or move. You can decide whenever. I wasn't sure what you'd be able to bring, so I got you a throw pillow." April indicated a fuzzy yellow pillow sitting on the otherwise bare bed. She was hovering, clearly wanting to know if the room and the pillow were okay.

"It's great," I said.

"Oh good," she said, exhaling. "Let me show you where we eat—and the bathroom. The bathroom is kind of an adventure. It's not in this building."

I didn't like the sound of the bathroom adventure and followed nervously. She showed me back to the tree, and pointed out that along with containing the stairs, it also concealed a curved door. This opened to reveal another set of steps, these being plain stone and going down into a stone-lined tunnel, wide enough for maybe two people to walk side by side.

"There are passages that can't be seen by the public," she explained as she switched on the light and led me down the steps and through the tunnel. "For servants, so no one would see them walking from building to building."

We walked about fifty paces and reached a door.

"Oh," she said, pulling some keys from her pocket. "Your keys. You'll need these to access the house and the bathrooms, but we keep a spare here . . ." She indicated a hook by the door. ". . . you know, in case you're in a hurry and forget."

The door opened into a cavernous basement with a high ceiling. It felt more like an empty warehouse, echoey and pleasantly cool. We walked around a mostly empty warren of large rooms, some with a few tools lying around—shovels, rakes, sledgehammers, racks of cleaning materials and paper towels and toilet paper.

"Over here," she said, "our bathrooms are behind the public ones. They're gender neutral."

There were single bathrooms, and then two showers with just curtains for doors, and hooks outside for clothes and a towel. I was thinking of the many ways this setup could be awkward (1. Someone opens curtain, I am naked. 2. I see a spider, jump out naked. 3. I accidentally open curtain, someone is naked. 4. Curtain falls down for no reason, I am etc.) when a ghostly sound floated through the space.

"Helloooooo . . ."

I turned around, but there was no one in sight.

"Helllllooooooooooooo, neighhboorrrrr . . ."

April turned in confusion as well.

"Van?"

"Who isss Vannnnnnn. I'm a ghoosttttttt."

"Van, don't freak Marlowe out. She just got here."

"I would neeevcrrrrrr . . ."

April zeroed in on the sound and found it was coming from the empty swimming pool that was at the edge of the basement. At the bottom was a lanky guy with a wild puff of brown curly hair and the widest mouth I'd ever seen outside of a Muppet. It looked like he could flip his entire head open. He was sitting at the bottom of the small but surprisingly deep empty swimming pool that was tiled in a vibrant aqua green, puffing cheerfully on a vape.

"You founddddd meeee," he said.

"Why are you sitting in the pool?" April asked.

"Privacy," he said with a shrug. "You're the new one! It's Marlowe, right?"

I nodded.

"I'm Van, as in, get in the."

"It's kind of early for that," April said, indicating the vape.

"Tours are gone by now," he replied with a graceful wave of his hand. "Best time of the day. Marlowe! Come down. Here . . ."

He held out the vape.

"I'm fine," I said. "Thanks, though."

He nodded graciously. "You burned a house down?"

"*Van* . . . ," April said. She had a look on her face that told me they all not only knew what I had done but had talked about how they were going to talk about it, and Van had just violated the terms.

I had practiced this too.

"It was a scented candle," I said, "and it . . . exploded . . ."

I was immediately off script as well, because talking about how you caused a house fire is hard. There is nothing casual about it.

"Oh, we know," he said. "It's fine. Shit happens. We get it. You've come to the right place for that."

"Seriously, Van, Dr. Henson is around. Don't let her see you doing that in the house."

"She doesn't care," he said, waving us off. "Anyway, Marlowe, come to me anytime for a kiki or an edible or whatever. It's lovely to have you."

April shuffled me off.

"He's *really* good at tours," she said as an explanation. "Van is the best, really."

She took me to the far side of the basement and opened a door onto a sparkling stainless-steel-and-white-tile kitchen, restaurant-sized, with a long wooden prep and worktable with a dozen metal bistro chairs set around it.

"The original kitchen was down here," she said, "but because this is going to be a retreat, they took it out and put this in. Obviously, no tours come here. We only do the upper levels. Anyway, the way it works is, everyone comes in and gets their own breakfast. There's cereal and bread and eggs and stuff. For lunch, you can come back here and make a sandwich, or if you want something from the refreshment stand, that's free, but just so you know, it's awful and it takes forever. For dinner, they did a deal with a restaurant in town and they make us up trays of stuff we can stick in the oven or warm up on the stove . . ." She opened a massive industrial refrigerator, where several marked tinfoil trays were stacked. ". . . so we have this roster. It's someone's job to come and warm one or two of these up. It's usually lasagna or a chicken casserole or something like that, and there are always vegan ones in there. And we have salad stuff. And we always have leftover hot dogs and hamburgers from the stand. We eat together, and we have a schedule for who cleans up and loads the dishwasher. And we have tons of ice cream from the place in town. There's always ice cream."

This was deeply reassuring to me, as I lead an ice cream–forward existence. I didn't start working at Guffy's by accident.

"What's your favorite?" she asked. "We can ask for it. We all request flavors. I like birthday cake."

"Moose Tracks."

"I don't think I've had that?"

"It's peanut butter cups and fudge in vanilla ice cream. Sometimes chocolate. They make extreme versions as well, but I like the regular one."

"I can see if they can do that," she said. "I mean, we have a lot of fudge in town."

April was doing all the heavy lifting here to make me feel welcome. This one hit home.

"So you've all been here for . . ."

"Two weeks," she said. "But we live nearby and we've been on the island a few times helping get things ready."

"So it's weird I'm here."

"Not weird! I was excited we were going to have someone new. We've all known each other forever."

"Seems kind of strange that they brought me in from so far, but . . . I guess she did it to be nice."

April cocked her head. "Dr. Henson isn't . . . she's not mean. But she's not nice. If she brought you here, there was a reason."

That sounded ominous, and April realized that.

"She's fine! I don't mean, like, she brought you here for a bad reason. It must have been a good one. We barely see her, anyway. She's working on a book about this place and the family, so she's in her rooms almost all the time. She comes out to have meetings with visiting students and historians, or she goes to town sometimes, but basically we run the place. Now you'll run it with us! We'll show you everything you need to know."

Her walkie-talkie crackled to life.

"Bring Marlowe up to the porch," said a voice.

"She's ready," April said, smiling broadly.

It was time for me to meet my new boss, the woman who had summoned me to Ralston Island.

July 8, 1932

Victory Ralston had always been embarrassed by her name. When the *Life* magazine reporter had spoken to her this afternoon, she could see him measuring her up, using *Victory* as the yardstick. It sounded like she should be riding in on a horse while carrying a flaming sword. At school, she used her middle name. Marie. A much better name. A real name, not the *concept of winning*.

She was glad that *Life* magazine thing was over. The whole thing made her self-conscious, all the photos they'd had to take out on the lawn. Now she was just trying to read her book, but everyone upstairs was being too loud.

All the Ralston children were well educated and multilingual, more or less fluent in German and French, with passable academic understanding of several other languages. To keep them on their toes, their father regularly had all the books in their library switched out. Sometimes they could read in English, but they might come down to find that only Greek was available. No one liked this except Unity. Unity was the linguist. She sat there now, with eight copies of *The Wizard of Oz* in front of her. Their father would regularly give her a new copy in a different language, setting her the challenge of trying to learn a bit of it. Along with a dictionary and a few books of grammar, she would use *The Wizard of Oz* as a baseline text, moving back and forth between various versions, comparing the languages, trying to break the code of how this new one used its symbols to communicate ideas. Today it appeared that she was trying to learn Russian.

"They're drunk again," Victory said to her sister. "Earlier than usual."

Unity nodded in reply, her eyes still on Oz.

"I don't care except I can't read," Victory went on, looking up at the ceiling.

As Unity was not having this problem and did not seem overly interested in her plight, Victory pushed herself out of her chair. She made her way to the tiny room behind the library where her brother Benjamin was at his easel in the process of copying a still life painting.

"They're starting early tonight," he said, delicately adding an edge of silvery blue to a flower petal. "It's like they're trying to get caught."

Benjamin's little studio had originally been a large toy closet. It had been given to him when he became serious about painting, as a storage space for his canvases and supplies. More and more, though, he hid away in here, copying Dutch masters by the light of the single window.

"It's really good," Victory said, standing by his shoulder to admire his work.

"It's all right," Benjamin said, squinting at the brush-stroke he had just applied.

"I can barely tell the difference."

"Well, don't tell that to Jan Davidsz de Heem."

"I'll do my best. When did he die?"

"Around 1680," he said.

"Oh, then no promises."

She looked around at the various prints that Benjamin had collected. The Dutch loved to paint mundane objects back in the 1600s. Flowers. Bread. Oysters. Cheese. Rotting vegetables.

"Why do you think they were so interested in painting these sorts of things?" she asked.

"Because they could—technical mastery. But they were also statements. Ars longa, vita brevis."

Art is long, life is short.

She envied Benjamin's painting; that he had something he could make that took his entire concentration. He was unbothered by the noise upstairs. When he painted, he was gone, off to a place he built stroke by stroke. She could tell he wanted to get back to it, so she drifted up the circular stairs, the ones carved to look like a tree. They opened into the studio that occupied the entirety of the top floor. William was at the piano in the corner of the room, his face flush and slick with sweat. He was playing Debussy, a piece that rattled and thundered through the room, that sounded like ten pianos playing at once. Clara was wearing a deep-maroon bathing suit with a white belt. Her copper-colored hair was heavy with sweat and clinging to her head like a shining helmet. Her bare feet pounded the floor. With every twist and bend she poured everything out of herself while wringing the music dry. It was almost frightening to watch her dance, like she had so much life in her that it was trying to get loose from her body, and she was wrestling it to keep it in.

Or she was drunk. Bit of column A, bit of column B.

Benjamin, William, and Clara all had ways of letting things out—on canvas, on keys, on the floor and in the water. Victory, Edward, and Unity had more academic interests. They had no outlet, no way to sweat it out, to pour it out. So sometimes, like Eddie did now, they poured it in. He was flopped on the floor on the far side of the room, drinking from a bottle full of brown liquid.

When William came to the end of his piece, Clara collapsed onto the floor, her face running with sweat.

"Pass it over, Eddie," she said.

Edward peeled himself from the chair and handed the bottle to Clara, who took a long swig. Clara held the bottle out to Victory, who shook her head.

"You don't know what you're missing," Clara said. "This is good. . . . What do you think this is? Whiskey?"

"Rotgut," Eddie said. "The finest rotgut."

Alcohol was illegal because of Prohibition—and Phillip Ralston believed the stuff was poison, so even if it became legal to drink, there would be no liquor on Ralston Island.

He was naive enough to believe that his staff and family felt the same, and that they would never seek it out. What he didn't realize was that there was no need to go anywhere—the booze came to them.

Where they were, in the middle of the Thousand Islands, was the great booze battleground. Canada was only a mile or so away from the mainland shore, and sometimes only a few yards away on another island or section of the river. Ralston Island was on the US side, but only just barely. All the islands in the St. Lawrence were a middle zone—a place between nations, and in some ways, worlds. Prohibition existed in some parts of the water, but drift another moment or two, and your cocktail was perfectly legal. This was why some islands were known basically as cocktail bars. More important, this was why bootleggers used this stretch of river as one of their main highways to get alcohol into the United States. Half the boats that went by during the day were loaded with it; all the boats at night were.

Some bootleggers took crates of booze out into the water and dropped them overboard, weighted down with bags of salt. As the salt dissolved, the crates rose and small boats would collect them as they bobbed to the surface. Sometimes when being chased, the bootleggers simply threw the stuff overboard. There was probably more booze in the river than fish. Clara simply swam out and grabbed some free-floating bottle, or she'd linger in the water with a silver dollar hidden in her swimsuit and buy one off a passing boat.

When you obtain free-floating alcohol in often unmarked bottles, you never quite know what you're getting. Sometimes it was weak and tasted like water with old nickels in it; other times, you got something like burning honey that warmed you all the way down and helped you melt into the sound of the lapping water. It was usually the first one.

"Go on, Vic," Eddie went on. "It'll put hair on your balls."

Clara cackled at that. Victory shrugged. Eddie always said stuff like that to try to be shocking, but Victory took a practical view of the human body and was not fazed.

"If I had testes," she said, "I think it might have the opposite effect, as alcohol is a depressant. There's interesting research going on in Chicago right now on bovine testicles from the stockyards. Father was telling me about it."

"She's raised you cow balls," Clara said. "Your move, Eddie."

"I'm going to go and piss off the roof," he replied.

He clambered out the window. William took this as a sign to leave the piano and the room. Victory and Clara remained behind, Clara flat on the ground, her chest heaving as she recovered her breath and took another swig.

"You can't drink all summer," Victory said.

"Can't I?"

"Come on . . ."

Clara rolled onto her stomach and turned herself to face her sister.

"Come on, what? What else is there to do? I should be

51

in dancing school, in New York. Instead, I'm here, dancing around the room. Doing the same thing, every goddamn day. No visitors. So yes, Victory, I am going to drink all summer, and if you had any sense, you would too."

She punctuated this with a long swig and a grimace.

"Looks tasty," Victory said. "Seems fun."

"So go sit with Unity and talk about the health benefits of yogurt and the importance of good breeding. She loves that stuff."

"She's trying. We're all trying. It's nice here."

This budding argument was interrupted by a loud rustling noise from outside, following by a heavy thud.

"There goes Eddie," Clara said. "That one sounded solid."

At a certain point in the night, Eddie would piss off the roof, then climb down the trellis on the side of the playhouse. He usually made it, but sometimes didn't. He hadn't broken a bone yet, but the summer was young. As the caretaker, the one interested in medicine, Victory was generally the person who picked up the fallen.

"I'm just saying," she said as she got up, "there's no point in getting drunk every night. It's not good for you."

"And I'm saying," Clara replied, "that something about this place has to give. We're not here because this is good for us. We're here to be controlled."

In later years, the few she had, Victory Ralston would think back on these words of Clara's. At the time, she put the remarks down to Clara's elevated sense of drama—her big emotions, wild swims, feverish dancing. But they had not been idle remarks. They were the key to everything, and she had missed their meaning.

Victory would never forgive herself for this oversight, right up until the moment, some ten years later, when the bomb fell from the London sky and made her a part of it.

5

My first impression of Dr. Belinda Henson was that she looked like a praying mantis—green, long, and strangely arranged, with big bug eyes. She was sitting on a chair on the veranda dressed in expensive athleisure—yoga leggings and a snug top in a bright, verdant jade. Her limbs were tangled together in a complicated position that looked uncomfortable to me. She had a face shaped like an upside-down raindrop— a wide forehead tapering rapidly down to a pointed chin. Her hair was a quiff of white gray, and she wore large sunglasses to hold back the late afternoon sun. Her attention was on the viewing screen of a camera she was holding. It was a serious piece of equipment, with a long telephoto lens. April and I stood there for a long moment until she finally tipped her head up in our direction.

"Marlowe," she said. "Marlowe Wexler."

I held up my hand in a sheepish *hello* gesture.

She uncoiled herself and stood. She took me in with a dis- passionate gaze, and the resulting look on her face suggested that while she wanted more from the situation, she knew better than to expect it.

"I'm Belinda Henson," she said. "And you're the one who burned down someone's house."

"Well," I replied. "Not all the way."

I am not only truthful—I am modest.

"I'm told you have a good memory."

I was probably supposed to say yes, yes I did. To nod. To show that in some way bringing me here was worthwhile. But I just stood there because I have no capacity to take a compliment. She waited for my reply for a moment, then shook her head gently. I looked to April, but she had tiptoed off into the shadows.

"Have you read the manual?" Dr. Henson asked.

I said that I had.

"Do you remember what year the house was built?"

"Between 1920 and 1922."

"Cost?"

"Four million."

"What kind of a diet did the family follow?"

"Natural foods," I said. "Following the prescription of Dr. John Harvey Kellogg, the family refrained from consuming meat, refined wheat, alcohol, caffeine, or sugar. A typical breakfast consisted of plain yogurt, stewed fruit, juice, boiled milk, nut cutlets, mushy peas, and prune toast."

"Verbatim from the guide," she said approvingly. "Good. People love those details about the mushy peas and prune toast because it's disgusting. Ralston was obsessed with health, which is funny, because his family came from tobacco. His family was very much a part of the Gilded Age scene in New York City, not the richest of the rich, but close enough."

She quizzed me for another few minutes, asking me about the members of the family, what kind of stone had been used for the house, who the architects were. I started to ease into the questions. I like a quiz—and it's easier to show people I can remember things rather than just say I can.

"All right," she said, nodding approvingly. "It seems Wren Gibson was right about your memory."

So Mx. Gibson's first name was Wren. It always catches me off guard when I find out that teachers have things like first names and friends. I know this logically. They're people. But it's always disorienting to find these things out and realize there's so much we don't know about the people we see every day.

Dr. Henson opened the massive front door. It looked like a door that should creak as you pushed it, and that bats should fly out, but it had a silent, well-crafted glide. My first impression of Morning House was that everything twinkled. The sun seemed to be everywhere, jumping from mirrors, refracting from crystal doorknobs. This huge room was made of wood—wood-paneled walls, wooden floor—but it all glowed.

"That's part of the design," she said, following my gaze. "The way the light comes into the house and bounces around. Phillip Ralston was a man who liked to control his environment, I think it's fair to say. Look up."

I tipped my head back and saw a domed ceiling made of stained glass. The center was a kind of sunburst—orange and yellow and brown and white—radiating and changing into blue and lavender. But every piece was a different shape. There were sunbeams and tendrils and waving lines, all of which ended in a ring of human faces, I think women, with golden hair. They were at the outer rim of the wild mosaic, looking down.

"It's a masterpiece," Dr. Henson said. "Made of over twenty thousand pieces of glass. It's incredible that it's lasted all these years and that it's in such good condition. The same could be said of this whole place. I'm sure you've heard, this is the first and only summer this house has been open to the public. It's been sitting disused since 1932. There was a local effort to try to buy it and preserve it, open it up for tours, but the town couldn't raise the money. As a gesture to the community, the group that bought it is letting the town run tours here for one summer."

Dr. Henson proceeded to give me a walk-through, not quite a tour, the names of the rooms tossed off as we walked past doors. The first floor of Morning House was composed of rooms for every time of day. There was a breakfast room with long windows; a sitting room for the afternoons with views over a garden; and a library with a massive fireplace for cool evenings.

Through a set of bottle-green double doors, there was a grand dining room. It was an impressive space, self-assured as a church, with a green marble floor cut through in geometric patterns in black and gold. The table looked like it could seat a hundred, so just the tail end had been covered in white and silver plastic tablecloths. Mahogany wainscotting hugged the room from below, while the top section of the walls was papered in a moss green, run through with fine lines of green and gold. It was too fresh and clean to have been original.

"When the family left the house, the furniture was put into storage. Some was used later or sold, but luckily for us, a lot of it remained. We got it out a few months ago, cleaned it up, and restored it to its original position, as far as we could determine. I'm not someone who usually does this kind of thing. I'm here because I'm working on a book about the family. I'm in charge in the sense that someone has to be, and being here helps me do my work."

We walked toward the back of the house, where there was a large room full of ancient gym equipment—gymnastic horses and rings, a wooden rowing machine, an old leather punching bag.

"The exercise room," she said. "A major part of the family's life. They had strange views about health."

She opened a door at the back of the gym, revealing a white-and-green-tiled room that might have been a bathroom, or maybe a lab. It had some health-adjacent purpose. It had things like a massage table and a large shower with lots of heads. There was a steam box with a stool in it and a space where your head would come out the top. I could sort of guess what that was for. I couldn't say the same about the object at the far end of the room, a kind of elaborate casket that was filled with lightbulbs.

"What was this for?"

"Some quackery," she replied. "It's a sunbed, but it seems designed to electrocute you. Nothing in this room seems safe. They were obsessed with digestion, so maybe something to do with that. Take this, for instance."

She nodded toward a boxy wooden chair with a hole in the seat. It wasn't quite a toilet, but I could see it was in the toilet family—a truly upsetting relative with a threatening aura.

"One strange thing about this house," she continued as we walked back into the main hall and started up the grand stairs that led up to a series of other floors, all edged in balconies that opened onto the space. "In most of the places along here on the river—the big houses—the whole point was that they were set up for visitors. You came here for the summer and you brought friends. Morning House had no dedicated guest rooms. This family needed a lot of bedrooms. Can you name the members of the Ralston family?"

"Dr. Phillip Ralston," I said. "He was the dad. He was married to Faye. He adopted six kids—Clara, William, Victory, Unity, Edward, and Benjamin. He had a younger son named Max."

"Good. They all had bedrooms here on the second floor. Phillip, Faye, and Max and his nanny over on the left, and the six older children this way . . ."

She pointed toward a hall with six identical white doors with ornate brass handles but did not stop her progress. She indicated a doorway on a landing halfway up the steps to the third floor.

"It's a half level," she said. "In the time Morning House was built, the higher up in the house you slept, the lower your status."

"That makes no sense," I said. "Aren't the views better from the top?"

"Don't mistake wealth for logic. The servants' rooms began on the third floor, though they also slept on the fourth and in the turret. They put in this halfway room for Dagmar, Phillip's sister. When the house was originally built, she had Max's room. But when Max came, they had to switch things around. Max was a baby and needed to be near his mother. It wouldn't be proper for Dagmar to be on the same level as the servants, so they built out a little and made this room, the second-and-a-half floor. It's a very nice room. It's my room, in fact, so it's not part of the tour."

She kept going to the top floor. We were almost level with the glass dome, and I could see the eyes of the glass women up close—luminous and blue, still clear as ice after a hundred years. Here, the walls were not papered or paneled in fine wood. They were simple white plaster with the occasional pane of clear plexiglass covering up some raw wood planking. While the space was empty, the walls were not. There was writing all over them, and some carvings as well. Names. Dates. Initials. In some cases, they had carved their initials into the plaster so deeply that I could get my finger into the grooves up to the first knuckle.

"This is also part of Morning House," Belinda said. "The people took it over long after the Ralstons left. When I was a kid, growing up here, we used to come to the island all the time. It was where we had parties and explored. Everything you can imagine, that's what we used this abandoned mansion for. People did that for years."

Clearly. The graffiti artists often dated their work. The dates ranged from 1944 up until around five years ago.

"You grew up near here?"

"Oh yes. I'm a local. Morning House has always been on my horizon. We all knew the stories. In fact . . ."

She scanned down the wall near the doorway until she spotted a small message in black ink.

"Here I am," she said.

I looked and saw a message: BELINDA HENSON WUZ HERE, WITH HER BEER, JUNE 4, 1977.

"Probably not the smartest thing to sign your destruction of private property, but we all did it. The general impression was if you only defaced the fourth floor it would be okay, and it was. As long as you didn't do it in this last room, which was Faye's favorite."

I followed through a set of tall French doors. This room had a vaulted ceiling and traces of silver wallpaper with trailing pink roses.

"She would sing up here," she said. "The sound would fill the house. There are cabinets built into the walls of this room. They used to store chairs so they could hold recitals here. In theory, anyway. No one ever came to visit, so there were no recitals, and now, no chairs."

She indicated a panel in the wall and gave it a gentle press, revealing a closet with a vacuum and some buckets, along with a yoga mat.

"I do yoga up here every morning at sunrise," she said. "I keep my mat here. But there's also something very important that you'll find in this closet and in all the rooms."

She pointed to a red box marked WINDOW FIRE LADDER. I got the message.

"I am *not* a babysitter."

I hadn't just asked, "Hey, Dr. Henson, are you a babysitter? Is that how you would describe yourself?" But she spoke like I had, and she was kind of mad about it.

"I care more about the family than the furnishings, but you can learn a lot about people from their homes, obviously. Morning House is Philip Ralston's creation, and it contains some glimpses into his mind. Come this way. I won't be breathing down your neck. As long as you all do your jobs safely, I don't care what you get up to. But no candles. The idiots . . ."

She seemed to want to correct herself, then shrugged.

". . . who bought this place are setting the fireplaces back up and I saw candles down there in their supplies, but do not use them. The fire ladders are in all the upstairs rooms. I'll have April show you. Van will forget. He's good with the presentation, less on some of the details. A child almost climbed up a chimney the other day. Do not let children climb the chimneys."

"No children in chimneys," I repeated.

She opened the doors that led out onto a massive balcony that was the roof of the floor below. It was trimmed in a crenellated wall, all unfurnished. From here, the water looked less glassy and green and more like a rippling muscle of steel blue. There were two islands right in front of us, one with a high cliff edge, and a smaller one with a single green house. More were in the distance, small and insignificant.

"This is the highest point on this section of the river," Dr. Henson said, walking to the edge. "You can see for miles. I take a lot of photos from here. I've gotten some amazing pictures of birds. There's a pair of bald eagles that sometimes perch on the oak on the far right. That's the best thing to see. The worst is what people get up to . . ."

She had a haunted air as she said this, and I had immediate visions of naked grandparent parties on boats with names like *I'm Knot That Drunk*. I may have been scarred by my own experiences in Key West. My grandparents' best friends are their hippie neighbors, and I accidentally got a look at someone's entire ass through the screen door as they bent over to get the remote. Sometimes, right before I fall asleep, it appears in my mind. The floating ass, wasting away in Margaritaville.

"This is the most popular thing visitors come to see on this island," she said. I immediately started scanning the view, but she shook her head.

"Look down."

I looked over the side of the balcony, to the ground four

stories down. Directly below us, in between the bit of garden and the other balconies and porches, was rubble and nothing else.

"Where is it?" I asked. "What is it?"

"You're looking at it. That's the death spot. You see, the story of the Ralstons is lore around here. It's what made this place so alluring, so mysterious."

I'd read the basics of this in the manual. It was a sad story. On the twenty-seventh of July, 1932, Max Ralston—who was four years old—slipped out of the house without anyone noticing. When they did, there was a massive search. It was his oldest sister, Clara, who found his body at the bottom of the lagoon. The family was in shock. Clara went off by herself for the rest of the day. She returned to the house that evening, seemingly intoxicated and wild with sadness, and fell from what must have been this balcony.

"The witnesses said she seemed to be dancing before she threw herself off," Dr. Henson said, adjusting her huge glasses. "She landed on the patio below, where the rubble is.

The family immediately left the island—within a few days—and they never came back. The only thing Phillip did to the house after he left was to have the patio where Clara landed smashed to pieces. People always want to see it, but they're disappointed that it doesn't make for a good picture. Anyway . . ."

Clara's death spot was summarily dismissed.

". . . you'll be getting the details a lot over the next few days. If you've learned what's in the manual, you should have no problem. I'm sure the others will help you."

She said this in a tone that suggested that the others may or may not help me and that she didn't care much either way.

"It's good to have someone from outside of town to keep an eye on things. And if anything is off, you'll come and tell me."

"Off?"

"Not off, but . . ." She stopped herself and cocked her head slightly, as if puzzled by her own remark. ". . . if you have concerns. As I said, I'm not the babysitter, but I want to make sure everyone's getting along."

I had no idea what any of that was about, except that it sounded like I was supposed to narc on the others if they did something wrong. Dr. Henson looked out at the view and the other islands in a dispassionate way, signaling that she had no more to say about the subject. She had made it clear: she didn't care about our creepy teenage problems. Not in a mean way. Just in a not-caring way. Frankly, that's how I like my authority figures.

"You must be glad they saved it," I said. "All this history."

I said this as an offhand remark—something you do to punctuate a conversation. Like *nice to meet you* or *have a good day* or *this concludes my TED Talk*. I wasn't thinking much of anything aside from that the view was nice, I missed Akilah, and I wondered how many nights in a row I could just eat hot dogs until everyone else here dismissed me as a dirtbag. So I was confused when Dr. Henson said, "No, not really."

"No?"

65

"No. That's not how history works. We don't save every monument just because it's big or because it's there. Lots of things are big, lots of things are *there*. Some things should be allowed to fall down. But this is still here, so we do the best with it that we can. Anyway, why don't you take the opportunity to look around. You'll start training tomorrow."

With that, she left me alone with the view of the river and my little weird thoughts.

6

When Dr. Henson left me standing on the balcony, I made my way back alone, retracing our path to the second floor. I stared up at the dome for a long time, until my neck hurt and I got dizzy. There was something about the colors, the *faces*. Identical faces of some woman with oversized blue eyes and a tumble of gently curling brown hair, all rendered from shards of glass. Only rich people would put a ring of light-beaming faces with wide, staring eyes on their ceiling. It was like an overcaffeinated audience of clones was watching everything from the sky. But it was the sun at the center that got me the most—the hard power of it, the way it was so orange that it was brown, like it had burned itself up. The overall effect was not soothing if you really looked at it, but the light was nice.

I walked down the hallway where the Ralston kids slept— six rooms, identical in size. The rooms were large and airy, full of ornately carved furniture, painted porcelain lamps, and funny little things. One had a massive armoire with pictures of cats carved into it, another a lamp shaped like a parrot, another a strange little clock shaped like a bear. One had an ornate desk, another a massive gilt mirror that took up a third of the wall. The girls all had those dressing screens that I've never understood. Why do you need a screen to change in your own room? Plus, these had a fine, transparent lace stretched over the frame, so there was no point to them at all. There was more lace on the bedside tables and the bureaus. Lace curtains on the windows and the glass door that led out to a balcony. Big Lace had gotten its dainty paws on this house.

I drifted around the rooms on the first floor, walking through the sunbeams that flooded in through the windows and illuminated the dust motes. There was the smell of a recent cleaning, a bit of must, and a current of summer air. There were sofas that faced sofas, arranged for a time where there was nothing else to do but face other people and talk to them. No television. No computers or phones or anything to filter out the relentless presence of other people you saw every day. There were cushions for days, all delicately embroidered in flowers and plants and patterns. More lace, of course, dripping over everything like sleeping ghosts. I'd call the style cozy castle.

I found myself in a bit of hallway where there were several cabinets that displayed photos of the Ralston family. They were a tall bunch, and very similar-looking in that way that people from the past all look alike. The girls had bobbed hair and the boys had the same cut, with a sweep across the forehead. They stood in a line wearing identical white shirts and shorts with the letter *R* over where a breast pocket would be. Only one stood out—a girl. While the others stood straight, she had a slight cock to her hip and she looked at the camera from under the fringe of her bangs. She didn't seem impressed. A man figured in several of the photos, usually in a pinstripe suit, extremely from The Past, with a pencil-thin mustache. That had to be Phillip Ralston. And the studio portrait of a woman in a tight evening dress, looking over her shoulder at the camera, her long blond hair floating down in a perfect wave—that was Faye, his actress wife. In a few photos, there was a severe-looking woman with dark hair, pulled back and tight to her head. She had an intelligent face. She looked like someone who didn't miss much. The plaque indicated that this was Dagmar.

There was one photo of a little boy with a wild tangle of curly blond hair and wearing a jacket with a massive bow around his neck, like he was a present. Max. The boy who died. I was looking at him when I realized I was covered in tiny rainbows that were coming from a doorway I hadn't noticed on the walk-through. I moved closer, following the rainbows. I could see a rack of sweatshirts inside.

The dancing rainbows were flying off the twenty or so prisms that were stuck to the large window, full of late afternoon sun. I had to shield my eyes against the onslaught, even as it appeared I was being refueled with pure, nuclear-grade queer power. Off to the side was a large display of Thousand Island dressing. There was a person in this room, partially concealed by the tower of dressing. They had their back to me and were refolding and piling some T-shirts on a table.

Their socks were dark blue with the outline of a creepy tree in black, and the words I LOVE CREEPY SHIT in yellow.

"Why are you staring at my knees?" they said, without turning around or removing their headphones.

I involuntarily backed up a step. The person had dark hair just past the shoulders, choppy, dark blue streaks that almost blended in. They wore loose black shorts and a draping, slightly faded black T-shirt over it.

"The only use for this thing," they said, pointing at a suncatcher made of tiny mirror disks. "It catches knee creepers."

"Not your knees," I said. "Your socks."

They looked down at their socks, as if it was news that they were wearing any.

"This is the gift shop?" I said.

"What tipped you off?"

I'd just been trying to make conversation, and sometimes conversations demand that you say obvious things. Part of me wanted to back slowly out of the room, but this person was regarding me with interest, and I wanted this person to maintain their interest.

"I'm Marlowe," I said. "I'm the new . . ."

"I know who you are."

"You don't have a name tag," I pointed out.

"I'm Riki. She, her. I don't do name tags. I don't need one. I don't do tours. I just do this, and no one needs to know my name when they're buying their dressing. No one works the gift shop but me. I'm an *independent contractor*. . . ."

"Oh."

"You burned a house down," she went on. "Was it fun? It seems like it would be fun to burn a house down. Cathartic."

I needed to change the topic. There was a book on the counter. It was open, face down to hold her page. The title was *The Daughter of Time*.

"You like fantasy?" I asked, tipping my head at it.

"Yes," she said. "I do. But that's not fantasy. It's a mystery. This is the twelfth time I've read it."

"It must be good."

"No," she said. "I've read it twelve times because it's terrible."

I got the sense that Riki wasn't entirely against talking to me—more like she was waiting for me to say something worth listening to. On that front, I was really going to let her down, because all I could think to do was point at the tower of Thousand Island dressing bottles and ask, "Do people buy a lot of dressing?"

This, it seemed, was a topic she was prepared to engage with.

"More than you will ever know," she said. "A depressing amount. Welcome to Morning House. Come for the excesses of capitalism, stay for the deaths. Get yourself some thick orange dressing at the gift shop. Here."

She unstuck a flat magnet from a display next to the tablet that served as a checkout.

"The recipe for Thousand Island dressing. On a magnet. Here you go."

It looked like she was giving it to me, though I didn't

know why, so I reached out for it.

"Eight bucks," she said.

"Oh. I . . ."

I didn't want a salad dressing recipe magnet, but it seemed by reaching out for it I had entered some kind of contract. At that moment, April appeared in the doorway and looked between me and Riki, toying with her monogram necklace, sliding the *A* back and forth on the chain.

"Marlowe, are you . . ." April didn't finish that question.

Riki retracted the magnet and slapped it back on the display.

"Hi, April," she said.

"Hey, Riki. Um, Marlowe? Did you need help unpacking or with your stuff? Because we're going to have dinner in the main dining room here in the house tonight, as a special thing, for you."

"A special dinner in the house," Riki said. "You're getting the celebrity treatment."

April's freckly face flushed pink and she compressed her lips, as if physically holding in a remark. Something was going on here, some issue that I was not privy to. It was like watching two cats quietly regarding each other, paws on the ground but the claws silently sliding from under the fur.

"I'm fine," I said. "I'll go unpack. I'm good."

"Oh." April nodded. I seem to have said the right thing. "Okay. Great. Dinner's at seven."

I got the impression I was supposed to go now, so I shuffled toward the door, where I was again splattered with rainbows. Riki smirked and returned to the pile of sweat-shirts she had been folding when I interrupted.

I often think back to this first meeting with Riki. Things at Morning House, I could already tell, were going to be complicated. I was so innocent then to think that *complicated* would cover the situation I had gotten myself into. I tell myself that the dominos were already set up before I got there—they only needed that little push to set them all going on their terrible track. But there I was, the unknowing, necessary finger, flicking the first one into motion.

July 14, 1932

Clara floated under the floor.

It's hard to keep a secret on an island. You need to find a private place, and if the island is small, this can be difficult. But Clara Ralston was good at finding solutions. They may look for you in every room or on the water or even on a roof, but no one ever looks under their feet.

She found her spot her first summer on the island. Their boathouse was large, and its slips housed their yacht and smaller boats. Clara swam under the dock, into the shadowy water. The stranger things of the river were here—the slimier sea vegetation, reaching up for her like a thousand slippery fingers, the smallest fish with the most to hide, the things that had no name that the river coughed up and spat toward the banks, the things that were probably rocks but you were never sure.

She would sometimes float here for an hour in the dark, the dock above so close at points that it almost touched her face, the crew or members of her family walking right on top of her, speaking and unaware of the person just under the floor, bobbing and smiling. She'd heard many things in her hideaway. She knew about their captain's mistress, Velma, who worked at Eddie's Bar in Clement Bay. The upstairs maid and the gardener would meet here when the crew took the yacht out and canoodle in one of the canoes. She always hoped to overhear something juicy either about or from Father, but he seemed to have no secrets. He was just as boring in private as he was in public.

"Clara?" a voice called.

William had come to meet her for a ride on her speedboat, *Silver Arrow*. She was not covetous of her boat and would allow her siblings to use it freely. She was, however, careful to guard her secret space, even from William, her closest sibling. She glided silently under the boards, swimming around the boathouse to the shore, emerging through the door as if she'd come from the open water.

"Are you ready?" she asked. "I want to show you something."

Silver Arrow was a magnificent little mahogany speedboat that had come in second in the powerboat races last summer. She could go almost sixty miles an hour. Clara opened her up and cut through the water, her bobbed hair flattening against her head. Sometimes when she went out in her boat, she thought about not stopping, not turning. With a flick of the wrist she could be in Canada. She could step onto its shore and hide in its wilds. Or she could ride the length of the St. Lawrence out to sea.

Today, she steered them toward Washington Island, one

of the most sizable islands, just offshore from the town of Clayton.

"Frankie told me about this," she said, slowing the boat down and turning into an inlet. "He said I had to go and have a look."

Frankie was a part-time worker on the island who had recently repaired one of their boats. He was ancient and smoked far too much, but he knew everything about the river. The St. Lawrence was famous for its shipwrecks—it had thousands. Most were deep, a hundred or hundreds of feet down. This one, however, was only about ten feet below the surface, beams clearly visible. She pulled *Silver Arrow* right on top of it and cut the engine.

"See that?" she said as they tacked gently in place. "Under us. It's the wreck of the *Elk*. Do you want to hear the story Frankie told me about this one?"

"I don't know if I believe any story Frankie tells."

"Listen. He said that the captain lived here, on Washington Island." She indicated the piece of land only a dozen or so yards away. "He was coming home, and he was drunk— so drunk he rammed into the island. He knew the ship was going to sink, but he thought he could get it in a little closer, so it would be in more shallow water in front of his house. The captain's wife came out and saw her husband outside, on his slowly sinking ship, so she got her paints and she painted it going down. That's how slow it was."

She stood up on her seat, stepped to the edge of the boat, and dove into the clear water. The ship right there—a hundred or so feet of her—the hull bizarrely intact, encrusted in vegetation. It was terrible and wonderful what the water did to the things it claimed. She reached out and tapped the rotting wood, then quickly withdrew her hand and shot to the surface.

"Touched it," she said.

"What for?"

"It's less scary that way," she said as she pulled herself up the back of the boat. "Shipwrecks are eerie, but I can't look away." She hooked her chin on the edge of the boat and looked down at the *Elk* as a large fish glided by. "This one, it's like us, sinking slowly, right in front of everyone. And they came from *Life* magazine and took pictures of us going down. I don't know what we look like afterward. No one's made that picture yet. No one wants to paint the curse."

"What the hell has gotten into you recently?" William said. "You're drunk all the time and you talk like Edgar Allan Poe. I half expect to see you walking the parapet at midnight with a raven on your shoulder."

"That sounds amazing. I should do that. Can we get ravens here? Can I paint a pigeon?"

"Clara."

He said her name crisply, and she sat up in mock attention.

"William," she replied.

"What is wrong with you? Why do you keep saying these strange things, like you think our family is cursed? We might be bored. We might be a little offbeat. But we're not cursed.

Cursed families don't get photo essays in *Life*, no matter what you say. You don't need to do this spooky act around me."

"*Think* our family is cursed?" Clara dipped her fingers into the water. "I know it is. There's nothing magical about curses. You just do a bad thing long enough, it takes root. No magic about it. You know it as well as I do."

If William knew what Clara meant, he wasn't prepared to admit it. He turned his focus to the wreck of the *Elk* below them, the view wobbling in the ripples on the water.

"You're in one of your moods," William finally replied, He put on a pair of sunglasses and turned his face to the sky. Clara continued looking at the *Elk* down below, in the strange world under the water. Only ten feet down but in another land. You could visit, but if you stayed in it too long the current would claim your lungs and the fish would eat your eyes. Your bones would settle to the bottom and turn to silt.

William was right. She was in a mood, haunted by a thought she could not express. Her soul cried for escape— just go, drive the boat and go—but she instead took the wheel and steered them back, inevitably, to Morning House.

7

It didn't take me long to empty my two suitcases. I put things into the rickety dresser drawers. I put the sheets on my bed, arranged the single throw pillow April had provided, put out my toiletries and the smattering of samples and mistakes that I smilingly call my makeup collection. And in a place of pride, on the middle of the bureau, the Midnight Rose lipstick Akilah had given me.

Maybe it was the bouncing vibes or just the fact that being new can sometimes feel like dislike, but I slipped into a funk. I had entered the time of day when, for some reason, I always felt depressed about Akilah. It was always just as the sun was going down that my mood would free-fall. It was like I could sense the ghosts of all the summer nights we were supposed to have had together. I should have called my parents, but they would have heard my bummed-out tone and worried. I texted. I sat down on the edge of my squeaky new bed and scrolled on my phone as the shadows fell over my room. I was so lost in my murky thoughts that I didn't notice it had passed seven. Only the little knock on the door shook me out of it.

"Dinner!" April said as she peered around the side.

I was surprised to find that, in my gloomy absence, April and Van had gone to some trouble to make the grand dining room into a proper little party for me.

I was ushered to a place at the mahogany table set with silver plastic dishes and a napkin that someone had attempted to fold into some shape. It was kind of a spiky triangle situation.

"It's a swan," Van said. "Napkin art is my passion."

"We just wanted you to have a good first night," April said. "And— Oh, hey! Good! Everyone's here."

Two new people joined us. The first was a stunning girl with short hair wearing a pair of white sweatpants and a cropped hoodie. From her posture and gait, it was clear that she was an athlete. She moved well, the way I think you're supposed to, head and hips and feet all properly aligned. I'd seen my reflection as I'd walked into the ballroom earlier and I looked like I was walking against the wind.

I straightened up.

"I'm Liani Harris," the girl said.

The other person was a guy, maybe two inches shorter than me, but built out by several inches. Every part of him had been worked out. Even his forearms were cut. He had a confusingly even tan and professionally white teeth. He reminded me of a potato, for some reason. A nicely baked potato, ready to burst with a little squeeze.

"Tom," the other person said, extending his hand. "Tom Keeting."

I'm not sure I'd ever done a handshake before, largely because I don't spend my time closing deals or greeting foreign leaders. Tom gripped my hand much more firmly than I expected, giving my hand a quick crunch and a shake. He was a polite potato.

"Marlowe," I said. "Wexler."

"It's good to have you here, Marlowe," he replied.

Was it? Liani seemed less convinced, and I agreed with her.

"Okay!" April said. "Let's eat! So we have the chicken thing again tonight. Do you eat chicken, Marlowe? This one is good. It's got tomatoes and onions and peppers. This mac and cheese is made with butternut squash, so it's vegan, and here's salad. And there's no nuts in anything . . ."

April rambled on about the meal while the others sat and began filling their plates. I was genuinely touched by all this effort. Here I was, some random weirdo who'd been thrust on them, and they were trying to make me welcome. Maybe I'd been wrong. Maybe this would be the best summer ever. I began to feel the lift. Yes. Though I had been brought low with the fire, perhaps I could rise. I could work my way back into polite society. I could convince Akilah that I probably wouldn't burn two houses down. It would be a funny story someday. And it all started here, at this table, in the room with the moss-green walls.

Do you ever get like this? Think a dozen thoughts at once

and go up like a balloon or sink like a balloon with a rock in it? Just ping around with no emotional middle point? If so, get in touch with me at once. We'll go have confusing times together.

"So," Liani said, "what do you think so far?"

I tried to think of something significant to say, something that would convey that I understood she was just being nice, but also that I was paying attention to what I had seen, and also that I was funny and altogether a pleasure to be around.

What I said was "It's big."

Tom passed me the mac and cheese. "Liani and I are the outdoor people. I handle boats and the dock side, and Liani is the lifeguard at the lagoon."

"I'm sort of the opposite of a lifeguard," I said.

It was meant as a joke, but Liani cocked her head at me. There is no delete button for real-life conversations, and that is most of my problem.

"What does that mean?" she said. "You can't swim?"

"I can swim," I said. "I mean, I won't sink. But I don't think I swim correctly? My strokes are . . . not right, but . . . I won't sink?"

No one wanted to hear whatever I was saying, so I stopped.

"We grew up here, so we can all swim," April said, helpfully ending this strange interlude.

"My family is in boating," Tom cut in.

"*In* boating," Van repeated. "Not into. In."

"Uncle Jim's? The boat you rode in on? My dad and my aunt own it. It's been in the family for fifty years. My grandfather started it. We do tours, fishing, boat rentals."

Tom reminded me of someone running for office. I wouldn't have been surprised if he concluded this by saying *I'm Tom Keeting, and I approve this message.*

"So," Van said. "You're from Syracuse, right? Why do you think Henson brought you here?"

He was saying what they must have all been wondering.

"My history teacher knows her. Maybe I could learn the stuff fast enough? I'm good at memorizing. And you're short a person or something?"

This had a strange effect on the assembled.

"Short," Van repeated, toying with his fork. "I guess we are. Short a person. It's a weird phrase, right? Short. You're short. Short . . ."

Liani drilled her gaze into her mac and cheese. April fluttered a bit and leaned in, about to speak, when someone else entered the room. Riki, headphones around her neck, leaking sound, dropped into a chair next to me.

"Riki!" Van said. "Joining us tonight?"

"There a problem with that, Van?"

"You know I have no problems with anything. I'm utterly *frictionless.* We never see you, is all. Not for dinner."

April's eyes went wide. Tom began forking up a massive amount of mac and cheese and shoveling it in with fervor. He ate like he knew something you didn't.

"So," I said, "I'm going to be an indoor guide? I guess I'll be going on tours for a few days. I learned a bunch of stuff from the guidebook. Dr. Henson was saying people like to see that rocky bit outside, where the girl fell? Clara?"

"People love damage," Riki said, digging away at her mac and cheese.

"Thanks for that," Liani said.

"It's true, though. People like to hear about crime, about war. They like to see the scars. People come here because they want to look at a big, expensive house where some people died."

"Not everyone is a freak," Liani said.

Everything was vibes. Vibes in all directions, bouncing around like sunbeams. I couldn't duck them.

"Nothing freakish about it, and nothing wrong with freaks. People love, have always loved, dark shit. And this place has a good story. Strange rich family, little boy drowns when no one is looking, older sister dances off the roof, house is left to rot, brother leaves a treasure . . ."

"Treasure?" I repeated. "That wasn't in the guide."

"Because it's bullshit," Liani said.

"Here are the facts," Riki went on. "Benjamin, the last surviving Ralston, used to come to the island every year until he died. He last came in 2002. He insisted on coming onto the island alone. As he got off the boat, he told the others he was going to bury a treasure, and he had something with him that he didn't have when he got back on the boat."

"Bullshit," Liani repeated.

"You're both correct," Dr. Henson said from the doorway. I hadn't heard her approach. It was unsettling. She had changed out of the green stick insect outfit and was now wearing a loose dress in light gray linen, with a heavy statement necklace made of gold beads with an owl pendant resting on her sternum.

"Riki is correct in that Benjamin is reported to have said it," she said. "Liani is correct in that I imagine it was a joke. You'll get to find this out quickly, Marlowe. Water people—sailors, people who live near oceans, rivers—they love a story. And these islands do have a lot of stories. My grandfather was a bootlegger. He smuggled whiskey in from Canada. He told me stories of how they used this island and this house, both while it was being built and when the family was here. In the fall and winter they had a free-for-all, but even in the summer, with the Ralstons in the building, they kept it going. The builders built in a little hiding spot in the house that wasn't on the plans."

"A hidden passage?" Tom asked.

"Nothing that exciting. More like a dank closet, far from anywhere the family might go. And there's no way that space is structurally sound, so I'm not telling you where it is. But it's also not very interesting. It's basically a closet. I've been in it. There's no treasure. It's full of old bottles and dead mice. Don't worry about the secret places. Look at what's around you, on display."

She waved her long-fingered hand around, indicating

the room we were in, but I didn't see any potential evils. Just chicken and vegan mac and cheese.

Dr. Henson squinted at something on the other side of the room.

"Is that mirror crooked?" she asked. "I can't tell. I had corrective eye surgery last year. Before, if I had looked at that mirror without my glasses it would have been a blob on the wall. Now I don't know whether to trust my eyes."

Everyone turned. I couldn't tell if the mirror was crooked either, as the irregular gold pattern on the wallpaper made it impossible to tell which way was straight.

"Sometimes I wonder if it was worth getting my eyes fixed," she went on. "The past looks better when it's a little blurry. Soft focus. That's how we like our past. That's why we never learn."

I got the feeling that we'd been set up for that remark, that she'd never cared about the mirror and this was her opener for everything she ever did—history lectures, general small talk, drive-through orders.

"As a historian," she continued, "a lot of times I find that people ignore the obvious. Evil, especially. People act like if a thing is in front of them—if people come out and say or do something in full view of everyone—that somehow it must be okay. Because how can they be doing anything wrong if they're doing it for everyone to see? Evil isn't always smart. Some evil deeds are done through complex maneuvers in secret, but the biggest evils, the ones people get away with most often, are the ones done right out in the open."

"Are you talking about the dickheads who bought this place?" Van asked.

"Oh. Them." Dr. Henson's phone pinged and she picked it up, glancing at it. "I think those particular dickheads, as you put it, work both in the open and privately. Hence buying a castle on an island. Public, private—the lines can be blurry."

"Well, they're continuing the Ralston curse," Riki said.

I don't believe in curses, exactly, but I'd had some bad luck this summer and it seemed like the universe was sending Marlowe Wexler a message to keep her head down and lower her expectations.

"Curse?" I said, turning to Riki.

"Nothing good happened to that family," she replied.

"What happened is this," Dr. Henson cut in, unable to risk hearing history told incorrectly. She pulled out the chair at the far end of the table, keeping a little distance from us, and sat down. "On July twenty-seventh, 1932, Max Ralston drowned in the afternoon when he was left unattended. His sister Clara fell off the roof that night, presumably jumping due to grief. Faye Ralston, Max's mother, didn't recover from the shock. A month or two later, Phillip Ralston sought the advice of his medical colleagues, and decided to take her to the first private psychiatric facility in the United States, Craig House. Craig House was a modern facility run by Dr. Clarence Slocum. It's outside New York City in the town of Beacon. It was a very fancy place—Zelda Fitzgerald was there when Faye was. Marilyn Monroe would stay there later."

"Fancy," Van said.

"That's where Faye was during Christmas 1932, just five months after the deaths. Phillip rented a large house in the woods nearby so the family could spend the holiday together. But on the twenty-eighth of December, Dagmar, Phillip's sister, and Unity took a walk through the snow. They didn't know the area, so they didn't realize the snowy ground they were walking on was a frozen pond underneath. They fell through the ice and drowned. That's four members of the family dead between July and December.

"So now there were four Ralston children: William, Victory, Edward, and Benjamin. Victory attended Yale University, where she graduated from medical school with honors. William studied music at Juilliard, and Benjamin studied painting at Beaux-Arts de Paris. None of them were slouches. Benjamin got out of Paris before the Nazi invasion in 1940 and encouraged Victory and William to join him in London to aid the war effort. They got a house together. Victory worked in a war hospital, William helped refugee efforts, and Benjamin worked with British intelligence. He was away on the night in 1941 when a bomb landed on their street and blew up the house. Victory and William were both killed. Phillip had a heart attack when he got the news. He survived that one, but not the next one, which happened five months later. So, in 1941 that's three more Ralstons dead."

This was a cheerful countdown.

"Meanwhile," she said, "Edward had been in New York. He had a serious alcohol addiction. Technically he worked as a banker, but really he spent his time gambling and partying.

He was driving drunk one night in 1944 and drove his car into a river and died. Faye never left the hospital and died there in October 1947. That left Benjamin as the very last Ralston. He was a decorated war hero and well respected in the art community. He came out as a gay man to his siblings quite early on. Benjamin was a champion for people with AIDS, long before the disease had its formal name. He poured much of his remaining fortune into housing and treatment programs for those with the disease. Moreover, he was known to help people on a personal level—going to hospitals, sitting with people who had lost partners, providing food, shelter, and comfort wherever he could. He paid bail for people who were jailed during ACT UP protests."

"Raise one to Benjamin," Van said, raising his can of Coke. "Here's to a real one."

"And the only one who made it to old age. And that is the story that the Ralston curse is based on. In reality, it was a strange family that made its own bad luck, though some members of the family tried to be beneficial to society."

Lecture finished, Dr. Henson stood to go, focusing on her phone and not looking at us again.

"Going to dinner in town," she said as she left the room. "Make sure to clean this up."

Suddenly, Riki's I Like Spooky Shit made a lot of sense. She had been following the story as it was told, hooked on every word, though she clearly knew all the details. She was into it. There was no missing it. Now that it was over, she too got up, leaving her dirty plate.

"Are you going to help clean up?" Liani asked.

"No," Riki said. "I'm an independent contractor."

"I can think of other things you are."

"Happy for you, Liani. Nurture that imagination."

As Riki walked toward the door, she stopped as she was about to pull her headphones over her ears.

"Oh, by the way," she said to me, "did anyone mention you're taking over for a dead guy?"

July 19, 1932

"They're arguing," Unity said.

She was at the window of the playhouse library, looking out from between the tangles of ivy and honeysuckle that squeezed the building.

"Who is?" Victory asked.

"Father and Faye."

Victory joined her sister at the window and looked out. They couldn't hear what was being said, but the gestures made it clear. Phillip was indicating the water. Faye was bundling a crying Max in a blanket and moving him back toward the house.

"Another failed swimming lesson," Victory said.

"Not a failure," Unity replied. "Max is a difficult student."

"Look at Faye's face. Look at Father's. That's failure."

"That's just Faye giving up," Unity corrected her.

They were supposed to call Faye "Mother," and they did in front of their elders, but when it was the six of them, she was always called Faye. Sometimes it was still so odd that she was here.

For the first ten years of her life, Victory didn't have a mother. Like her siblings, she had been adopted almost from the very moment of her birth. She came into the world and went directly into the hands of Phillip Ralston. She would ask her friends at school what mothers did, and she got vague answers about planning meals and parties and taking care of the house and telling them to listen to their father. The Ralstons had a housekeeper to take care of the running of the house. They had a cook, and servants who made their beds and laid out their clothes. They had their aunt Dagmar to sit silent and knowing at the opposite end of the dining table and weigh in on domestic matters. There were loads of women in their houses who sounded like they did things mothers did, so Victory felt herself perhaps a little superior to people who had only one woman to do all of that. Plus, she had her five siblings to talk to, to help her when she had problems, to support her. She needed nothing else.

Then, when they came home for the winter break from school six years ago, their father sat them all down in the living room of their Fifth Avenue house. Next to him was a woman. In Victory's memory, she was like a picture of a goddess from a story—tall, finger-curled and bobbed hair that looked like it was spun from platinum. She was wearing a stunning green velvet dress.

"This is Faye," he said. "Faye Anderson."

"You were in that film we saw," William said. "*The Silver Cuckoo*."

"You have a good memory," Faye said, smiling.

"Faye has been in many films, and many shows here in the city. Children, I am so very glad to tell you that Faye has agreed to be my wife, and your mother."

Victory took this in stride. So another woman was joining the staff. Not everyone felt the same. Clara came to her room that night, wrapped in her red dressing gown and clutching a pillow.

"She's going to be our stepmother," Clara said.

"So what?"

"So what? Our mother, Victory. Our *stepmother*. Step-mothers are always mean in stories."

This was an unusual display of distress from the normally fearless Clara—the Clara who pinched out matches with her fingertips and dove in any body of water she saw. The same Clara who saw a group of boys abusing a stray cat and punched the ringleader in the face, knocking out his two front teeth and rescuing the animal. (Father paid for the boy's dental work and privately elevated Clara to the highest rank within the household for her courage. The lucky cat went to live with their neighbor, Mrs. Elsmore, who named him Lorenzo, installed velvet cushions on every windowsill for his comfort, and fed him poached salmon twice a day.

"She's not our stepmother," Victory replied.

"Of course she will be. She's marrying Father."

"But you have to have had a mother for someone to be a stepmother, and we've never had one, so she can't be. She'll just be Mother."

Victory had no idea if what she'd just said was true, but it sounded solid. Clara calmed a bit and thought it over.

"Whatever," Clara finally replied, letting that part go and hugging her pillow closer. "She's still going to be mean. She won't like us."

But Faye Ralston was not mean. In fact, she was kind. She had presents for each child that reflected their interests. Faye loved sport as much as the Ralston family did. She was an excellent skier and swimmer. When they fell ill, she sat by their bedsides if they were sent home from school. She was nothing at all like the stepmothers in fairy tales. Victory thought Faye was entirely acceptable, and she seemed to make Father happy. This may have been heightened by the fact that they only spent school holidays and summers together, but those summers were idyllic.

Two years into the new arrangement, Faye started throwing up after breakfast, and then she got a little bump at her belly. Phillip Ralston, being a man of science, did not dance around the subject with his children. There was a child growing inside Faye—his child, their new sibling. He pulled out a medical textbook and showed them what was going on inside Faye's body.

"Faye is working hard right now," he went on. "She is growing organs and systems. She is providing nutrition to the new child through the food she eats."

"The baby eats nut cutlets?" Benjamin asked.

"Not exactly. But the nutrients in the nut cutlets are transformed into the material the baby needs to grow and develop. So we must all be very good and kind to Faye and thank her for working so hard. It is not easy. That's why she feels tired and ill sometimes. But she is perfectly healthy. You have no reason to fear."

Unity burst into tears. Unity was like that.

"But you'll still love us?" she asked. "Won't you?"

"Unity! Come here." He reached out his arms to his daughter. "Everything will be the same. It will only improve."

Unity did not budge. Her concern began to affect the others. Clara also began to cry. William patted her shoulder and looked extremely concerned. Edward looked askance, and Benjamin appeared mildly terrified. Only Victory was unmoved, but this was mostly because she was still digesting the anatomical implications of what she'd just learned. It was fascinating stuff, growing babies.

"What's wrong?" Phillip said, saddened by the response of his children. "What is it?"

"The baby will be different," Unity said. "Everything will be different. If the baby comes from you and Faye, that means he will be more connected to you than we are. You said that's how heredity works."

"Ah." Phillip Ralston nodded. "Yes, of course. We have discussed the concept of heredity. Of breeding. Animals have offspring, and we, as humans, are animals. We are simply the highest form of animal. And when we breed selectively, we produce the highest form of human. But our case . . ."

He indicated all the children and himself.

"Our case is quite special," he began. "I delivered you all. I knew your mothers, and I also knew who your fathers were.

All died in the war—all good, strong men. The women who gave birth to you were also strong and good. It was the war that made it impossible for them to care for you, the loss of their husbands, the struggle to feed their families. I took you all with me, one by one, because I had the resources to care for you."

Unity sniffled and stopped crying, and the mood calmed.

"You promise we're just as good?" she asked.

"My dear Unity, do you think that I—an established expert of eugenics, who understands the importance of biological purity—would be careless? No. I met you at your birth. I knew you all to be quite magnificent. I chose you. Isn't that wonderful? You are all quite, quite perfect."

Unity nestled her head into her father's chest. Victory watched, unsure of how she felt.

"That means that some babies are not as good," she said.

"Exactly so."

"How can you tell?"

"Through looking at the parents. Race, of course. Their economic state . . ."

"You just said they couldn't afford to keep us."

"I did, and well spotted, Victory." He nodded approvingly. "That was because of the war. Wars cause scarcity. Come now. I think you all could use some cheering up. I think a trip to the pictures is in order. And perhaps we'll stop at FAO Schwarz and see what new toys they have."

All was made right with that. Everyone jumped up and cheered at the thought of movies and toys. Victory did as well, but her mind always lingered on the idea that some people might not be as good as others. It didn't make sense to her, no matter how many times her father explained the science (which was constantly). After all, they were Americans, and they were always told how this was the land of the free and everyone was equal. She saw many people on the street in New York, and they all seemed fine to her. Father had to be right, because he was a doctor and knew about these things, and yet she was dissatisfied. She was young and knew little, but she knew her heart, and her heart said no to this idea.

Eugenics was wrong. She kept this thought locked away. It was hers, and hers alone, because it might be taken from her if she showed it to the others. She would keep it and grow it. A little seed.

Max was born in New York City in February on a freezing-cold morning during an early frost. Phillip had kept the children home from school for the last two weeks of the pregnancy so they could be there when their new sibling was born. There was a frantic happiness all around the house, then the high wail of a baby. This little thing—red, almost purple at times, eyes screwed shut and tiny fists—this was Max.

Things were not the same. It was like the Ralstons had been living on a finely balanced platform that was, ever so slightly, starting to tip. Max was Faye's baby, always in her arms. There was a connection there that was unlike any other in the house. Faye was good to all, but Max was small and needed her and her alone. He needed her milk, her warmth. He needed to be carried from room to room and held. On the piano in the music room (the one that was really for guests and show—William mostly played the one in the playhouse), there was a lace cloth and an array of framed photographs. There were two group family photos, three of Clara, Unity, and William by themselves. Two of Edward, Benjamin, and Victory. One of the three sisters and one of the three brothers. There were eight of Max.

Right now, Max was nearing the house, wrapped tight in Faye's embrace, his arms around her neck, letting out a piercing wail that sent the birds scattering. Victory and Unity stepped back from the window so they would not be seen staring out.

"He's going to be a nightmare today," Clara said, coming into the room, sweat dripping down her face. "God, listen to that. They should stick him on a lighthouse island to warn off ships."

"He didn't want to swim," Unity said.

"Clearly. He never does. And now someone's going to pay."

Victory turned away from Clara. She was right, of course, but Victory didn't like talking about it. Talking about it made it more real, more immediate. She peeled back a bit of curtain and watched the sobbing Max go inside with Faye. Father stood alone for a moment, hands on hips, staring up at the sun. He had a look on his face that Victory had never seen there before: defeat. The wriggling, screaming four-year-old had defeated him.

"Lock your doors," Clara said as she went back toward the stairs.

8

"Well, that moves things along," Van said, tipping his chair onto its back legs and pulling his vape out of his pocket.

I knew immediately this was no joke, because Riki's words had the effect of someone dropping a hissing bomb with a lit fuse on the table. There was a second of paralyzed confusion, then Liani jumped up and left. Tom swore under his breath and went after her. April's mouth twisted up into a strange little bow, like she had swallowed a bunch of bees.

"What's happening?" I asked. I think this was a fair question. In reply, April grabbed me and got me out of the room in a kind of Secret Service hustle.

"Oh god," she said as we made our way through the echoing main hall, under the watchful gaze of the women in the ceiling. "I'm so sorry. God. This isn't your fault."

I hadn't known that anything in this would be my fault, but I allowed myself to be moved along, feeling guilty anyway. As I've said, I'm good at feeling guilty. It's my natural resting state.

April couldn't decide which way to take me, starting first

for one of the reception rooms on the first floor, then taking me outside. We saw Liani and Tom moving quickly down the lawn, so April took me around the veranda, opting for an isolated section that wrapped the side of the house.

"*I* wanted to tell you," she said in a low voice as she sat down on one of the Adirondack chairs. "I thought you should know that something happened. I mean, someone was going to tell you. I *told* them that. I said that you would find out."

"What is going on?" I asked again.

In reply, April reached into the pocket of her hoodie and got out her phone. She flicked through some photos until she came to one that showed her and a guy with a deep tan.

"Chris," she said. Her voice was thick with suppressed emotion. "Chris Nelson."

I've never been attracted to guys, so I'm not sure what I'm supposed to be looking for when assessing them, but I think Chris was handsome. He had black hair, prominent, dark brows, deep-brown eyes, and a soft smile. He was posing with a pit bull wearing a dog jacket that read ADOPT ME. I had to assume that Chris was the dead guy Riki had referred to because I couldn't say to April *So, this is the dead one, huh?*

"It happened seven weeks ago," she went on. "The second of May. Prom. There was a party. It's a tradition. It's a different island every year so that they can't stop it. The whole thing is you stay until dawn and you come back to town for breakfast. It's kind of more important than the prom itself. Every year the school and the cops say they're going to shut it down, but no one does because they all went to it when they were in high school. It's that kind of thing."

April looked to see if I was following, and I nodded.

"There were always six of us," she said. "Me, Chris, Tom, Liani, Van, and Riki. We've known each other since we were—I don't even know. We all grew up basically on the same street. We were always like brothers and sisters when we were little, but that changed. Chris and Liani started dating in junior year. They broke up last fall, in November. That's a whole other story. Then Chris and Van got together around Valentine's Day. So when prom came, Chris went with Van, and the rest of us went single. I mean, except for Riki. She didn't go to the prom itself."

She gave me a little nod as if to say, *you know what I mean*. And the thing was, I did. I'd only been on this island for four hours and I already knew that no, Riki wasn't going to the prom.

April needed a moment to steady herself before she got to the next part of the story. She rubbed the heels of her hands on her thighs and blinked several times. I braced myself.

"That night," she began, "we all met up at eleven thirty to ride out. Van and Chris went together on one of Chris's family's Jet Skis. Tom, Liani, and I went on one of Tom's family's small boats. I don't know how Riki got out there. She was there when we all arrived. Here . . ." She scrolled through her phone for another moment and held up a photo. "This was us earlier in the night."

There was Liani in a stunning long red dress with a slit up the leg. She was with Tom, who wore a dark suit. Chris

101

and Van were next to them. Chris was in a black tuxedo. Van wore a gray one, with tails and a top hat. April was in a blue dress with a full skirt. Riki was not in the picture.

"There was so much happening that night," she said. "We were all dancing, taking videos. Pretty much everyone was drunk. At some point, Van and Chris went off to be alone, and then Van was back, all upset, because he and Chris got into a fight. But that happened a lot. Then, as the sun came up, everyone started to get ready to go back for breakfast. Van was supposed to be riding back with Chris on Chris's Jet Ski, but Chris was still off somewhere.

Van said that Chris could just stay on the island for all he cared and he would ride with us on the boat. So we were packing up, and I was going to go look for Chris, but then someone started screaming. Then lots of people were screaming, saying Chris was in the water . . ."

April seemed to drift away from the veranda where we sat. She was remembering, and she tucked her knees into her chest and hugged them.

"We all ran to where the screaming was coming from," April said. "I can still see him there, in the water . . ."

She shook her head and closed her eyes, willing the image away.

"Liani tore off—she ran so fast. She got down to one of the shore points. She didn't even take off her dress, she just pulled it up to her waist and jumped in. I can always see her, swimming in that dress. She flipped him over and pulled him to the shore and started CPR, but it was too late."

Liani, swimming in a prom dress to pull her ex-boyfriend from the water. It was all so extreme. So intense.

"When Van saw him—I remember he just started laughing like crazy. He couldn't stop. He was actually hysterical. We had to stop him from jumping in the water too. He started saying he was going to swim to shore. I grabbed him. Tom grabbed him. We had to hold him down."

"What happened?" I said. "Did Chris fall?"

"I think so. No one knows. Everyone was at least a little drunk. I think Chris was a lot drunk. I don't know if he jumped in to swim and didn't think about the rocks, or if he was close to the edge and he lost his balance. It just happened. But he hit his head and drowned."

April put her phone into the pocket of her fleece.

"We talked about whether we should tell you. Liani made the case that we shouldn't, and she had maybe the worst trauma, aside from Van. Van . . . you noticed he's a little high? He's been like that since it happened. He's self-medicating all the time. It wasn't his fault."

I hadn't suggested it was, but April was just talking at this point.

"Chris was the one who set this all up for us. Chris was big into organizing things and working for charities. Chris was the best. He used to work at an animal shelter. And he was a big part of River Rescue, which is an environmental group that protects the river. He was one of those people who went to community meetings and made speeches about stuff. When this island went up for sale, and the town got it for the summer for tourism, Chris made the pitch that the guides should come from our high school. He actually went to all these meetings about educational grants. He helped set up the whole thing where the town would hire the six of us, and Dr. Henson would have to teach us for a semester, and we would get school credit for it and then get summer jobs. That's what he was like. He was going to go to *Princeton*. Anyway, all we want to do is be with each other, and we are, you know? We're here. And it's a job. And we have to do it for Chris."

I nodded. I had one more question, but I wasn't sure whether to ask: *Hey, what the hell is the deal with Riki?* Sometimes if you want to know something, you have to ask around the question.

"Riki lives here too?" I said. "She's not in the playhouse."

"She stays here, in the house," April replied. "Riki tends to operate by a different set of rules than the rest of us."

She slid the charm on her necklace back and forth, ticktock, ticktock.

"You saw there's some tension," she said.

"Hard to miss."

"Yeah . . ." April rubbed her right hand down the side of her face. "Riki's kind of the reason Chris and Liani broke up last fall. It was . . . bad. I'm surprised she decided to go through with it—to take the class with us and come here. But that's Riki. She's going to do what's she's going to do."

She held up her hands, indicating that these things were out of her control.

"You know," she said, "sometimes I think, at least it happened in May. If it had been in April, I would never be able to say my name without thinking about him. But I always think about him anyway. I should get back and check on Van. Are you okay?"

"Me?"

"Yeah. You've been through a lot this summer, right? And this was a lot."

She reached out her hand and put it softly on my elbow. I have to admit a light flutter—I'm not immune to the charms of a cute redheaded girl. But that wasn't where my head was at, or my heart. This was all too grave, too much.

"I'm fine," I said.

"Oh. Good. Okay."

She stood, lingered an uncertain moment, then nodded and left. I stayed on the veranda for a moment, watching an orange-and-black butterfly meander past on a soft current of breeze.

Chris had entered the chat. Chris, the dead guy.

9

It wasn't lost on me that this was something interesting I could message Akilah about. At least, it seemed like an interesting idea at first glance. But what would that message look like? *Hey, guess what? I'm subbing for a dead guy. He fell off a cliff. How's the Cheesecake Factory?*

No. I couldn't be the one who just started a fire and now had random dead guy stories. You can have one of those, but not both. Not in a matter of under two weeks.

I returned to my room for the rest of the night, shuffling around and rearranging things, listening for noises, voices in the fairy-tale house. The walls were thick but the floorboards sang. I heard Liani and April walking up the steps. I went online and searched the name *Chris Nelson*. I got five hits from local sites.

CLEMENT BAY TEEN DIES IN ACCIDENT
A local teenager has died after falling from a rocky point on Mulligan Island last night, authorities say.

Christopher Nelson, 18, of Clement Bay, was at a party with many other students from Roosevelt High School. Somewhere around 5:00 a.m., he fell from a sixteen-foot cliff into the rocky bottom of the shallow waters below. His body was recovered by a fellow classmate, Liani Harris, who swam out to provide aid. A rescue boat arrived soon after, but Nelson was pronounced dead at the scene. . . .

ALCOHOL AND DRUGS INVOLVED IN LOCAL TEEN'S DEATH

The autopsy of local teen Christopher Nelson revealed that he had a blood alcohol level of 0.12 and traces of marijuana in his system, which potentially led to his fall. . . .

I searched socials and found Chris's accounts were still open, though there had been no activity since the second of May. I looked at pictures of Chris at the prom with the others. There was Van, tall and dapper. Liani, simply gorgeous. April, adorable in a cobalt-blue dress, her hair swirled into a flaming red updo studded with pearl accent pins. I scrolled back through Christopher Nelson's life. I saw him posing with dogs wearing RESCUE ME! jackets. I saw him with his arm around Van, kissing him on the cheek, Van smirking goofily, eyes squinted shut. I rolled back through the year, watching him pose, seeing his impassioned posts about the river and the environment. He took several shots of wildlife, of the river itself, with long captions about how it needed to be protected and preserved.

When I look at the river, I realize how lucky I am to live here, and how important it is to do everything in my power to protect this place for my generation and for generations to come. We aren't the only ones who live here either. All the life that depends on this river needs to be protected as well.

Lots of likes on that one. April left a caption with a dozen hearts. Van wrote: *Look at my sexy wildlife warrior.* More hearts.

I went back in time through the winter and saw April, Van, and Chris flopped down in the snow. Liani appeared in the feed as I moved back into the fall. The pictures were more romantic—so many studies of Liani. Liani with longer hair in Bantu knots, puckering her mouth for the camera with shimmering copper lipstick on her lips. And there was Riki, sliding into the group shots in October, smiling, her smudgy kohl eyes staring down the camera. Riki always seemed to wear oversized black T-shirts. She went through a deep-blue lipstick phase, which I found very attractive on her. She always seemed to be in the middle of saying or doing something when the picture was taken, never posing.

I kept scrolling, watching them all grow younger. I saw them doing tricks on Jet Skis, playing for the camera. I saw Van shrink in height, Tom in muscle. Liani was gangly. April had chipmunk cheeks. Riki sometimes wore blue. I went all the way to the end, to a picture of a puppy in a laundry basket, then refreshed to go back to that final photo, the group shot at the prom. The last night Chris Nelson was alive.

Then I switched over and started scrolling through Akilah's feed. I did this most nights. Wiggle that tooth. Salt that wound. Make sure it hurts. I knew every photo on there by heart, and I studied new ones like they were the Voynich manuscript. No new ones of her, just one of her big orange tabby, Scrambles. So I did my other new painful hobby—I scrolled the Cheesecake Factory menu. I replayed our date. I imagined Akilah taking orders for avocado tacos and grilled chicken salads.

By the time I looked up, I realized it had grown dark. It was almost eleven. I'd been scrolling for over two hours, and I really needed to pee. The bathroom was so far away. This was going to be terrible.

I got up and opened my door cautiously. All was dark and quiet in the little fairy-tale house, with the thick walls and the exposed beams that crossed the ceiling with measured haphazardness. It was a hunk of concrete whimsy—a big toy.

I stepped out onto the stone front step and looked up at the wide expanse of sky, scattered with all the stars not visible from Syracuse. The sky had a blue glow, with just a bright curved needle of moon piercing through. Next to me, squatting silently, was Morning House.

I'd never gotten the creeps before. I didn't really know what the *creeps* were. That night, I got them, and I understood. It's a cold, nervous prickling—an overwhelming sense that something in the environment isn't right. That there is a danger, but the danger is pretending to be something else.

There is something that you don't want to be around, and the need to go back to somewhere you understand, that's warm and secure, where you can be away from the thing you can't name.

And yet. There was something about the cold, uneasy feeling that also made me want to look at it a moment longer. Something darted through the sky above me. A bat. Looping, sweeping in circles. I read a book about bats when I was a kid and have always had a lot of affection for them since. Bats are just here to eat insects and use sonar. They don't know we made it weird for them. They've never heard about vampires. (This is sort of the same logic I use when I can't watch animals under threat in movies or on TV. I know they're fine—they're getting a treat for doing something—but *animals don't know what acting is*. No matter what's going on, they're telling the truth.)

Now I really had to pee, which meant facing that trip through the door under the tree stairs, down the steps, and through the tunnel to the basement. I was going to have to get used to this. I stepped quietly back inside, pulled open the strange little door, and switched on the light. Just an ordinary basement passage. I decided to walk with a confident stride, like I loved walking through dark basements—the fake-it-till-you-make-it approach. The short tunnel was no problem. I got the key on the other side and opened the fire door that led to Morning House's basement.

This was different. In the passage, all was lit; the walls were reachable. I could hear the hiss of water in a pipe, the

110

wind on old walls, the echo of thousands of tons of house above me, shifting in its sleep. Creepy shit, as Riki's socks would say.

There was another light switch that illuminated the way to the bathroom. It dumped industrial, orange-tinted light on the path I needed to take. I hustled, bare feet on cold concrete floor, not caring about what I might be stepping on. I was on a mission. Pee and get out. Maybe this would grow on me in time, but that time was not now.

Mission accomplished, I gave my hands a quick wash and rubbed them dry on my shorts as I hurried back. I was an arm's length from the switch when I heard it, the distinct shuffle of feet on concrete. There was someone else down here, moving through the bowels of the house.

"Hello?" I called.

I heard a soft scrape, then movement stopped. Maybe it was Van, sitting at the bottom of the pool?

"Van?" I said.

Nothing. I stood, arm outstretched toward the light, gulping down the bile that jumped up my throat.

"Okay," I said, "well, I'm going back to the playhouse, so . . ."

No need to murder me, creeper! Nothing to see here. Marlowe Wexler is not going to get up in your business.

I put my back against the wall and moved along, sideways-crab style, toward the door that led to the passage and the house. I heard it again. A definite movement.

I'm not proud to tell you that I didn't bother to turn off

111

the light. I tore that door open and ran—ran through the passage, ran up the steps, ran back through the little door under the tree, which I slammed shut. I went to my shadowy room and turned on the overhead light. There was nothing there but the bed, my stuff, and a lone moth that was twiddling around the ceiling and banging into the shade.

Every single time I had to pee I was going to have to make that trip, and I did not like that at all.

Someone had been in the basement with me, which was *fine*. So why hadn't they answered? Unless it was a stranger on the island, someone who snuck on after closing? Or someone who took the tour and hid for the night? Maybe people did that for fun? As a goof? As a dare?

Possibly it was a rat. River rats, actual rats . . .

But it wasn't. I knew that much. Someone had been down there.

10

The next morning, I shuffled down that same basement passage to the bathroom in my rubbery slides. A few hours had vanquished the bad vibes completely. It had returned to being a benign space, kind of pleasant on a summer day. The showers were as basic as they came—a cheap showerhead in a concrete stall with a drain on the floor and a plastic curtain. The first shock of warmish water came tinkling from the showerhead with all the urgency of a sleepy toddler. Then it suddenly became alert and power washed me, sending me flying against the vinyl curtain with a yelp.

"Showers are weird here," I heard a voice say.

I did a quick body wash while dancing against the tips of the spray. I wrapped a towel around myself and peered out to see Liani standing outside, wearing a short blue terry cloth robe.

"It takes a minute," she said, putting her caddy down on the floor of the next stall. "But the pressure is pretty strong once it builds up."

I hadn't thought to bring a robe. It had never occurred to

me that the bathroom would be so far from where I slept. I only had the slightly too-short towel to cover me as I gave her an embarrassed nod and then hustled, wet-footed, through the basement, the tunnel, back up the stairs, and to my room under the magical tree.

I had been issued three maroon Morning House polo shirts and one fleece. I pulled one polo out of the plastic packaging. It hung loose. I'd been told to bring some kind of bottoms in khaki or gray. I'd gone with gray shorts.

When I got to the breakfast table, April, Tom, and Liani were already there. (Liani was obviously quicker than I was at showering—and probably most things.) Tom was working his way through his Froot Loops with the determination of a marathon runner who'd just passed the twenty-sixth-mile mark. Riki floated into the room, dressed in black, her headphones on her head, blocking out any possible conversation. She opened the fridge, removed a bowl, and was gone.

"Morning," Liani mumbled, smirking in the direction of Riki's retreating figure.

"We'll show you around outside this morning," Tom said. "Get you familiar with the grounds."

When I stepped outside, I understood why they called it Morning House. The eerie, toothy building of the night before was transformed. In the afternoon, it was imposing. At night, disturbing. In the morning, it had a glow. Light seemed to drip down the facade. The red peaks and spikes of the roof had a cheerful tone, like jaunty little caps.

Tom showed me along the dock area, where I had come

in the day before. There were sections we didn't have to think about, like the ticket booths, the refreshment stand, and the landing dock for the big tourist boats. He walked like a determined Muppet, as if there was a string coming from his sternum, pulling his chest toward an unseen hand in the sky, his legs bobbing in strides that were just a few inches longer than they should have been. It wasn't the walk of someone going places as much as it was the walk of someone who watched some videos of someone going places and was attempting to replicate it at home.

"Is it strange to be here?" he asked. "On the island for the summer?"

"I don't know," I said. "I just got here."

"But it must be really different for you. You're from near Syracuse, right?"

It was and I was, and clearly Tom wanted me to acknowledge that it was going to be maybe a little weird for me. I nodded, and he seemed satisfied.

"My family has lived around here for over a hundred years. Boating, fishing. My uncle was the mayor of Clement Bay until the last election. So, we're pretty . . ."

I waited for the rest of the sentence, but it never came. I was left to imagine what Tom and his family were "pretty" like. Pretty powerful. Pretty well-off. Pretty good at fishing. Pretty close to Canada. Or maybe they were just all very pretty.

He pointed at the concessions stand at the dock and the small booth with border control.

"They got a company to do all the tickets and food," he said. "I guess the government sent the guy who does border control for Canadian boats."

Border control for this little island seemed grand and silly, like three kids in a trench coat.

"This is technically America," he went on, "so Canadians have to pass through border control, but there's nothing to it because all they do is walk around the island and leave. The line between Canada and America is just somewhere in the water. Boats cross it all day long."

I had noticed this on my ride out, when my phone kept telling me I was in Canada, then that I was back in America.

"Anyway, we basically have nothing to do with the things that happen on this part of the dock. We never even talk to the people who work here very much. They come in for the day, go home. They often don't even come up to the house. I do this bit over here where the private boats come in."

Tom walked me down a small rocky strip that formed a tip off the end of the island, to a stone arching bridge. Ahead of us was another stone building, nowhere near as large as Morning House, but easily as big as the playhouse. Probably bigger.

"This is the boathouse," he said as we crossed over the tiny bridge. "It's technically on a different island. The big one is Ralston Island. This one is Sunbeam Island. But it's all one property."

The boathouse door opened onto a large area that stretched out over the water. The walls were covered in what home renovation shows call shiplap. I guess the whole ship part of that is real. It was rustic and serious-looking, with ropes and tools and a stack of canoes on one side. There were two large docking slips, but only one was occupied, and barely at that. A single Jet Ski bobbed there sheepishly.

"This is our Jet Ski," he said. "Life vests are in here."

He swung open the cabinet doors and revealed a stack of wearable orange life vests, then swung it closed again just as quickly.

"And over here . . ." He indicated a small padlock box hanging from a bolt in the wall. ". . . is the box for the keys. The passcode is 1932."

"The year everyone died here?"

"Well," he said, "seemed easy to remember."

He punched in the code and the box swung open, revealing a key on a long piece of red retractable cord.

"Everything you need for the ski is in this box under here." He pulled out a plastic box from a shelf. "Everything is in here—flares, PLBs . . ."

"What's a PLB?"

"Personal locator beacon."

A big rule for me is this: never go anywhere where you need to bring your own beacon. Pro tip.

"Key's on a lanyard," he said. "Put it around your wrist when you're on the ski. Most important thing. If you come off the ski, the key will pull out and the engine will cut off."

He demonstrated attaching the lanyard to my wrist using a Velcro band. Tom seemed to genuinely believe I'd be coming here often for all those Jet Ski rides I loved to take.

"You ever ridden one?"

I shook my head.

"They're basically our cars," Tom explained. "Or our bikes."

Well, the joke was on them because I don't like bikes either. This Marlowe likes to move around on land in the safety of her tiny Smart Car. She likes her water shallow and not full of five million shipwrecks.

"It's easy. I'll show you later. We have to put out the cushions now, though. That's the first job of the day. We store them overnight in the living room."

I followed Tom around Morning House, to the rubble pile that had once been a patio. He stepped across this and opened the double doors, pulling out a blue tarp stacked high with cushions. We carried these around and put them on chairs, tying them in place.

"By the way," he said, "see the big island in front of us? That rock face right there."

He pointed at another island, with a cliff face cutting out of the water.

"That's Mulligan Island," he said, pointing at the closer of the two nearest islands. "That's where it happened."

"Where what happened?"

"Chris," he said simply. Just like that. Oh, that's just where Chris fell to his death. I *think* he was trying to be casual about it to make it less weird, but it had the opposite effect. Either that or he was a sociopath. But I'm bad with people

118

too sometimes, so I tried to ride along.

"Oh," I said. "Right."

"I thought we should tell you," he said, turning back to the cushions and tarp. "But it affects me less than the others. Liani dated Chris. And Van was dating him. I think April too, at some point. I was the only one who didn't."

Riki was not included in the list, I noted, but seemed to be swept into the group.

"It's . . . so close to here."

"Yeah. Some people were saying we should have the party here, on this island, but—it's an illegal party. We're not supposed to have it, but everyone turns a blind eye. It's a tradition. If we had it here and messed the place up, that would be huge trouble for the people who need this place for tourism money this summer. So we decided to do it over there, on Mulligan."

"He was drunk?" I said. "He fell?"

"I guess. Maybe he jumped. We all know that spot has rocks right under it. He would have known that if he was sober, but who knows? Fell, jumped, it ended up the same." He had put the last of the cushions on and began folding up the tarp. "The thing is, Liani is still having a hard time. So are the others, but Liani . . . I'm just saying."

I didn't know what he was saying, but now I would certainly be aware of the rock in the distance and Liani in general. And I was heading her way now, to the lagoon, for my next bit of the tour.

The lagoon was on the shallower end of the island. It

119

looked much like the rest of the shoreline, except that there was a low rocky wall that came up about three feet out of the water. This was dotted with ladders, stone benches, and urns. Liani was also putting out cushions, but she did so in a red bathing suit and shorts, a whistle around her neck.

"This is the lagoon," Tom said. "The outdoor natural swimming pool, basically. The Ralstons sank a wall down to the bottom to block this area off from the rest of the river. There are holes in it, too small for people to pass through, that allow the water in, along with some small fish. This is where Liani takes over."

"The shallow part here is four feet deep," she said. "The deepest part is over by that bench on the far right. That's about thirteen feet. The average depth is eight feet. It's a hundred and sixty feet long, so the dimensions of an Olympic pool."

"Phillip Ralston wanted his daughter Clara to be in the Olympics," I said, recalling the piece from *Life* magazine that had been in the PDF Dr. Henson had sent me.

Liani shrugged, indicating that this was true, but that was then and here we were now, standing in front of it, and only one of us was qualified to take care of anyone swimming in it.

I may have been reading more into her shrug than she intended.

As we stood there, three black swans waddled down the lawn and hopped into the water.

"I've never seen black swans before," I said.

"The Ralstons brought them in here, I guess because they're uncommon and they look cool."

Liani showed me into a small stone building by the lagoon edge. This was sort of a large shed that contained a paddleboard and oar, several pool noodles, a backboard, and a first aid kit.

"And this," she said, dragging out a metal detector. "I've used this almost every day. People drop things constantly. They take off their earrings to swim or whatever and drop them in the grass."

She patted the metal detector like it was her faithful dog.

We stepped back outside, where Liani began to indicate the circular life preservers hanging from posts and fencing.

"If you see anyone fall in the water, throw them one of these and call for me. Don't try to go in yourself."

"Then you'd have two people to get out of the water."

I meant it as a joke, but the expression on her face let me know that I had blown it. No one around here thought there was anything funny about water safety, and knowing what I knew now, I should have remembered not to make that joke.

"Drowning people can take other people down with them," she went on. "That's what makes rescues dangerous."

She turned away, and I noted that she shook her head faintly, like she couldn't believe this is who she had to work with now.

By lunch, I'd learned everything I was apparently ever going to learn about the outside operations. Lunch was a premade sandwich that I ate alone in my room, because I didn't want to face anyone for a few minutes, then Van came to whisk me off on my first proper tour of the house. I followed him down the sloping path to the dock. He was long and lanky; his maroon Morning House polo shirt hung off his frame.

"Like we said at dinner last night, people just like to look at fancy stuff," he said. "That's basically all this is. Show them fancy stuff. Who doesn't like fancy stuff? They also like the death stuff because the house is supposed to be cursed. Mostly fancy stuff, though. It's like Disney World! But real. And bad. And with no rides."

"Disney World is real," I pointed out.

"That's what they want you to think. What I'm saying is that this is like Death Disney World. We're here to give the people what they want. You came here to see expensive shit and places where people died? Then follow me, tourist. Some tip. This is key information. More on that later. We're not supposed to take the tips, but we all take the tips. They go toward the community weed and booze fund, which is oper-ated by me. Dr. Henson does not know about the tips or the fund because we never see her. She's more or less imaginary, for our purposes. She mostly sits in her rooms and works on her book. If we need her, we get her on the radio, but we've never needed her. It's a beautiful situation."

There was something grand about Van—he had the air of recently deposed royalty and now he worked here at Morning House as a tour guide, but he was fine with it. Van seemed fine with everything, and I think by fine with everything,

I mean he seemed kind of high. Friendly. Aware. But high. Possibly.

A group was getting off one of Uncle Jim's cruises—at least fifty people were ambling through the gate.

"These people have just been sailing around for two hours," he said. "At least one will be someone who has a social media channel about tourism. Anyone under twenty is here under duress and wants to take selfies or make content. We let those people be. They don't need us. And there have been five engagements so far. That was exciting. Watch. I'll show you how it's done."

Van had up to this point been the human embodiment of vape smoke and Dorito dust, but when the tours rolled up in front of him, he became a different person. He was a talkative guide, breathlessly describing all the things Phillip bought for his children. There was William's customized Bösendorfer piano from Vienna, a speedboat called the *Silver Arrow* for Clara, a painting by Dutch still life master Willem Kalf for Benjamin, an antique rolltop desk that had come from Austria for Unity. Van rattled off the prices—ten, twenty, thirty thousand dollars here and there. Two kids got things that were harder to store. Edward got controlling stocks in a jute company so he could learn how to manage a business. Victory wanted nothing for herself—instead, she was the namesake of an entire wing of a charity hospital.

Again, I was psyched as hell to get my grandparents' Smart Car.

The playhouse, where we were staying, had been designed

and built by a guy who made fantasy-style houses for people in Hollywood. Apparently, that was a thing for a while. Before all the open-plan stuff you see on home renovation shows, somebody was out there building Snow White's castle or fake peasant houses for movie execs.

"And here . . ." He indicated one of the sunny rooms on the second floor that I knew was used for sitting in the afternoon, because this was the kind of house where you moved around all day to rooms designed to catch the sun. ". . . is where they used to keep their prized collection of pet pythons. The Ralstons were avid collectors."

"They were?" someone said.

"Kidding! Now, you'll love what we're going to see next . . ."

Right after touring with Van, I looped around to tour with April. April's tour was bright, with lots of conversations with the tourists. She didn't go into the same level of detail that Van did—she gave the basics and gave people a lot of time to make videos and take pictures, which appeared to be what they really wanted to do. Sometimes people had questions. April did not make up answers. If she didn't know, she said so, which was reassuring. I toured with each of them two more times until the patter started to run through my head and I was tired of hearing about the dome and the furniture.

"At the end of the day," April explained as the last tourists left, "we take sections and clean up a little. We sweep, wipe the glass cabinets down, check the bathrooms. I'll do it. It's your first day. You can walk with me, though. We'll do the

124

bottom floors. Van will do the top two. We'll start with the bathrooms downstairs. That's the worst part."

I followed her to the basement bathrooms. There was a nook full of cleaning supplies next to it. She put on gloves, and I did the same. I couldn't follow her and do nothing. Together we dumped out the trash, swept the floors, and ran a mop over them.

"Don't worry about Liani and Tom," she said as she squirted a ring of bleach gel around the rim of the toilet.

I hadn't been worried, but now I was. "What do you mean?"

"They're just . . . It's fine."

The more someone tells you that things are fine, the clearer a signal it is that things are not fine but they are not going to tell you what's wrong, and the thing that's wrong will eventually make itself known when it's sneaking up behind you with a baseball bat and a crooked smile.

So we mopped up a bit, and the pungent smell of bleach filled the air. Morning House glowed again in the late afternoon sun. It collected the light, like some kind of mystical temple. It rained down through the thousands of pieces of glass above us in the dome. Light disinfects, I've heard. Obviously, it illuminates. It feels like security and truth, but what Dr. Henson said about bad things often being out in the open—that was gnawing at my thoughts. There was too much light, beaming down through faces leaded to the sky. It was like the house itself was trying to convince you of something, trying to make anyone who managed to get inside understand the straightforward glory of wealth. And yet, almost everyone who lived here burned too bright and fast. I idly wondered about the ethics of capitalism while I looked up whether or not you should wear sunscreen indoors if there are too many windows. The modern world makes us hold a lot of worries in our minds at the same time, and right now, I wanted to know which kind of danger would burn me up first—wealth inequality or UV rays. Which took me back to fire, and candles, and Akilah, and the merry-go-round went on.

July 19-20, 1932

At dinner that night, there was a bit of a chill between Father and Faye. She sat primly at his side in an elegant baby-blue twinset. Everyone was expected to attend dinner at Morning House, including Max, who sat in a modified chair next to Faye. Max's nurse was ill tonight, struck down by a stomach problem.

The kitchen staff brought out the dishes of macaroni with tomatoes and nut cutlets, along with a crusty, somewhat impenetrable loaf of whole-grain bread that had to be hacked apart with a big knife. It was always served still warm, and the family cut their own fresh slices as it was passed.

"Clara," he said. "I was thinking you might give Max a swimming lesson tomorrow afternoon, teach him how to jump into the water."

Clara could not hide the disappointment on her face.

"It would be extremely appreciated," Phillip said.

"How appreciated?"

This was a bit of a daring question, but Clara was a daring person.

"You've mentioned this dancer you think so much of, Martha Graham. Would you like to meet her?"

Clara lifted her chin. She was listening.

"She will be visiting the Alberts on Mercy Island in the beginning of August. I can arrange for you to go there and spend some time."

This offer was too good to resist. The next afternoon, Clara dutifully accepted charge of Max and headed to the lagoon. Victory and Unity came along, maybe for support, maybe to be entertained. It was probably a combination of the two.

"Come on, Max," Clara said, lifting the little boy up and climbing into the water with him. As soon as the gentle, clear water hit his skin, Max began to shriek.

"Max, don't scream in my ear. I'll hold you by the middle. I just want you to kick your legs."

Max continued to scream in Clara's ear.

"He doesn't like it," Victory observed.

"I know that," Clara said, looking over her shoulder, wincing away from the noise. "All right, Max. How about you hold me around my neck and I'll take you for a ride!"

"Cold," Max said.

"I know it is. But doesn't it feel nice?"

"Cold."

"Just put your feet in, Max."

"Cold!"

"He thinks it's cold," Unity observed.

"How about just your toes?"

"No!"

Max swung up his foot, catching Clara in the jaw.

"Max, stop it. Stop it, Max. *Stop.*"

It was like Max had a dozen limbs. He clutched for her cheek, digging in his nails right below her eye. She reflexively let him go, and he dropped into the water. It was not a long drop—his toes had already been skimming the surface, and the water was only about four feet deep. Max screamed so loudly that birds flew out of a nearby tree. Unity and Victory waded into the water to help get him out, while Clara sat on the side, winded and frustrated.

Once out of the water, Max wriggled free of his sisters and paced off.

"That went about as well as I expected," Victory said. "I think . . . No!"

Clara saw Victory's focus and moved with speed. She ducked just in time to miss the rock that Max had hurled directly at her face. It clipped the side of her head as she turned. Her ear was ringing. Max tore off toward the house and Faye ran from it, toward them, catching him up in her arms.

"What's going on?" she said.

"Clara pushed me, Clara pushed me . . ."

"I didn't," Clara said, clutching her ear. "I was holding him up and he kicked me and scratched me. I dropped him by accident, then he threw a rock at my head."

Faye looked to Victory and Unity for confirmation and

found it in their grim expressions. She looked despairingly at Clara.

"Are you all right?"

"Fine," Clara said unhappily. "I turned in time. It would have taken out an eye, or my nose."

"Please don't tell your father, Clara," Faye said. "Please. I'll make sure you won't have to do this again and you'll still meet Martha Graham. I know her. I'll take care of it. Please. Say you scratched your face by accident."

Clara looked down at her lap and nodded.

"Thank you," Faye said, looking at all the girls. "Thank you. You won't have to do this again. I know it's hard. He doesn't want to swim. Phillip is . . ."

She didn't finish the sentence. She wrapped Max back up and hurried him inside.

"You gave up too easily," Unity said.

"So you teach him," Clara said.

Unity stalked back to the house, leaving Victory and Clara at the water's edge. Tiny droplets of blood gurgled from the cut on her face. Water mixed in with the blood, and pink drops fell to her leg.

"It's only another month or so," Victory said to her sister.

Another month here, maybe. But nothing would change. Ralstons didn't change.

"Tell me about your day, everyone," Phillip said at dinner as he passed the bread. "How did the swimming lesson go?"

Clara looked over to Max, who was trying to use his fork

to pick up some mushy peas and he kept failing and reaching for them with his hand. Whatever had befallen his nurse still kept her upstairs, so it was left to Faye to draw his hand back each time, gently returning it to the fork. Aunt Dagmar kept her gaze down on her mostly empty plate. Aunt Dagmar never ate much at dinner. She had a tray of what she privately referred to as *normal food* brought to her room at six every evening. Her appearance at the table was purely ceremonial.

"It was a start," Clara said.

Faye gave her a thankful smile and the slightest of nods.

"It didn't go that well, Father," Unity said.

"How so?"

"Max was . . ." Unity kept her eyes steadily on her plate as she spoke. ". . . upset."

"It was a start," Clara said again.

Max was stabbing down at the plate, unable to get to the peas.

"He became *very* upset," Unity went on. "He struck Clara."

William looked at Clara across the table. She kept her head down.

"Max," Phillip said. "Did you hit your sister?"

"Clara dropped me in the water," Max said. He spoke clearly. A full sentence. "I hit her with a rock."

"I didn't *drop* him in the water," Clara said in a low voice.

"Max." Phillip set his utensils down. "You must never, ever throw a rock at someone. Especially one of your brothers or sisters."

Max continued to noodle with his food.

"Stop that and listen to me, Max."

William's stare penetrated the top of Clara's head. She had to look up at him. There was a flash of something in his eyes. Worry. Warning? There was a feeling hanging over the table now, some kind of sword of Damocles. A pulsing moment that trapped her breath in her rib cage.

"I think Max was frightened by the depth of the water," Unity said, trying to cut the tension. "Though Clara had the situation well in hand. He was upset."

The issue of the rock was important, but Phillip took the note from Unity. Unity was his little lieutenant, always keeping things in order. It brought a measure of peace. It would have been easier, of course, if she'd never brought it up in the first place.

"I was there," Faye said quickly. "It was nothing."

"Hit her good," Max added.

"Max!" Faye was pleading now.

Phillip looked to Faye, half closed his eyes, and sighed.

"If you say it was nothing," Phillip replied, "then it was nothing. Max, apologize to Clara. Tell her how sorry you are, and how you will never do anything like that again."

"Sorry," Max said halfheartedly.

"And when you are in the water with your brothers and sisters, especially Clara, you are safe. Swimming is important. We will set this aside for now, and it will not happen again. You will continue lessons with Clara tomorrow. Everyone, let's finish with dinner before it gets cold. Max, eat your peas."

"Can I have custard? I don't like peas."

"Agnes," Faye called, "would you mind, some baked milk custard . . ."

"You need the peas," Phillip said. "You will eat the peas, Max. Peas are a fruit. Does anyone know why?"

"They contain seeds," Victory said. "And they develop from the ovary of a flower."

"Correct. They are a good source of protein for those who do not eat meat and are full of vital nutrients. They are excellent for the digestive system. So, Max, eat your peas and then you can have a custard."

"I don't like peas."

"Everyone, please put your forks down," Phillip said.

Once again, dinner came to a halt.

"We will all sit here, Max, until you eat your peas. No one else can eat their dinner, or have a milk custard, or enjoy their evening until you do—and I am sure you don't want that. I want you to eat them, yourself, holding your fork."

Max seemed to rumble internally. Clara could see him holding down his temper. His little face went red, and he balled his fists. Phillip stared him down. Clara had no idea who was about to win this contest of wills. Max picked up his fork. For a moment, Clara was sure he was about to stab his father in the hand. He turned it on the plate instead, jabbing relentlessly, spearing one or two peas, but mostly sending them everywhere in a ferocious effort, a mockery of eating. This went on for one minute, two . . .

The dining room clock ticked away. Clara heard Edward

mumble something under his breath. Victory went utterly blank and stared at the curtains. Unity watched Max. William kept his eye on Clara, and Clara imagined she was swimming away from here, through the dark water, in the direction of the moon.

"All right, Max," Phillip finally said with a sigh. "That's good enough. Agnes, you can bring the milk custard. Everyone, eat."

Clara ate automatically, barely tasting the gluey nut cutlet or the tart raspberries. Now that Max had gotten what he wanted, he was suddenly a master of the fork and spoon. He had defeated his father. Everyone knew it. There was a general air of deflation, and of something new. A bit of chaos in their otherwise orderly system of things.

No one wanted to stay at the table when the plates were empty, so dinner was dismissed. Clara slipped off the light cotton sweater she was wearing. As the dishes were cleared, she reached for the bread and cut herself a last, small slice.

She dropped the knife quietly into her lap, folding the sweater over it, and carried it away.

11

For my first few days at Morning House, I followed a routine. I woke up, got beaten up by the shower, had breakfast, and then followed tours over and over, until the script stuck to my neural pathways and I could spit it back out again.

From April, I learned which places were the best for taking pictures, what parts people liked to hear. From Van, I learned how to keep the group moving. (The trick: randomly throwing in "You're going to love what we're going to see next!" It's genuinely that easy as long as you sell it.) I began to think of Morning House as my house. Well, not my house that I lived in, but a place I was part of. I got to know which boards creaked when you stepped on them, which way to turn to keep from being blinded by the light streaming in. I knew the musty smell of the basement differed from the musty smell of the upper floors. I got used to people oohing and aahing over the domed ceiling.

Tom gave me a terrifying lesson on the Jet Ski, which I resolved never to use. Imagine riding a horse on a wild, powerful river. It's like that. This was going to be an issue, maybe, because Jet Skis were the major mode of transport around the islands and the shore.

The dinners were cordial. I got a spot on the roster and helped warm up our trays and leftover hot dogs. We always got vegan butternut mac and cheese, which I ended up loving. Liani swam every morning and night in the lagoon. Tom often went with her, and it became clear that while they were not yet a couple, that was going to happen at any moment. Van puffed his vape and made enigmatic jokes. April would chat with me nonstop in an onslaught of friendship.

Riki was almost invisible back in the gift shop. She was like a cat that you know is in the house but never comes out from under the bed. Dr. Henson would walk through the house sometimes, usually on the phone, always in her pristine yoga gear and a pair of green Hokas with yellow soles. I assume they ate, but I saw no concrete evidence of this.

I still had a sucking hole inside, a place where Akilah had been and was not. The routine of the place helped, but generally I just wanted to get through the day and be on my own so I could think repetitive thoughts about the texts I wanted to send to Akilah. I wrote them in my head all the time. I wanted to tell her everything that was going on and make it seem like I was interesting and fun and not just someone who set fires and ran out of town. I could win her over with some stories, I thought. But each time I even thought about typing something out, I ran completely cold and clenched in on myself.

This was how it went, more or less unchanging, for a few days. A constant carousel of tours and obsessive thoughts, punctuated by the warning squawk of a black swan. At night, in bed, I made mental movies about what it would be like to get back with Akilah. I had so many scenarios planned out. I imagined her coming to the island by surprise. She would arrive on a tour boat. I would turn, and there she would be.

"I guess I can't stay away from you," she would say.

Or sometimes she said, "I was passing by."

Or sometimes she ran to me across the lawn.

I kissed her everywhere. On the front porch. In the ballroom. In various bedrooms. Most often, I took her to the magnificent balcony where Dr. Henson did yoga and the line between the United States and Canada was blurred. Up there, well, that was the scene of my most detailed imaginings. They carried me to sleep, and the next day I woke up in the fairy-tale house again and followed more tours.

The next real event in this story occurred about four days in, after the tourists left for the day. I was showing the last ones where they could stand for a good picture, when Tom came past, striding his purposeful stride.

"Liani and I are going to town after this, if you want to come," he said. "We're going to pick up food for the next few days."

The idea of town sounded like an exciting change from my new routine of playhouse to Morning House and back again; the same thirty feet.

"Sure."

"Twenty minutes at the dock," he said.

Twenty minutes later, I was at the dock with my bag.

Liani was sitting in a tiny motorboat bobbing in the water, her eyes hidden behind massive sunglasses.

"Hop in," Tom said.

I inelegantly clambered down into the little boat, which teetered in a way I actively hated. This was truly the Smart Car of the water, except that as soon as Tom pulled it away from the dock, it took off at speed, nose coming out of the river, water spitting in the sides. It was too loud to talk, and my hair was whipping in my face. I gripped the seat with clawed hands. Five minutes later, we pulled up to one of the piers right in the middle of town. I got out with quivering legs, and Liani bounded out after me.

"Okay, so we'll meet you in an hour at the Blue Anchor," he said. "It's at the end of the street on the river side."

I guess I'd thought that Liani and Tom had asked me to come to town with them so that we could do stuff together, or just to do this one thing. Liani was already walking off, and Tom followed. I was in Clement Bay alone.

I had seen a little of Clement Bay when I came in with my parents, but we hadn't spent any time there. It was your classic river rat town, very small, focused on things to use in and around the water. Like any self-respecting vacation town, it had more than the required number of fudge and ice cream places. I stood in front of one that had a large plastic ice cream cone in front, along with a hilarious large chair for people to take pictures in and tag the shop.

I decided to get ice cream because I am not a complete fool.

The girl behind the counter had pink hair and was cute. I considered trying to tell her about the hot bottom and maybe breaking the ice a little, but it was too soon. I wasn't ready to share a hot bottom joke with anyone yet. They didn't have Moose Tracks, so I got one scoop of butter pecan and one scoop of honeycomb and tried to numb the crushing loneliness.

This was the kind of thing I was supposed to be doing with Akilah this summer—ice cream at sunset as the summer day cooled off and the smell of grass swelled in the air. I could vividly imagine her in this white romper she often wore with a black tank underneath, maybe with a bit of gold shadow frosting her eyelids. I sat for a minute in a small park facing the water and got out my phone and took a picture of Morning House in the distance, the sun behind it, giving it an otherworldly glow. I kept going back and forth about sending it to her.

This is where I work now! Different from Guffy's! Not on fire, just looks it, lol

The ice cream dripped down my hand, sticking my fingers together. God, it hurt. It felt like there was a hole in my chest, slightly to the right, under the breast, right there in the ribs, a sucking hole made of anxiety about the extreme amount of nothing in my future, because my future had been filled with her, and nothing and no one was like her.

I started to tear up, but then a man came by with a ridiculous black Labrador who sensed trauma and bounced up to save me. She licked the ice cream from my hand and thumped me with her tail, and for a minute, everything was okay again. I pushed myself up and walked down the street. I passed a small Victorian house, painted green with red trim, that housed an organization called River Rescue. There was a Pride flag hanging in the window, along with several posters, the largest of which read STOP THE KEETING FISHING AND BOATING EMPIRE FROM DESTROYING THE BEAVERS' HABITAT.

Keeting caught my eye, because that was Tom's name and this was a small town. There probably weren't two Keeting families with large fishing businesses. I stepped closer and looked at a photoshopped picture of an older version of Tom clubbing a beaver. Apparently, his family was trying to build a new marina on top of a valuable wetland.

Next to the River Rescue house was an identically structured one, this one painted gray with purple trim. Gold lettering in the window read THE BOOK GARDEN. In a window display along with an assortment of popular mysteries was a copy of *The Daughter of Time*. That was the book Riki had been reading.

I stood there, eating my ice cream, wondering if this was a hugely popular book that I had simply never heard of. I finished off the cone in a few bites and went inside. My arrival was heralded by the small tinkle of a chime. I found four copies of the book right by the front, in a small display marked STAFF PICKS. Nearby, there was a rack full of socks—the gifting kind that cost more than socks normally do but they're funny so you pay double. Prominently displayed, right in front, was a blue-and-black pair that said I LIKE SPOOKY SHIT.

The girl behind the counter was reading a graphic novel called *The Chuckling Whatsit*. She had it propped up in front of her and everything about her posture and expression said that she didn't want to be disturbed while reading. I apologetically set the book I wanted to buy down on the counter. She looked at the copy of *The Daughter of Time*, then up at me. Her hair was longer, but it was the same deep brown, almost black, just without the dark blue streaks.

While I had been making those connections, she had been evaluating me.

"Are you at Morning House?" she asked.

I had changed out of my maroon polo shirt, so I didn't have any visible markers of Morning House on me.

"This is the only copy of this we've ever sold," she explained. "And you look like the person Riki described. The one with the fire."

Riki had mentioned me. More than that, Riki had *described* me.

"Does Riki work here too?"

"Well, yeah. We own it. I mean, our parents own it. I'm Juhi. I'm her sister."

Things clicked into place. Riki was an independent contractor—she was the only one who worked in the gift shop.

"Yeah," she went on. "It was her idea to ask the committee if we could be in charge of the store, since we're a local business and we have all the stuff. She's smart like that. It makes *way* more money than this place. What's it like up

141

there? Is everyone being weird?"

"Kind of," I said. "I heard about Chris."

"Oh yeah," she said. "Chris Nelson. That was a lot. For a minute it looked like they might not open the house for tourists because all the people working there were friends of his, but everyone needs that money, you know? Eleven seventy-five. Tap or swipe."

I tapped, and Juhi forged on.

"They seemed to be doing okay, but they brought you in, so I guess they needed someone else. I don't know why they didn't bring someone from town. I would have done it. You're not from here. Why do you think they brought you in?"

Like Van, Juhi had been direct with her questions. I was about to say that it was because my teacher knew Dr. Henson and all that, but the truth was, I had no idea why the hell I'd been brought here, really.

"What happened with your fire?" Juhi asked. "You burned some house down? On purpose?"

"No! No."

"Did you get arrested?"

"No."

"I thought they arrested people for starting fires."

"It was an accident," I explained, feeling my face flush. "A candle."

"Oh." Juhi seemed disappointed and switched topics again. "So, is Riki talking to everyone now?"

"Not really," I said.

Juhi leaned back, nodded, and took a long sip out of a

heavily stickered water bottle. I had confirmed some suspicion of hers, clearly.

"I told her it would be bad," she said. "But there was no way she wasn't going to go. She's obsessed with that house and the story—she loves true crime. Even if it completely sucked, she was going to go."

Since I was here, and since Juhi seemed to love gossip, it was worth trying to get some.

"What happened?" I asked. "Something about her being the reason Chris and Liani broke up?"

Juhi continued sipping and shook her head once.

"It wasn't Riki's fault," she said. "Well, it was, but . . ."

With that, she turned her gaze down, like she'd said too much.

"Hope you're having a good time," she added. "Tell Riki to bring back my silver sandals. I know she took them."

The Blue Anchor was a small café on the river side of the street. It was inside an old building with a large front display window filled with a few dusty model boats and a partially rusted anchor. The inside had a similar vibe, with an array of mismatched tables and chairs that may have been a design choice or from a clearance sale or both. In a nod to the nautical theme, the floor leaned to the right like a ship in a storm. The walls were covered in framed sayings like, "I don't need a river to be lazy" and "Did someone say rosé?"

Liani and Tom were sitting at a table on the back deck, huddled in conversation. I watched them for a moment from the screen door. It didn't seem romantic. Tom kept running his hand over his short hair, like he was making sure it hadn't crawled off his head. Liani was tapping a finger on the table insistently. Tom nodded and then cast his gaze over and saw me watching. I immediately moved, like I had just gotten to the door and hadn't been standing there watching them, but I don't think I fooled him.

"You see some of the town?" he asked.

"Yeah," I said. "Looked around. Got some ice cream. Bought a book."

Liani raised an eyebrow when I mentioned a book. I understood that this had to be about the people who worked at the store, not the concept of books. I'd seen Liani reading a lot—at breakfast, when no one was at the lagoon, on the porch after dinner. She pounded books.

"Then let's get the food and go," Liani said, sucking down the last sips of her iced tea.

At the counter we were handed several sheet pans covered in tin foil. I helped carry these to the boat, and soon we were on our way back, my jacket pulled tight to avoid the spray coming up and over the side of the boat as we sped along. Tom steered us past Mulligan Island as we went—I don't think intentionally. It was just another one of the 1,800 islands, but a close one, with a high edge of rock on the side facing Ralston Island, dropping to that glassy green water studded with stone.

A bad place to take a fall.

12

That night, after dinner, I went back to my room and pulled out the copy of *The Daughter of Time*. I rippled the edge of the pages with my thumb. Why had I bought this book?

Riki. I bought this book because I wanted to share some mental space with Riki.

I decided to acknowledge something, that little tickle in my abdomen. The prickling feeling on my arms. The sensation that my brain was opening itself, demanding to consume the book. Riki. Like a cat in the dark Riki. It wasn't what I felt about Akilah, that overwhelming rush. The breakup made everything more muted. I felt *something*, though. A soft buzz. Or not as dead inside.

At first I wasn't sure if the book and I would get along, because it opens with a complicated family tree of ancient royals in England. All of them are named Richard, Edward, or Elizabeth. I decided to let this slide and get into the story. It's about a detective in England named Grant who falls through a trapdoor and ends up in the hospital, unable to do anything until he recovers. I related to the stupidity of his circumstances. Trapdoor, scented candle . . . you fall down the hole or go up in flames.

The story took place in the 1950s, so there was no TV or internet. Grant is stuck in the hospital staring at the cracks in the ceiling, ignoring the pile of books people have brought him. A friend suggests that he try to solve a historical cold case, so he tries to solve the mystery of whether Richard the Third murdered his two nephews in the Tower of London.

Apparently, there were two princes in a tower, two little kids in line to the throne, and they vanished in 1483. Everyone seemed to think—maybe still seems to think, as Wikipedia told me—that their uncle, Richard the Third, murdered them because they somehow messed up his plans to become king. This is a cold, cold case. How do you figure out what may or may not have happened in 1483?

Well, in the book Grant does this by comparing historical accounts and asking over and over who is telling the story. A lot of this involves something called the Wars of the Roses, which I imagined to be people jabbing each other with flowers. Old English history appeared to be a ball of Richards, Elizabeths, and Edwards rolling around various battlefields.

I set the book down.

I had the strange feeling that I was being set up for something. I had taken the place of a dead guy, as Riki had put it. Dr. Henson had hinted at something odd, that I was supposed to be a pair of eyes in this group. Riki was clearly an outcast, and it felt like she was leaving me a trail of crumbs in her looks and pauses, her book suggestions, and her too-casual comment. Like this detective, I was sitting in my bed looking at images, taking in little pieces of some bigger story. Unlike the character in the book, I could do something about this.

Even though it was after nine o'clock, there was still a drape of bluish light hanging over the horizon. Morning House was hunkered down, the stones darkening and the windows blank. The sunrise over the doorway had been extinguished for the night as I entered the door beneath it. The massive dome above created more shadow than illumination, but it was still easy enough to make my way up the stairs.

I didn't know where Riki nested inside this massive house, but I could make a few educated guesses. I tried the door that led to the gift shop. It was locked, but it was unlikely that Riki was sleeping under the table of salad dressing bottles. She had to be somewhere up on the third or fourth floor, where there were a few locked rooms that had already been converted for new use by the owners.

As I crept from the second to the third floor, I noted the light under Dr. Henson's door, and I could hear her on the phone with someone.

". . . that's what I thought," she was saying. "I'm not sure it's possible. Not now . . . No . . . No, I'm not sure . . ."

I walked gingerly by, even though there was no rule about my being here after hours.

Just like there had been no rule about me using the cottage.

I checked all the doors on the third floor, getting down

to look at the crack for light, listening at the door. All were quiet and still. The fourth floor was the same. This left the tower at the back of the house, the one with the roped-off winding stair. She was nowhere else. She had to be up here. The steps up the tower were extremely steep, and I had to hold on to the rail to steady myself on the way up. There was a tiny landing, maybe just a foot wide, at the door at the top. I took a deep breath and knocked. I had to take a few steps back down, otherwise I would have been about an inch away from Riki when and if she opened the door, which she did. She stood above me in cutoff jeans and a massive black hoodie.

"I was wondering when you'd finally show up," she said. She left the door hanging open. I took the final steps up and went inside.

Being a turret, the room was circular. Circular rooms mess with the mind. We expect corners and angles, flat walls that hang things neatly. Also, this room was massive, and the ceiling high and domed. The area near the door was given over to cardboard boxes, a few stacks of loose shirts, plastic-covered pallets full of Thousand Island dressing, and a clothes rack with a few wind chimes and suncatchers hanging from it.

"This was one of the maids' quarters," she said as she walked past the stock. "Eight people lived here. Now, just me and these fucking wind chimes."

She flicked the nearest wind chime with her finger and it made a muted noise, as if it knew not to annoy her.

The far side of the room, near the other small round window, was her domain, and unlike ours, it was furnished with what looked like original furniture. She had a larger bed with a heavy wooden frame, covered in a purple quilt. There was a desk with a slightly crooked leg and a patterned rug that looked like it had stories to tell. A pile of books snaked up the wall. Next to this area, there were unused bed frames stacked against a wall, along with some threadbare upholstered items and three rickety wooden chairs.

"Not all the furniture was in good shape," she said. "They let me have my pick of some of the rejects. Here . . ."

She pulled over the least decrepit chair and indicated I should sit in it. The room was drafty, making the wind chimes quiver but not ring out, and causing me to shiver involuntarily.

"It's cold up here," she said. "Notice there's no fireplace. Even though this place was only used in the summer, the other rooms have fireplaces. But this is where they kept the cheap maids, the ones who had the worst jobs. No fire for them. They did get one sink, so that's nice."

She nodded toward a small sink under a window, loaded down with all her toiletries. They spilled onto the floor around it. She had big palettes of eye makeup, a scattering of brushes. The closest window was draped in overlong curtains. They were a wild mishmash of dark velvets—electric blues, deep purples—along with silky bits of what may have been old saris, and touristy dish towels.

"Did you make those?"

149

"Oh yeah," she said. "Last year, I decided I was going to get into sewing. I bought a used sewing machine off eBay and learned from some videos, but all I ever made were those curtains. I used clothes I found in a thrift shop and cut them up for material. Turns out I didn't like sewing. I just needed something to do. I like those, though."

She dropped into a furry beanbag and looked up at me. We were doing everything at weird angles—me looking up at her from the tight turret stairwell, and now me looking down from my wobbling chair as she sprawled below. "You were in the bookstore," she said. "You bought a copy of *The Daughter of Time*."

"Well, you said it was shit and I love pain, so I went for it."

This almost got me half a smile.

"I met your sister," I said.

"You did. Her name is Juhi. It means jasmine in Hindi. My full name is Rikisha, which means rose. My family is into flowers. That's why it's called the Book Garden."

"It's a nice store."

"What it is," she said, leaning back, "is a small bookshop in a tourist town that's empty over half the year—and if people read here at all, they buy stuff online. I had the idea to basically open up a branch here, inside Morning House, because this is where the tourists will be this summer. I'm here to make money, because we need to or the store will close. So I sell wind chimes."

"They say if you do what you love, you never work a day in your life."

I actually got a short laugh for that.

"Did you start the book?" she asked.

"I read a few chapters."

"What do you think of it?"

"I'm not sure," I said. "It's a lot about royal lineage and everybody is named Richard or Elizabeth."

"That's hard the first time," she said, nodding. I was glad she thought that was hard too. I wanted to sound smart about this book that I only partially understood. The truth was, I did like it, even if it was rough going and I couldn't track all the Richards and Edwards and Elizabeths. There was something under all that. I grabbed for the parts I knew.

"The thing I really liked was, he would ask everyone who came into his room to look at a copy of the portrait of Richard the Third and tell him what they saw. A doctor saw a polio patient. Another cop saw a judge. Everyone sees what they want to see in his picture. And then after that, the detective has people bring him different history books and he realizes things don't add up if you look at all the stories side by side. It's all about who tells the story. It reminds me of this place for some reason?"

"What do you mean?" she asked.

I wasn't sure what I meant. That had kind of popped out of my mouth.

"Just . . . there's no mystery here, but there's this story of two kids dying. We have pictures of them. And Dr. Henson is in charge, but she seems to hate this place? She said something about not caring if it fell down."

"She has a point."

Riki seemed to like to lead me only so far in the conversation, then watch me make my way to the next step. But I wasn't sure where this path was going. I switched to more solid ground, something I needed to say.

"Thank you," I said. "For making sure I knew about Chris."

"It was the right thing to do," she said. "I was going to explain it all myself, but I'd get so much shit for it. I figured if I brought it up, April would take care of the rest. That's sort of her job. Van might, but . . . not the others. Liani is treating it like a state secret. And who the fuck knows what Tom thinks. He'll do what Liani is doing. But you can't *hide* someone's death." She plucked at the tufts of synthetic hot-blue fuzz. The air crackled with things unsaid.

"I know there's some kind of problem," I said. "With . . . I mean, among all of you."

"Oh?" She smirked. "You noticed?"

"April said it was because . . . of Chris."

"What did she say?"

"That you were the reason Liani and Chris broke up."

"Well," she replied after a moment. "That's true. Not everyone loved him, no matter what April tells you. April is the only one who's still a true believer in Chris. April wants everyone to be happy and in love with each other. Everyone else knows the truth. Chris was an asshole. But I need this job—the store needs it—so I'm here. And I have stuff I want to do."

"Stuff?"

"Personal stuff," she said.

She leaned back into the blue fluff of the beanbag and looked at me harder than maybe anyone has ever looked at me. I felt like she could see my bones.

"Let me know what you think of the rest of the book," she said. I was being dismissed from her tower, back down to fantasyland. I hesitated for a moment, surprised by the sudden change in the conversation, then got up and left.

MARCH 1932

Max Ralston wasn't quite like his siblings.

What had worked so brilliantly with the older six children would not work with Max. He didn't climb up onto the piano stool with William's eagerness. He didn't sit on the floor for hours with a book like Victory, or pick up on languages like Unity. He didn't draw like Benjamin, or even rattle off his times tables like Edward. He couldn't swim like Clara.

And it wasn't just that he didn't excel—he was, well, difficult. The other children had never been permitted to leave their toys about, but Max's stick hobbyhorse could often be found on the lawn, or even sitting in the middle of the great hall. And his toys broke so often. The jack torn from his box. The arms pulled from the stuffed bear. The toy piano missing its keys. The heavy metal toy train that went flying between the rails of the third-floor balcony, only to scar the floor below.

Then there were the little injuries. He kicked Clara in the belly when she tried to brush his hair. When William played the piano, Max might smash the keys—or even William's fingers—with his tiny fists. He took Unity's book out of her hands and threw it in the fire. He dumped ink over Benjamin's drawings. He snuck up on Victory with a pair of scissors and snipped away a large lock of her hair. The only older sibling he tended to avoid was Edward, and that was probably because Edward once flicked him between the eyes with a spoon.

Little unpleasantnesses. Tantrums. Nothing Clara dwelled on until that day last summer, when she was floating in her secret spot under the boathouse floor. Someone came running in and plunged her hand into the cold water of one of the slips. It appeared a few feet in front of Clara's face, a strange visitor to her grotto. Another person came running in. Clara remained very still, allowing her toes to touch the slimy bottom to maintain her position under the dock.

"Mabel!" a voice cried. It was Annie, one of the maids. "What's he done to you?"

"Scalding hot tea," Mabel said through tears.

"Little monster. Little beast. Let me see your hand."

The hand was withdrawn.

"He did it on purpose," Mabel said, through tears. "I saw it in his eyes. He looked right at me and grabbed the teapot and poured it right over me."

"Beast. Evil little beast. And he's getting bigger. He's only going to get worse. It's why they can't have a pet, you know."

Max was why they couldn't have a pet? It was true that they had all come together over Christmas to make an official petition for a dog. This was denied, with apologies, because Faye was allergic. (Which seemed odd, when Clara thought back, because there were photographs of Faye from before her marriage to Father in which she was holding a small dog.) And then there was the cat Clara had saved from the boys on the street, the one they gave to their next-door neighbor. Clara had lobbied to keep him, but again there was a vague mention of allergies and a promise of an upgrade to her dancing studio. *Max* was the reason?

"He'll kill someone yet," Annie went on. "The others are all right, but God only knows how. Keep your hand under, there."

The hand was plunged back into the water, almost touching Clara's face.

"Scalding hot tea," the girl cried.

"The doctor will look at it. He'll take care of you, but don't bother trying to tell him the boy is responsible. The doctor lets it all go. High spirits, he says. High spirits is why they can't keep a nurse for longer than a month or two."

This tallied with Clara's experience. Nurses came and went. Clara and the other children never bothered to learn their names, they changed so often. That was typical of nurses, their father had explained. They specialized in certain ages, or they wanted to see somewhere new. Clara hadn't thought about it much because she didn't care. All six older siblings were away at school for much of the year, so it wasn't like she got to know any of them very well.

That would change. When they returned to New York

City at the end of that summer and the nurse did not come with them, she watched. A new nurse appeared at their Fifth Avenue mansion. Her name was Miss Danforth. She had a thick Scottish brogue, bright red cheeks, and styled her hair in a tight bun. She also appeared physically capable of pushing a trolley car off its tracks. Clara liked her at once. She watched Miss Danforth work with Max in the few days she had at the Fifth Avenue house before they were shipped off to school. Max seemed suitably cowed by her. She was still there at Christmas, her bun still tight and high on her head, still knitting calmly while watching Max play. Fewer toys broke that Christmas season. Clara was impressed.

When the six came home for a week in the springtime, Miss Danforth was gone. Clara asked her father where she was.

"Home to Scotland," he said. "Family matters. This is Miss Ellis."

Clara decided to get to the bottom of this at once. She had six days at home, so there was no time to waste. She watched the servants for the first day. No one would talk to her directly about the matter. She would have to find a way in. Her bedroom in New York faced the back of the house and their small walled garden. If she sat in her window and looked straight down, however, she could watch the back entrance where deliveries were made and staff came out to smoke and chat. It was from this perch that she noticed a boy about her age delivering groceries and other supplies several times a day. He had an easy way about him, leaning casually against the wall that separated the garden from the servants' passage, talking and sharing cigarettes with the staff. Once he looked straight up at her, gave her a lopsided smile, and lifted his cap. He had big, bright eyes with a look in them that Clara could clearly pick up from three stories above. It gave her a little sizzle of excitement, and an idea.

That afternoon, she lingered in the front parlor, keeping an eye out the window onto the street. When she saw the boy approach, she hurried out with a brown paper package under her arm.

"I need your assistance," she said to him. "Could you leave the box and help me carry this down the block?"

She held up the package, sagging as if it was heavy. (It was just her dressing gown and weighed nothing at all.) The boy looked at the package, and at the folded ten-dollar bill Clara discreetly displayed between her fingers. Up close, Clara could see his luminous, laughing brown eyes and comically heavy eyebrows. His overalls were clean but wearing through in patches, and his right shoe came away from the sole, revealing more hole than sock underneath. He smelled of sweat, but Clara did not find it unpleasant—in fact, she preferred it to the scent of cloying lily of the valley soap that clung to her.

"You're upstairs girl," he said.

"Clara. What's your name?"

"Lenny."

"Well, Lenny, can you put it down and walk with me or not?"

"For that, I will, upstairs girl."

Lenny quickly deposited the box in the recessed area

158

by one of the basement windows and relieved Clara of her feather-light package and ten dollars.

"So where are we taking this sack of rocks?"

"Just across the street."

The Ralston mansion faced Fifth Avenue and Central Park, just opposite the Arsenal and the zoo. They passed into the park and descended the stairs that led down to the zoo. Clara sat on a bench and Lenny sat next to her.

"So," he said. "If you've come to propose, know that I have other offers. But you just gave me more than I make in a week, so you're moving up the list."

"I need you to find out what happened to my little brother's last nurse," she said.

Lenny leaned back on his elbows and whistled.

"Didn't expect that. I thought you wanted cigarettes or something."

Clara would have loved a cigarette, but she would never dare while with her father. He could smell cigarette smoke at thirty paces. She only smoked at school.

"I'll take your money," he replied. "But why can't you ask someone yourself?"

"I did. They said she went home to Scotland for family reasons, but I don't believe it. And no one of the staff will tell me because I'm family. I need you to make conversation and find out whatever you can. That ten dollars is the first payment. Five more every time you can get me more information about what happened. I'll meet you here tomorrow morning after you make your first delivery. Nine o'clock. Deal?"

She took her dressing gown back from him. He tipped his cap.

"Pleasure," he said. "See you in the morning."

The next morning Lenny was leaning against the front of the Arsenal eating a doughnut. Clara eyed it hungrily.

"The nurse fell down the stairs," he said. "A bad fall. Cracked her skull. Someone found her at the bottom of the steps. Thought she was dead. The doc—your dad—got her to the hospital. Sounds like it was a close thing, you know?"

"But they didn't tell me that," she said. "Which means Max was probably involved."

"They said something about a little boy. Max. That was the name. No one saw her fall, but they all seem to think he pushed her."

Clara chewed a thoughtful cuticle while the zoo's sea lions barked in their nearby pool.

"I need you to find out everything they're saying about Max, or anything else you can find out about things they've seen and heard."

Every morning of the rest of that spring week, Clara left the house in the morning to take a walk through the park. She'd cross Fifth Avenue and take the stairs down toward the zoo. Lenny was there, sometimes a little late, but always with some new tidbit of information. In five-dollar increments, she pieced together what happened in the house when they were gone, or just out of their view.

Max, it seemed, had been treating the staff much like he

160

treated his toys. It was common knowledge that Max would openly urinate on any staff member who displeased him. One nurse had the soles of her feet sliced to ribbons when Max left broken glass in her shoes, another found pins in her bread, a third woke to find him holding a pair of scissors above her eyes. And Lenny had things to say about Clara and her five siblings.

"Everyone thinks you guys eat weird," Lenny said. They were by now on familiar terms. He even brought warm jam doughnuts, which they ate overlooking the sea lion pool enclosure. "You're not supposed to have stuff like this."

Clara nodded as she stuffed jam doughnut into her mouth.

"Mostly, everyone thinks you older ones are okay," he continued, licking powdered sugar from his fingers. "They think your sisters are nice. They seem to like you too, but I get the sense that they can't work you out. The main problem is the little kid. I hate to say this to you, but I think there's something wrong with that brother of yours."

Clara chewed her doughnut and listened to the bark of the sea lions. Lenny was right. There was something wrong with that brother of hers.

13

The first part of this story begins with the petrichor candle. The second starts with the Midnight Rose lipstick. My two cylinders of doom.

Both were associated with Akilah Jones, but she was innocent in all ways. The candle wasn't her fault, and what happened at Morning House on Ralston Island had nothing whatsoever to do with her except that I was there, and I owned a tube of Midnight Rose lipstick she had given me because she thought it would look nice on me and my weaselly thin lips. It's like when they were making me in the workshop, they were about to ship me when they realized they hadn't given me a mouth and someone said, *Just draw a straight line. We gotta send this one. Her mom is fully in the hospital with her feet in the stirrups.*

I know this is not how babies are made. Or mouths. But hopefully you understand. I like my thin lips. (I know I just called them weaselly. It's just that if I ever try to put on lipstick or anything like that, my margins for error are literally very small, and if I get it wrong there's lipstick everywhere and I become Big Marlowe Clownface.)

The lipstick had stood on the crooked dresser in my room for that first week, a tiny monument to my pain, a reminder of all that was lost and all that could have been. Every day, when I applied the scant amount of makeup I wear, I considered picking that lipstick, but I couldn't face it. But that late June morning was juicy. You know how some summer mornings are just so ripe, so full of warmth and scent and sunlight that it stirs a deep evolutionary impulse to live out loud, as the inspirational signs say? Or just say rosé?

That day, I decided, I was going to try harder to be perkier. I would do my best with my regulation cargo shorts and maroon polo shirt. My hair is about as long as April's so I tried putting it up in bunches, but it ended up looking like a lopsided pair of Mickey Mouse ears. When I took it down, I'd accidentally given it a little bump in the middle, a beachy wave. I was getting some sun on my face and a smatter of freckles over my nose. I didn't hate what I was seeing. Without thinking too hard about it, I snatched up the Midnight Rose, pulled off the cap, and *nailed it*. I flipped my wrist in the right way and there it was—the ideal Marlowe mouth. I spent five minutes trying to take a good picture, five more picking out and editing the picture, and then probably ten convincing myself it was a good idea to text Akilah, before deleting the text at the last second.

The lips were so good, I was determined not to waste them. I even skipped breakfast so I wouldn't mess them up.

I should not be trusted with good lips. They gave me *swagger*.

I walked outside, into the cheery June day, the light soft, buttery yellow with a pleasing hint of gray. Liani sat in one of the big green wooden chairs by the lagoon, dressed in her red suit, reading. I decided I should go and talk to her, make an effort to be more friendly. I came around the side, looking out over the water like I had just come to admire the view.

"What are you reading?" I asked.

"*The Fire Next Time*," she said, tapping her tablet to the next page. "James Baldwin."

That was one of those books that I knew everyone really had to read, but I never had. I would. I mentally put it on the list.

Liani, not a fool, knew I had come over to make conversation. She set her tablet down on her lap and looked at me. Why had I come? Just to talk. But about what? What could I do to reach out to her?

She was a bold and strong person, a smart person. I would be direct. I sat down on the ground by her and picked at the grass.

"I'm sorry about all the stuff you've been going through," I said.

"It's not your fault. You had nothing to do with it."

It was kind, but she was making it clear that I shouldn't insert myself into this. It was truly not about me. But she accepted the effort.

"You really can't swim?" she said.

"I can," I explained, "just not properly. I don't do laps right. But I can be in the water and I'm fine. I just kind of . . ."

I modeled my strokes, which involved tiny dinosaur paddling arms followed by windmills. Liani cracked a hint of a smile.

"But I wish I did," I said. "You swim every morning and night, right?"

She squinted and looked into the distance.

"I do," she replied. "I swim more now than I did before. It helps with the anxiety. When you get in the water, everything else goes away for a while, and it's so much work, you get out tired, clearer."

I suddenly thought, looking at her in her red swimsuit, of the red dress she had been wearing that night when she jumped into the water to pull Chris Nelson's body to the shore. No matter how you felt about your ex—jumping into a river, pulling them out, trying to revive them—that had to be brutal. Liani was traumatized, and she stayed by the water, always ready to pull someone out.

"Is it easier to be here on the island this summer?" I asked. "Away from town?"

She regarded me curiously.

"Yeah," she said. "It is. I'd rather deal with strangers in the lagoon than see everyone from town."

While it wasn't the same for me—she'd dealt with death—I understood the feeling of wanting to be around strangers, away from the town where I was the one who burned down a house. We were both hiding away on Ralston Island.

"We're going to have a massive storm," she said. "You heard?"

I'd seen the headline, but I hadn't read the articles.

"This is going to be huge," she said. "Like a hurricane."

"Are we going to leave?"

"No reason," she said, shaking her head. "This is the most solid structure for miles, and it's higher. This place is a fortress. We have water and food, plenty of batteries. It's safer to be here for a day than a lower building on shore."

The first Uncle Jim boat was puttering up to the island. I got up and wiped the grass from my legs.

"You look nice," Liani added as I went to go. "Nice lipstick."

It was the talk we had, not the lipstick, that turned things that evening. But it was the lipstick that gave me the swagger, and the swagger took me to Liani, and it was Liani who proposed the group swim that evening, after dinner.

"Get one in before the storm," Liani said. "It turns out she *can* swim. You want to come?"

She nodded to me.

Swimming sounded cold, to be honest, but I was being invited.

"Definitely," I said.

We cleaned up and I went back to my room to put on my bathing suit. It was a black two-piece, with boy shorts and a tank that I'd scored on sale at Target for about ten bucks, and I loved it. I felt like a cat burglar in it, like I should be climbing over roofs and sneaking into windows to steal the prized diamond necklace. Sometimes outfits give you *ideas*.

166

I considered reapplying the lipstick, but I wasn't going to chance it. The perfect lips that morning had been luck.

I trailed out of the playhouse with April, who I was sure was going to have a pink two-piece or something like that. She surprised me by wearing a blue one-piece that was all business. She caught me by the hook of the arm and half skipped down to the lagoon. I'll admit to a little heart flutter. Not that I liked April that way. Still, I was responding to the gesture. If a cute girl hooks your arm and wants to skip, you have to skip at least a little.

Liani and Tom were already down at the lagoon. Tom was looking at his phone while dangling his feet in the water. Liani was testing the sturdiness of one of the ladders.

"Pool noodles!" Van yelled. "We need pool noodles."

I didn't see him, but he emerged a moment later from the stone lagoon hut, arms full of noodles. He dumped them into the water, save one.

"Just put them back," Liani said. "I'm not dealing with your noodles."

"I love noodles!"

Van ran around in a circle for a moment, waving his noodle around. The pool noodle.

"We know," April said with a smile. She dropped her towel on the grass and took a running leap in, letting out a high-pitched yowl of temperature shock as she entered the water. Van went soaring in after her, in one long-legged leap. He immediately started swimming for the noodles. Tom slid in, and Liani dove into the back.

I stepped over to the shallow edge of the water. The surrounding walls of the lagoon were made of flat silver-gray stone, with some jagged, uneven edges. The water was a clear green, and I could see the silt and stone of the bottom, with its questionable black frondy things. I put in a toe and found that it was exactly as cold as I thought it would be. Didn't matter. I was going into this cold, frondy water.

I jumped, feetfirst, and had no time to scream from the icy sensation—I had been hit in the back of the head with a pool noodle.

"I fight you for control of this Queer Kingdom!" Van said. "Take up your weapon or forever be straight!"

I grabbed a nearby pool noodle and commenced battle with Van.

It was stupid. It was fun. Even with the wall, it felt like we were fully in the river. I'd been in the ocean before, but I always felt a bit guarded. This felt wild, so different that it seemed like I was being rebooted. Maybe even being restored to factory settings. Everyone was in the battle. Pool noodles everywhere. We were laughing, ridiculous tour guides playing games in the pulsing river, the wobbling line between the United States and Canada. After maybe twenty minutes or so, we all flopped on noodles and floated around in a loose circle.

"It's going to suck when they take this over," Liani said, adjusting her red swim cap. It had almost gone over her eyes.

"Who bought this place?" I asked.

"It's called something like the Liberty Pals," Van said. "Freedom Jags. Something something Freedom Liberty

Superfriend Jamboree Emporium. Big money, so oil or tech or something like that. We get the place for one summer. After that it turns into Castle SuperPacula and they'll use this place to do their keto and racism. Oh, that's a first . . ."

Something had attracted his attention. We all turned. Riki was crossing the lawn, heading for us, wearing a pair of black tank shorts and a matching rash guard top that zippered up the front.

Goth girls swim too.

Everyone else got a bit still, except for Van, who back-kicked around on his throne of noodles. Riki walked up to the stone edge of the lagoon and dropped a towel, then pulled off her shoes.

"What are you doing?" Liani asked.

"I'm going to swim," Riki said plainly.

"You've never come down to swim before."

"Well, I'm coming down to swim now," Riki answered. "Is this a private lagoon?"

Liani waved a hand, indicating that Riki should do what she liked.

The mood had frosted over. I'd liked that feeling, of being in this group of people. I wanted it back. But I was also glad that Riki was in the water with us. I wanted it all—the juicy June warmth and my lipstick and my new friends and Riki in the water with us.

It was time to open up to them.

"I guess I should explain my fire," I said.

This had the desired effect. The attention was back on

169

me. Van splashed closer. Riki took a few long strokes out, but was within earshot, I noticed.

I told them the whole story—about Akilah's yellow sweater and Guffy's and petrichor. I told them how many reviews I had read and about the thirty dollars. I explained that I'd worked for Juan and Carlita.

"I wasn't trespassing," I said. "I *was* allowed to be there."

"That doesn't sound like your fault at all," April said. "That sounds like, I don't know, a manufacturing error or something?"

"That's what the fire department said. But the house still burned down. Mostly."

"What happened with your girlfriend?" Van asked.

It was presumptuous to call Akilah my girlfriend, but I didn't correct him. I dug my nails into my palms.

"We just went back to work," I said. "We didn't talk about it. People said stuff to me about it."

"Dicks," Van said.

"And then Akilah got a job at the Cheesecake Factory. And I came here. That was it. We broke up."

Riki was pretending not to listen to all this, but barely.

"Some people would take that as a compliment," Van said. "If a guy burned a house down for me, I'd probably marry him. This is my problem."

"You really would," Liani said. "And it really is."

Dr. Henson passed by on the lawn above us, camera in hand. She looked down at us curiously, all swimming together, like we were exhibits in a museum.

170

"I respect the way she despises us," Van said. "When I get to be however old she is, I'm going to despise people like me too. It looks fun."

"She doesn't despise us," April said.

"Disagree. It must be good for her too, because look at her. All that yoga and history and resentment of the youth."

"Do you think she doesn't like you?" I asked.

"You should have seen her face the first time she came into our school to teach our seminar," Riki cut in, floating closer. "It was like she was a famous chef and someone was making her work at McDonald's."

"I thought she seemed fine," April said as she bounced gently off the bottom of the lagoon.

"Remember how we had to explain to you that Cruella de Vil wasn't a nice lady?" Riki said.

"I was seven. I thought she liked puppies."

This was as close as I'd seen to a normal interaction between any of them and Riki.

"She's coming," Tom said.

"Act natural!" Van tipped his head over his noodle throne, sticking his head into the water and his ass into the air. Dr. Henson glanced at this but didn't deign any other reaction.

"I have a research student from Yale coming tomorrow," Dr. Henson said. "When she arrives, bring her up to my room. She should be here on the first boat."

She looked over all of us again, making some mental calculation, and walked back up the lawn to the house.

Van had pulled his head out of the water and turned,

water flying from his tangle of long curls.

"Bring her to me," he said in a deep voice. "Bring me the student! Bring her to my chamber!"

"She doesn't hate us," Liani said. "She's here to write and research. She just doesn't care what we're doing."

"Well," I said, "she kind of does."

Five faces turned to me.

"I mean, when I got here the first day, she told me to kind of keep an eye on everyone and tell her if anything was weird."

"Like a spy?" Liani repeated. "She said that? Dr. Henson?"

"I thought she meant it as a joke," I said. "But I don't know. It was strange, how she said it."

"Aw," Van said. "So *that's* why she brought you here. She wanted a mole."

"No," Tom said. "She doesn't give a shit about what we do as long as we do our jobs and no one drowns. She just wants to work on her book."

Riki suddenly swam to the edge and climbed out of the water. She grabbed her shoes and towel and, not bothering to use or put on either, walked back toward the house. Liani noted my look of uncertainty as I watched Riki go. Van kicked water at April, and she laughed. Tom broke into some laps. Liani came up beside me.

"Word of advice," she said. "Be careful there."

I didn't have to be Sherlock Actual Holmes to figure out she had noticed me looking over and that "there" meant "with Riki."

July 23, 1932

Four days before the deaths at Morning House

"Something we need to discuss," Phillip Ralston said as lunch was served.

It was another perfect afternoon at Morning House, with the same platters of nut cutlets and mushy peas.

"I want you all to have a choice," he said. "The International Eugenics Conference is going to be in the city next month, on the twenty-second and twenty-third. I'll be going down for it, but I wanted to know if any of you wanted to come along. I think Alexander Graham Bell will be in attendance. It's sure to be fascinating. What do you say? Should we close up the house a bit early to go?"

"It sounds amazing," Unity said.

"I've been reading some G. K. Chesterton," Victory said. "He is against eugenics, and . . ."

Phillip waved a kind hand. "He's an otherwise decent writer, but eugenics is accepted science and plain good sense. It's up to us to ensure that the human race is healthy and strong, and we do that by good breeding. If you don't stop the unfit from breeding, what will happen?"

"But who determines the unfit? There's an argument that really what this does is target people who are poor, who aren't white, who just don't fit into an arbitrary category."

"Hardly arbitrary," Phillip replied. "But I applaud your intellectual rigor, Victory, as always. Come to the conference. Listen for yourself. I think you'll find it very stimulating. If you want to be a doctor, you'll need to understand eugenics. It is the future of health."

Victory nodded and looked down at her plate, her expression flat.

"And we'd leave here?" William said. "And be back in the city?"

"Yes. We'll return to Fifth Avenue and stay in the city until you return to school. But I don't want to cut your time here short. I know you all love it."

"I think we should go," Clara said quickly. "Back. To the city. For . . . the event."

"I'm for it," Edward added.

Only Benjamin looked a bit bereft.

"I suppose I could spend a few days at the art museum," he finally said.

"All right, then! We'll leave here on the twentieth. Which means we have to make the best use of our time here."

"Instead of swimming, I was thinking of taking the motorboat out this afternoon," Clara said.

"Boat!" Max shouted. He'd been left out of the eugenics conversation and was playing with his piece of bread, but he'd heard something that interested him.

"You want to go on the boat?" Phillip said. "With your sister?"

"With Victory."

Victory looked up.

"How about it, Victory?" Phillip said. "You, Clara, and Unity, as well. The three girls on the boat."

Faye looked up, brow furrowed. "Phillip, are you sure . . ."

"It's a good idea," Phillip cut in. "A very good idea. He'll be perfectly safe with the girls. That would leave us men with four for tennis. Edward, William, Benjamin. Tennis for us, boating for the girls. Two o'clock. And for your afternoon studies, Victory, I have an excellent book I want you to read. A new guide to eugenics. I'll get it from my office when we're finished eating."

And so the plan was made.

After lunch and their early afternoon work, the groups separated. The cook prepared a basket for the girls to take with them on the trip. The sky big and blue and bright, with a few puffs of solid white cloud for contrast. Clara took the wheel and sped down the St. Lawrence, past their fellow islanders on their porches or in their boats. They reached a beautiful bit of glassy green water near a rocky shoal.

"Need to take a quick swim," Clara said, stripping off her shirt and revealing her swimsuit underneath. "Back in a second."

"Taking a delivery?" Victory asked.

"There's good fishing here," Clara said with a smile. "Break out the snacks."

She dove off the boat and cut through the water with long, powerful strokes. Within a few minutes, she climbed back on board with a wide grin and something bottle-shaped clearly stashed down the front of her suit.

"Strange fish," Unity said.

"A delicacy," Clara responded with a smile. "What did Elisa send for us today?"

Victory had unpacked their basket on a blanket. Today, along with sugarless graham biscuits, apples, and mint leaf tea, she had sneakily provided sweet lemonade, shortbreads, and blueberry cake. Clara helped herself to the latter, while Unity carefully poured herself a cup of the tea from the flask and took a biscuit.

"You should really try this," Clara said to her, holding out the cake.

"No thanks. That stuff is poison. It's got sugar in it."

"If sugar is so dangerous then how is everyone else alive?"

"There are steps between good health and actually being dead," Unity said primly. She looked to Victory for backup, but she was reaching for a slice of the cake as well.

"It's really good cake," Victory said, shrugging.

"I want cake," Max said.

"You're not supposed to have cake, Max," Unity said. "None of us are supposed to have cake."

"I want it."

Unity looked at her two sisters as if to say, *See what you've done?*

"I'll tell you had cake! I'll tell you had cake!" Max was now jumping up and down, causing the boat to tack back and forth. "I'll tell Daddy, I'll tell Daddy . . . give me cake . . ."

"Max, stop jumping," Victory said, reaching for his waist to hold him still. Max wriggled out of her grasp and climbed up on the side of the boat.

With no warning, Clara reached out and knocked him into the water.

Victory screamed, but Clara held out an arm to keep her from moving. Unity watched, her expression frozen. From the water, Max let out a godawful yelp and flailed.

"Swim, Max!" Clara called. "Swim! Like we showed you. Kick. Kick your legs."

"Clara," Victory screamed. "What are you doing?"

"*Kick*, Max!"

Without waiting another second, Victory swung herself to the edge of the boat and dropped into the water. Max had drifted a few feet away and was still above the surface but was wailing and starting to sink. Victory scooped him under her arm and guided him to the boat.

"Grab him!" she yelled.

Both Unity and Clara lifted the inconsolable Max into the boat. Victory went to the back, where it was easier to pull herself on board. Clara wrapped a blanket they'd brought with them around his shoulders and tried to soothe him, but he cowered on the floor of the boat and coughed. Victory was a tower of rage. After climbing onto the boat, she went up to

Clara, swung her hand back, and brought it down hard on Clara's face.

Clara recoiled from the blow but seemed to take no offense.

"He has to learn how to swim," she said plainly.

"Are you *out of your mind*?"

"I wasn't going to let him drown," Clara said. "There's no current here."

"He can't swim," Victory snapped back as she bent down over Max. "And the water here has to be thirty feet deep."

"I was going to get him out, Vic. I was trying to teach him."

"Unity?" Victory said. "Are you hearing this?"

It wasn't clear if Unity was hearing this. Her expression was distant, like she had detached from the scene and floated into the sky like a balloon.

"I think she's right," she said after a moment. "We were all passable swimmers by four."

"By four I could do laps of the lagoon," Clara added.

"*Who cares?*"

"He's all right," Clara said, bending down and examining Max. Max gazed at her with wide, terrified eyes. She smoothed his hair back from his forehead. "You're all right, Max. I learned by jumping off boats. And I always watch out for you. You're safe with me."

She cupped her hand under his chin and looked him in the eye.

"You can trust me, Max," she said. "I'll always come and get you."

Rage had rendered Victory unable to speak. She took control of the boat and steered it back toward Ralston Island. No one said a word. Max huddled in his blanket, tucked into Unity's arms. Clara turned her sunburned face to the sky.

Victory steered *Silver Arrow* to the dock and stormed off, leaving someone else to tie her up. Unity was holding Max, who had gone completely silent.

"I'll take him in," she said.

Clara tied up the boat. As she walked back toward the house, she found Victory sitting in one of the little scenic spots along the path, the swan fountain, waiting for her. She took the seat next to her furious sister.

"He *has* to learn," she said in a low voice, after a moment's silence.

"Not by throwing him off a boat."

"Then how? He's the golden boy, Victory, but he can't swim like we could at his age. He can't read like we could. He doesn't know much German or French like Unity. He's not dancing like me, or doing times tables like Edward, or playing the piano like William, or learning all the names of bones like you did."

"Because he's *four*," Victory hissed.

"And he's *difficult*," Clara replied. "He's not learning because he's a brat and he doesn't want to learn his lessons. But he's *got to learn to swim*."

Victory held her sister's gaze for a long moment. She was about to speak, but then noticed that someone was walking toward them from the direction of the house. Aunt Dagmar was moving in their direction, taking long, determined strides. There was something chilling about seeing Aunt Dagmar move with such focus. She wore a navy-blue day dress with a wide red belt, giving her an almost military air. The sharp angles of her face, her silver-streaked chestnut-brown hair with its center part, riveted back from her face in well-policed waves—she herself was like the hull of a ship, breaking through the water.

"You threw Max off the side of the motorboat," she said. It was not a question.

"I wasn't going to let anything happen to him," Clara said. "I was trying to get him to swim. You know I would have pulled him out."

"You threw Max off the boat," she said again.

Aunt Dagmar looked to Victory. To Victory's credit, she didn't throw her sister to the wolves. She looked away, at the black swans nearby, at the pink roses, at the gardeners making sure the lines in the lawn were perfectly even.

"I was watching him," Clara said. "Aunt Dagmar, I swear . . ."

Aunt Dagmar carried authority—a correction from her carried as much weight as any from their father. She could issue a week's prohibition from the playhouse, or a thousand lines of Latin. Unlike their father, whose behavior could be easily predicted, it was hard to know what Aunt Dagmar was going to say.

"Do not throw him off boats," she finally replied. "Stay in the shallows. Be more careful, Clara. Both of you. Be more *careful*."

14

It happened the next morning.

The juiciness of the previous day was replaced with a relentless sweatiness. The air felt like a sour kitchen sponge, the kind that's been sitting by the sink for a week and never really dried. The river air, which normally smelled fresh, had a tang to it that spoke of blooming biomes. A swampy, farty smell. Everywhere there was talk of the storm that was coming within a few days—one of those once-in-a-hundred-years kinds of storms that seem to happen every year.

The first tour group came ambling up the path toward us, phones up, recording the first sight of Morning House.

"Showtime!" Van said to me, giving a little jazz hands. "Welcome to Morning House! Come up this way. I'm Van, that's my actual name . . ."

The group followed him in clusters—the eager ones who were going to win the tour, the ones with children came next, and last were the people who were already narrating their videos. One person held back at the end. She wasn't dressed like a tourist. She had on a deep-blue shirtdress, a voluminous one

182

that I would have loved to wear, except unlike her I would look like a demented toddler in it. She had the air of a casual professional, with a leather tote on her arm. She approached me.

"I'm here to meet Dr. Henson," she said. "I'm Makoto, the PhD student from Yale who's meeting her today."

"Sure," I said, unclipping my walkie-talkie from my cargo shorts. "I'll let her know."

I held it up to my mouth, tilting it just slightly sideways in a way I thought it might be done in an action movie, and called Dr. Henson.

I got nothing back.

By this point, I looked less like an action hero and more like that meme from *Die Hard* of the idiot who grabs the walkie-talkie and acts like he knows what he's doing and immediately gets killed.

"She knows I'm coming," she said. "Makoto Shimada. She said to take the first boat at Uncle Jim's River Cruises? She's going to show me some architectural drawings from the Morning House archive and walk me around? She's expecting me?"

I knew that tone—the one where you feel guilty for having to ask, but also annoyed for having to ask because you haven't done anything wrong, so everything is a question.

"I'll get her," I assured Makoto. I moved away a few steps to try again.

"Does *anyone* know where Dr. Henson is?" I asked into the walkie.

No reply at first, and then Liani said that she didn't know, then April, then Tom. Van sang a little bit of a song.

"I'll find her. I think she's just doing something." Like that meant anything. Everyone is doing something.

Van was taking his group up the main stairs, so I headed to the servants' staircase in the back and ran up to Dr. Henson's room. There was no answer to my knocking. I shuffled from foot to foot. The decision to open someone's door is a heavy one if it's someone you don't know that well, who is your boss. I tried the knob and found it was unlocked. I opened it a crack, called in, heard nothing. I inched it wider until I found myself in a large, sunny room. Whatever color it had been originally, it was now painted clean white, which made it feel enormous. There was a grand sleigh bed covered in a distinctly nonperiod bedspread patterned in sea-green swirls.

She was not in the room. There were two doors with large windows in them, each dressed in a light lace curtain. These opened onto a small private stone balcony. This was empty, as was the bathroom, which had two small windows that let in a creamy, soft light that would have brought any self-respecting influencer to their knees. As I came out, I identified a key problem—her walkie-talkie was charging on her desk. Her laptop was closed, with a pile of photocopied pages sitting next to it. There was a phone charger, but no phone. I texted her. I should have done that at the start. I saw the message was delivered, but nothing indicated it being read.

"Shit," I said out loud.

I left the room and went up to the third-floor hall,

checking every room. I continued up to the fourth floor, to the top balcony. I looked out over the wide view of the river and the sky, all the islands around us. No Dr. Henson. We'd had some passing rain that morning, I guess, because there was a dry rectangle where her yoga mat must have been.

A clue, at least. Not a tremendously helpful one.

By this point, I was due to take a tour. I called down to April to explain what was happening—that they should hold the tours and do one every thirty minutes instead of twenty until I found where Dr. Henson was hiding.

I went down to the gift shop, where Riki was ringing up a sweatshirt and a bottle of dressing.

"I can't find Dr. Henson," I said. "And there's somebody from Yale waiting for her."

Riki looked at me, reading my face to find out why I thought this was her problem.

"I've looked for her everywhere," I said. "The whole house."

"Did you look *outside*?"

"I've asked Liani and Tom."

Riki shrugged. "It's a mystery, I guess."

This was not a problem for the gift shop.

I wove through every room in the house again, including the basement. I even looked in the pool. I had worked up a sweat by this point. I found Makoto and updated her.

"I have to go back to New Haven tonight," she said. She sounded sad, not angry.

"I'll find her," I said with more confidence than I

possessed. This was rapidly devolving into one of those customer service moments where the situation has escaped your control but it's your job to catch the flak. I decided I would not fail Makoto. I went everywhere—up and down the dock, checked with the ticket takers, the refreshment stand employees, the people who worked the boats. No one had seen her.

By this point, April was bouncing along in her Morning House fleece like a happy maroon bunny, bringing the next group inside.

"What's wrong?" she said. "You still can't find her?"

I shook my head.

"Did she go out on the Jet Ski to town?"

The Jet Ski.

I ran down the lawn toward the lagoon and the docks beyond. Liani saw me coming and frowned in concern.

"Do you know if she took the Jet Ski out? Or the boat or something?"

Liani unclipped her walkie-talkie from her pocket. (Unlike me, she looked amazing doing that. I made a mental note to study her technique.)

"Tom," she said, "are the Jet Ski and the boat here?"

After a moment's pause, he replied that they were.

"She can't be off island, then," she said. "Unless someone picked her up on a boat. But she wouldn't just leave if she had an appointment. She's not like that. Or she'd tell us."

Her eyes went wide, and she turned on her heel and went to the stone shed at the edge of the lagoon. She opened it up and vanished inside for a moment. When she emerged, the look on her face caused my insides to twist.

"The paddleboard," she said. "When I went in here earlier I noticed it was gone, but I didn't think about it. I thought Tom had it or something."

"Whose is it?"

"It's no one's. It's just part of the swimming supplies. I've never seen her use it, but it's gone. . . ."

Liani stepped back inside, into the dark coolness of the lagoon shed, and I followed. It was a tiny space with no nooks to hide in. There were floats, noodles, a first aid kit, all of that. No paddleboard.

"And the oar is gone," she added. "Maybe she paddled to town? But the current here is too strong, and this is a shipping lane. I wouldn't paddle here. No one does. The board is for the lagoon."

Then I saw it happen—I watched Liani transform from Liani, a person who worked here with me and did basically the same job, to Liani, a first responder. She seemed to grow taller, like someone had inserted an extra vertebra into her spine. In one motion, she pulled off her Morning House shirt as she moved to the water. She took only a moment to unclip her walkie and pull off her shorts, so she was down to the one-piece red swimsuit. She jumped into the lagoon, feetfirst, causing the swans on the far side to flap in protest and make their way out. Tom saw this and ran his stiff, meaty run in our direction, removing his Morning House shirt as he moved.

I watched them make efficient sweeps of the lagoon,

weaving their way back and forth to the edges, occasionally stopping to look up and around and signal that they'd seen nothing so far. When they reached the sides and had found nothing, they decided to do it again, this time swimming side by side to make sure nothing had been missed.

"She's not in there," Liani said, pulling herself out of the water and catching her breath. "She's not . . ."

Liani sat down on the ground and stretched her legs in front of her, bending toward her knees and gripping them hard. She took long, sucking breaths.

"She's not in there," Liani said, breathless and hoarse. "It's okay. She's not in there . . ."

She didn't cry, but her breath was jagged and she kept nodding, as if trying to convince herself that all was well. Tom climbed out and sat next to her on the ground and rubbed her leg.

"It's okay," he said.

"I know, I know . . ."

But this left us with a problem. Dr. Henson was missing.

15

The jump from someone who can't be found to someone who is missing is long and short at the same time, because nothing has changed except your perception of the distance.

April finished her tour and joined us. We sat, the four of us, trying to make sense of what kind of a situation we had here. Liani seemed calmer now that she knew Dr. Henson wasn't at the bottom of the lagoon. The problem was, she also wasn't on its surface. Or in any room or building I looked in. Her texts went unread and calls went to voice mail.

"What should we do?" Tom asked. "She could have just gone off on the board. She could have gone to town."

"She told me she doesn't like going out in the open water," Liani said. "But she's gone, and the board is gone. And the longer we wait . . ."

Liani stood with her hands on her hips, staring at the grass below her feet. I looked out at the St. Lawrence. It was so wide and strong. So much water, dotted with boats and Jet Skis and islands.

"Wouldn't someone have seen her?" I asked.

"Maybe," Tom said. "There's no way of knowing."

April now had a frightened, quivering bunny energy as she played with the zipper of her fleece.

"We should check the house again," she said. "She has to be in there somewhere. You probably just missed her. We'll all look at the same time. Should we put a hold on tours?"

Holding the tours meant something was wrong. We looked at each other. Was something wrong? The level of wrong that we needed to put a halt to a day's worth of admissions?

"I can look again with Riki," I said. "That's two of us. You and Van can do the tours."

"I'm going to close the lagoon for swimming," Liani said, "and I'll take the Jet Ski and have a look around the island and out on the water. We meet back here in an hour. If we haven't found her, we call the police."

Makoto was still sitting in the window seat. She had stretched out a bit with her laptop. I ran around to another entrance to avoid her and went upstairs using the back staircase, taking the stone steps two at a time.

"What is going on?" Van said. "And who is that person who's been sitting in the hall all morning? Every time I walk past she looks like she wants to jump on my back."

"That's the grad student from Yale who's here to see Dr. Henson."

"You still can't find her? Maybe she went to town?"

"And missed her appointment?"

Van cocked his hip against the wall and chewed pensively at the antenna of his walkie-talkie.

"That doesn't sound like our Belinda," he said. "Not that I know her that well, but she doesn't seem like someone who misses appointments with people from Yale."

He didn't sound convinced.

"I'm going to search the house one more time," I said. "But keep an eye out?"

I returned to the gift shop, where Riki was reading at the counter.

"What's wrong with you?" she asked as I rushed in.

"Dr. Henson is missing," I said. "*Missing*-missing. Liani and Tom even swam the lagoon looking for her, and the paddleboard is gone. Liani's out there now, checking the waters around the island. We may have to call the cops. So we need to do one last serious look around the house. I need your help."

"Okay," she said, calling to two women who were noodling by the wind chimes. "Store's closed."

We started in the basement, going through every bathroom and shower stall. We looked in all the rooms with mechanical equipment, the storage rooms.

"You said the paddleboard is gone?" Riki asked, peering into the pool. "I don't think she took the board. This isn't the part of the river for that. We're right on the channel."

"Maybe she doesn't know that?"

"She's from here. She knows that."

April came down the steps and joined us, shyly coming into the conversation.

"Nothing?" she asked.

I shook my head.

"Maybe we check the boathouse again? She has to be somewhere."

I hadn't gone in the boathouse very often, not since Tom had shown me the Jet Ski. The boats it had been built to house were in the local boat museum. It was like a massive shed with a floor made of wood and water. The Jet Ski was still gone, so Liani wasn't back yet. April walked up and down the docks of the three slips, then she got down on her stomach and craned her neck to peer underneath.

"I doubt she's under the dock," Riki said, leaning against the post.

"But we should check under," April said. "Properly."

"I'm not getting in there. It's dark and weird under the building. There's all kinds of crap down there."

"I'll do it." April yanked off her shorts, fleece, and her polo shirt, so she was down to a sports bra. I turned demurely, but April wore very practical underwear—pink hip-huggers and a white sports bra, so it was basically a bathing suit. (Don't get me wrong—I have no objection to cute girls in their underwear, but there is a time and a place, and April was doing it for safety reasons. I follow a gentlewomanly code.) She jumped into the water feet-first, bobbing, then dipping under the surface and slipping beneath the dock.

"She's not under the dock," Riki said.

I agreed this was probably true, but . . . where the hell *was* she?

"So she never does this, right? Just go to town without saying?"

"I have no idea." Riki examined her black nail polish on her right hand, feeling out the middle nail for a possible chip. "Maybe someone came and picked her up and she forgot her appointment."

The shade of the boathouse suited Riki, the way the light slanted through the openings of the slips, partially honeycombed by the netting that kept other boats out. The deep-blue streak in her hair was more pronounced, a bolt through the smooth black. And the way she cut it—so blunt, to her shoulders, sharp bangs, ever so slightly pointed at the center of her forehead, marking an arrow down past her nose, to her lips. She wore dark-blue lipstick that had worn off a bit. She reminded me of the hydrangeas that surrounded the house—at twilight, their purples and blues turned the color of electric smoke.

She looked up. I had been staring too long, and I almost turned away, but she was staring straight back at me, a smile slowly twisting on those blue lips. So I admit I didn't notice the banging from under my feet for a moment.

"Shit," Riki said. She unzipped her hoodie and dropped it, then hit the water headfirst. April bobbed up to the surface, heaving and shuddering, gagging up water.

"I'm okay, I'm okay . . ." she said in a not-okay voice.

The whole thing happened so fast that the shot of adrenaline hit me a moment late, and I had to recover my senses. Riki went to April and nudged her over to the ladder on the side, then supported her as she climbed up. April had a long slice down her right thigh and arm, running watery blood down her body. I reached for her wet hands and helped get her onto the dock, Riki coming up behind, her T-shirt and shorts sopping wet, her hair cemented down to her head.

"I told you," Riki said, stepping onto the dock.

April shivered and looked down at her arm and leg.

"I know, I know . . . I had to ch-ch-check. She's not . . . I got my foot stuck in the net-t-ting."

Riki stomped over to the first aid kit on the wall and returned, opening it on the floor, dabbing the long scrape with gauze.

"It's not too deep," she said. "Here."

She passed an antiseptic wipe so that April could clean the blood from her arm. April was bandaging her leg as Liani steered the Jet Ski into the open slip and cut the engine.

"What happened?" she asked. "Are you okay?"

"She looked under the dock," Riki said.

Liani came over to have a look at April, who was now

putting on her fleece in an embarrassed fashion, hugging her arms into her body.

"I'm fine," she said. "I got my foot caught. I . . ."

She reached for her neck.

"My necklace."

She looked back at the water, seemingly considering another dive to find her missing necklace, but Riki cut that off.

"Don't," she said. "Are you kidding?"

"My grandma gave me that."

"Fuck's sake, April, you just got stuck under there."

"Did you see her?" I asked Liani.

Liani shook her head grimly.

"You didn't either?"

"No."

"Then it's time to call the cops," she said, pulling out her phone.

Again, I know this wasn't the time or the place, but I had to note that seeing Riki jump in like that had been absolutely hot as hell, and I would dwell on it for a long time.

The police boat came in from town about fifteen minutes later carrying two officers. They pulled up on the main dock, where the tourist boats came in. I guess someone had made the call to pull the tours, because the Uncle Jim boat turned before it reached us, leaving us to talk to the cops.

"So what's going on here, Liani?" one of the officers asked.

"You can't find Belinda Henson?"

There was a familiarity there. Of course—they all must have known each other, small town, and Chris's death only months before.

"When was the last time you saw her?" the officer asked.

"Last night?" Tom said. "When we were swimming. We were all in the water and she came down to tell us she had a grad student coming today."

"What time was this?"

"It was right before eight, I think?" April said.

"It was," Riki said. "I came back in around eight and I saw her downstairs."

"So you all saw her around eight last night. After that?"

General shaking of heads.

"And what about this morning?"

"I know she was doing yoga," I said. "Someone came to meet with her, so I looked around the house. I went up to the top balcony . . ." I indicated the high balcony. ". . . where she does yoga every morning. I saw a spot where her mat had been. It must have rained. There was a clear mark that her mat had been there."

"But you didn't see her."

"No," I said.

"What time was this?"

"Right after the first boat came. Ten?"

"So the final time you all actually saw her was last night. How did she seem?"

I didn't know Dr. Henson well enough to know how she

seemed. She seemed like a person walking by with a phone.

"Normal," Tom said. "Busy."

"Our paddleboard is gone from the shed," Liani cut in.

"What does it look like?"

"It's purple," Liani said. "Blue and purple. It has a wave pattern on it."

"And there's nowhere else it's stored?"

"It's been in there every time I've been in there," Liani said. "And I go in there at some point every day."

"All right," the officer said. "Take me up to her room."

Her gaze landed on me, so it seemed like I would be guiding this tour.

The sun was lower in the sky than when I had been in Dr. Henson's room that morning. It cut sharply through the windows, slashing the green bedspread and ricocheting off the mirror.

The officer made a note of all the things I had also noticed: the walkie-talkie on the charger, the phone being gone. But her search was more intrusive than mine. She opened drawers and shuffled through the contents. She went into the closet, had a look under the bed.

"Here's something," she said as she looked in the bedside drawer. "Her keys. She didn't take these with her."

She considered the bed for a long moment, then the desk.

"You didn't find anything in here this morning?" she said. "No messages? No notes?"

It took me a moment to realize what this question implied.

Within a half hour, a search boat with two divers was at the edge of the lagoon in the open part of the water. A glass-bottom-boat operator was recruited to circle the island. Out of a desire to do something useful, we cooked up a few days' worth of our food trays and brought them outside to feed the police officers and various other people who had come to assist in some way. We milled around as the police went through the house again. They walked from floor to floor, as we had, but came up with nothing. They were out on the lawn standing around when there was a sudden burst of activity.

"Something's up," Van said as the police moved down the lawn away from us and conferred. They talked together, looked up at us, talked again.

"That doesn't look good," Liani added.

The police officer I'd taken to Dr. Henson's room strode back up the lawn toward us, her face grave.

"What's going on?" Tom asked. He had that professional tone in his voice, the one that sounded like this whole weird event would mess up his reelection campaign.

"A boater found a paddleboard floating near Mulligan Island. They thought it must have fallen off another boat, but just in case, they turned it in this afternoon. Does the one here look like this?"

She held up her phone, which displayed a picture of a purple paddleboard with a wave pattern.

"That's it," Liani said. "Or one just like it."

198

It was in hearing those words that it dawned on me—and maybe some of the others, because I saw everyone exchange a look. Somewhere, in that expanse of dark water, was Dr. Henson, and sometimes people don't come back from that dark water.

16

Until Dr. Henson vanished, I hadn't taken much of an interest in my employer. She was the woman in the house, the professor, the one writing a book. A little supercilious, not terribly interested in teenagers.

A search told me she was born and raised in Clement Bay. Attended Syracuse, got her master's from Boston College, her PhD from Columbia University. She taught at Vassar, then Boston College, then Syracuse. She wrote papers and articles about the fascist movement, the Works Progress Administration, and a lot about the Nazi party in America—Nazi summer camps, Nazi rallies in New York, at Madison Square Garden . . .

She'd chosen to come back here, to the place where she was from, to help manage a house built by someone she clearly didn't like. Because of the yoga mat, I was the only person who could establish when she was still alive.

Eventually, my brain spun out from going down rabbit holes about terrible things. I don't remember falling asleep. I was only aware that my arm was being shaken.

"Hey . . ."

I peeled my eyes open and found that Riki was squatting next to my bed.

"Marlowe, wake up," she whispered. "I need you to do something with me."

I blinked. I was still holding my phone. Riki was tousled, her hair perfectly unruly, her cropped faded black T-shirt hanging just so over her midriff. She grabbed my cargo shorts from the chair where I'd left them and tossed them to me.

"Get dressed," she whispered.

"What time is it?" I asked, dragging the shorts under the blanket and pulling them on.

She flashed her phone in reply. It was 3:57 in the morning.

"What are we . . ."

She put her finger to her lips and signaled that I should follow her. This was when I noticed she was holding a bucket.

We crept out of the playhouse, me on actual tiptoe, like I was in a cartoon. I've never done much sneaking in my life. We were out on the lawn, under the velvet dark of the night sky, the grass slick with dew and the river softly hissing around us. She went straight up the front steps of Morning House, which was stern and dark and clearly didn't approve of what we were doing. She paused on the stone front porch to finally speak to me.

"I need your help with something," she said.

"Sure," I said. "What? Whatever . . . what?"

201

"Dr. Henson has a lot of research materials in her room. She's done work on the Ralstons for years for her book. And look . . . if she's missing and her board is floating out there on the river, that doesn't seem good. I think . . . I think she's not okay. If something happened to her, they'll probably take her stuff off the island—like, just box it up and send it away. We need to *preserve* what she did."

"What?"

Riki sighed in frustration, but softly.

"I know how much work she's put into getting all her research materials. Years and years of searching and talking to people and digging through archives, and if something has happened—what if that all ends up in some police evidence room? Or in some closet somewhere? It's not right. So we need to go and record it, for safekeeping. And I need your help. The others . . . we have issues. But I thought you would help me."

Did I mention that her hair was tousled just so? And her eyes—luminous, big and brown. She *needed* me. The girl with the big brown eyes and the spooky shit socks *needed* me.

Also, it was 3:57 in the morning. I wouldn't call that prime decision-making time.

"What . . . ," I added as coyly as I could muster with my groggy voice, "is the bucket for?"

We went in through the front door, Riki opening it. The house was a dark, sleeping beast. She was more familiar with walking around it during the night, so I followed. As we went

202

past, the Ralstons seemed to peer out at us judgmentally from their frames in the display case.

"Where are the cops?" I asked.

"They're staying on their boat for the night. No one's in the house but me."

I had the feeling that we couldn't be somewhere that big without *something* else being alive in there. Whatever was in Riki's bucket clanked around as we went up the steps.

"So you need my help—with what?"

"They locked the door," she said. "I need your help to get in."

"That seems . . . illegal?"

"What's illegal about it? Going into one of the bedrooms of the building we work in and you give tours of and I run a shop out of is not illegal. And I'm not going to take the stuff. I'm just going to take pictures so that it isn't lost."

She sounded so sure that I decided I believed her. It was probably illegal, though. Maybe? But probably in the way that you could argue that we didn't know was illegal, because I definitely didn't know. Did you have to know that something was illegal to get in trouble?

Look, I'll admit it. I wanted to be convinced.

"No one is going to know," she said. "Or care. They care if she's okay or not. They don't care if I see her notes about menus served here in 1932."

"So we're just going to go in, take pictures of research, and leave?"

"That's it."

That sounded all right.

"How are we going to get in if the door is locked? Do you have a key to her room?"

"There's another way in."

We went past Dr. Henson's room, up to the floor above. We stopped in an empty room that seemed to be above Dr. Henson's.

"Where's the passage?"

I looked around at the walls, trying to work out which panel we would push to reveal a staircase that went down to that room. I resented that no one had shown this to me yet.

"What passage?"

"You said there's another way in."

"There is," she said.

She pointed out the window to Dr. Henson's balcony, which was beneath us. Except Dr. Henson's balcony wasn't *directly* underneath—it was a few feet over to the left. But between us at this window and that balcony was a solid five feet of empty space and a long drop.

"But how do we get from here to there?"

"We do this . . ." She held up an emergency fire ladder. "This is the one from my room," she said. "No one will miss it."

Unfolding it, she tied the last rung of the rope ladder to the handle of the bucket, which, along with the ladder, had rocks in it.

"I'll swing this over to that balcony," she said, "and climb over."

"Yeah, I don't think that's going to work. That's not enough weight."

"It doesn't have to be enough weight, just some weight. It's not that far."

Riki unfurled the top of the ladder, grabbing the loose straps to secure them. The windows had been outfitted with firm handle grips for this purpose. She looped them through and tied them four times, then tugged and tested them. She leaned out the window and swung the bucket to Dr. Henson's balcony. The sound was about as loud as a shelf full of pots and pans landing on a pile of cymbals, and I reflexively ducked to the ground and put my hands over my head in surrender.

"It's fine," Riki said. "Marlowe, it's fine."

I tried to release the breath I was holding, but that wasn't happening anytime soon, because Riki was tossing the ladder slack over to the balcony and giving it a shake in preparation for climbing.

"What if the balcony door is locked?" I asked.

"Why would it be? Who's going to get in? It's not like anyone would use a rope ladder and swing down from the balcony above to try to get in."

She said this as she was backing out the window, hands firmly clawing the ladder. As expected, her weight caused the slack of the ladder to slip over the edge, and the ladder instantly flipped. She had wrapped her arms and legs around it, winding herself in it, so she was upside down but still secure enough. Somehow she skittered down a rung, then another, getting to the point where her knees were by the rail. She used the rail to pull herself closer, then with a final, nauseating lurch, dropped herself onto the balcony.

"See?" she said, pretending she was not freaked out at all.

"I'm not doing that," I said.

"Of course you aren't. I'll unlock the door."

I fought back nausea and ran down the steps, where Riki was waiting for me, door wide. She was wearing, I noticed, a pair of vinyl cleaning gloves and extending a pair in my direction.

"Gloves?" I said.

"There are boxes of them all over the place."

"But why are you wearing them? This isn't illegal, right?"

"It doesn't hurt to wear them," she said.

This didn't fill me with confidence, but she wasn't wrong. I put on the gloves.

Riki pulled the heavier curtain over the balcony doors and switched on the overhead light. I was in Dr. Henson's room for the third time in a day.

"So we're preserving her work," I said. "Which means . . ."

"I'll do the documents on the desk. Have a look around to see if she has more research stuff anywhere."

"What does research stuff look like?"

"Documents. Boxes. Folders. *Research*."

She shook her head, then turned to the desk and began sifting through the papers there. I spun in place, trying to see if there was anything that screamed of being research material. She had loads of books. I took a picture of those, in case that mattered, or maybe just to do something.

"I don't see anything . . ."

"Check the wardrobe," she said, looking over her shoulder.

Now I felt like I was doing something wrong. I couldn't have explained what. I wasn't trying to take anything from Dr. Henson, or damage anything. I was here to help, really. But then again, I had bad luck being in other people's places. I balled my hands into fists, then opened the wardrobe.

I found what I would expect to find in there—half a Chico's, a fancy tartan wool wrap, shelves full of neatly folded yoga clothes, two more pairs of Hokas, rain boots, a box full of wires and chargers, and a rolled yoga mat. No boxes marked RESEARCH!

I was about to close the door when I had a second look. That was the yoga mat she had shown me, the one she kept upstairs. Why was it here? Maybe she had two. She seemed like the kind of person who did enough yoga to warrant two yoga mats.

Over by the desk, Riki was snapping pictures.

"Help me with this?" she said. "There's this whole pile to do."

She handed me a stack of photocopied documents. They were all clearly old. Some looked legal. There were some handwritten ones that I could barely make out. I took pictures of them all.

"Okay," Riki said as she finished her pile. She leaned over and examined the laptop. "Almost done with this too."

"With what?"

"Her hard drive. That's where most of her stuff is."

"You copied her hard drive?"

"I uploaded it," she said. "Because I'm trying to make sure we protect all of it."

"And what are we doing this for again?" I asked. It's important to ask these questions well, well after you've broken into the place and have filled your phone with evidence that you were there.

"I don't know. The university? Or the museum in town? Her family?"

"Wouldn't her family get this anyway?"

Seriously, I had not taken the time to go through this logically. Four in the morning. That's when you should ask me to do stuff, especially if you are a goth girl with remnants of smudged eyeliner. Apparently, I'll follow you right to hell.

"Like I said," Riki replied, barely hiding her annoyance, "in case the cops sit on it or lose it."

It was hard to imagine Dr. Henson's stuff getting lost in the vast evidence lockers of Clement Bay, New York, home of fudge and Jet Skis. But I was here, and again, *this was not illegal*. I was a staff member. Maybe this was my duty.

I would go with that.

"Okay," Riki said, closing the laptop. "Time to leave."

She went out on the balcony and got the bucket. Then she turned out the light and walked with me toward the door. I went out into the hallway, but she remained inside. She handed me the bucket.

"What are you doing?" I asked.

208

"Meet me on the balcony under this one. Bring the ladder that's in the closet next to the living room."

"Wait, what?"

"I have to lock this door behind you. They'll notice if it's open."

"Are you taking that ladder from upstairs?"

"No," she said.

"Then . . ."

She indicated I should come back inside so she could show me the thing she had planned on not letting me see. She had untied the bucket from the rope ladder and tossed the ladder over the side of the balcony. It still hung free from the upstairs window.

I didn't see how this was a solution.

Riki looked around for a moment, finally getting on the floor and looking under the bed. She emerged with another rope ladder box. She tied the loose ends of the new ladder to two of the stone pillars of the balcony.

"*We're not doing anything illegal,*" I reminded her. "We can use the door."

"It'll be fine. This isn't that far off the ground. The ladder will reach."

Riki shuffled me in the direction of the door, and then out of it. I heard the snick of the lock.

I was alone in the vastness of the house. For the first time since I'd been here, I felt the presence of the Ralstons. They were somewhere in this air, in the squeak of the floorboards. I was a stranger in their house, a stranger with a bucket with rocks in it. Meanwhile, another stranger was outside, climbing like a spider, invading their windows and balconies.

Maybe this house didn't like interlopers. Maybe this wasn't a well house. Maybe it had a sickness that killed children and teenagers, that caused its makers to run from it. The ring of faces in the ceiling dome was dimly visible, but I could tell that their expressions weren't happy. I hurried outside into the enveloping dark, to find Riki already on the ground. The ladder swung from the balcony above her.

"Now we just have to take that down," she said. "I cut the top parts of the rope through halfway before we started, so it was strong enough to let me get down but would break if we pull on it hard enough."

I was out of words for Riki and her plan. I grabbed the ladder with her and we pulled with all our might, our heels cutting into the grass, sliding, swearing.

"It's not working," she said, putting her hands on her hips as she caught her breath.

"Did you really think it would?"

"Kind of," she said. "Or that it would break when I was halfway down. Halfway wouldn't be too bad."

"Oh my god."

"Look, all we need to do is cut it. The room below is Unity's. We'll get something long with an edge on it. There are long poles in one of the cabinets up here used to paint the ceilings. We'll get one of those and put a knife on it."

I was too far in to get out.

It took a bit of time to find the cabinet with the painting

210

supplies, but we finally located it. We went down to the kitchen for the sharpest knife we could find. A search around the storage room for some duct tape was unsuccessful. We did find some twine, so we tied the knife to the end of the pole, like we were fashioning weapons to have some kind of battle. We climbed the grand Morning House stairs with our weird spear and entered Unity Ralston's pristine bedroom, with its lace screen and elaborate desk. Riki opened up the window and peered up and over to the balcony.

We had opened the telescoping pole to its longest length, which was about twenty feet. That is a ridiculously long way to try to maneuver a knife in the dark. I held the flashlight as Riki poked and sawed and swore (I also kept an eye on Riki, who was leaning farther out the window than she should have been). This knot was not giving up without a fight. Riki retracted the pole and sagged with exhaustion.

"Persist," she said, possibly to herself.

"Let me try," I said.

I took the long pole and leaned from the window. The ladder was dangling at an angle from the balcony. This was a stupid task, but not an impossible one. I could see the knot, and I didn't need the full length of the pole to reach it. I hacked at the knot until my neck was sore from looking up. And then, against all odds, the rope gave and the ladder tumbled to the ground.

We made a last circuit of the house, removing all the evidence of what we had done—the first rope ladder, the pole, the knife—everything was put back as it was. As we came down the steps, the dome above us began to glow in the first morning light. I sat down on the floor of the great hall and looked up at it. I could sense every dust mote, smell every floorboard waking up, expanding gently in the heat and releasing its ancient odors of forest and polish.

Riki dropped down next to me. "That is some locked room mystery shit we just pulled off," she said, her lips twisting ever so slightly into a grin.

"You have insane plans," I said.

"You did it too, though."

"That's because I also have bad plans."

"We make a good team."

Have you ever seen a goth girl in pure, soft sunlight? It rained down over Riki, saturating her oversized black T-shirt and shorts. I noticed for the first time the tiny glimmer of a nose stud. A new note had entered the aromas.

"Do you wear perfume?" I asked.

"No. It's Mysore Sandal Soap. My grandma always brings it to us from Chennai when she visits. They sell it here, but she's committed to making sure we always have about six thousand bars. It's good, though. I like the smell. Chennai has the best street food in the world. We go every few years and I eat dosa and kulfi until I get sick. Kulfi is like ice cream, but way better. It's thicker. You get a cream one, a pistachio one . . . you have another dosa, which is a super thin lentil pancake. My favorite ones are filled with potatoes, and you have a cup of sambal on the side."

Riki tipped back her head and imagined her perfect street

212

food meal. Had she moved closer to me? Had I moved closer to her? I honestly couldn't tell you, but the space between us had lessened by a solid three inches.

I felt the tingle. It wasn't exactly like the night of the candle. Akilah was not here. But something sizzled inside me, and I was suddenly aware of my lips, of the air between us, of a lull in conversation.

Was this about to happen? Was I about to kiss Riki, or was she going to kiss me, or were we going to move at the same time, here, under the dome of light with thoughts of crispy pancakes full of potatoes on our brains? Were we just hungry?

"I'm . . ." She lingered on that statement. ". . . going back to bed."

She gave me a light pat on the shoulder as she rose and ascended the steps, back to her tower.

July 27, 1932, around 4:00 p.m.

The light filtered through the lace curtains on the windows, tickling Victory's eyelids. She opened them slowly. Everything was in soft focus, the edges smeared. That was possibly her dressing table and mirror across the room. Across the room? It might as well have been a mile away. The world was her bed, the gentle cotton of the coverlet, the sweet softness of the pillows.

Wasn't she supposed to be awake? She scowled at the question. Inertia took over. Victory flicked in and out of awareness, dreaming her room, dreaming the motes dancing in the sunlight. This sleepiness that had taken her over was luxurious. Her body wanted to participate—wanted to give in to the kindness of gravity and melt into the milky sunlight.

No. This wasn't right. It was day. Victory Ralston was too well drilled in her routine to accept this. With some effort, she pushed herself up onto her elbows.

Something was wrong. She blinked and looked at the clock on the table next to her bed. It was almost four o'clock in the afternoon.

Why was she asleep? No one slept through the afternoon in the Ralston family. She looked down and found that she was still in her exercise clothes from the morning. She hadn't even taken off her canvas running shoes.

Was she ill? She had to be ill. She felt her forehead, checked her pulse. Nothing seemed to be wrong with her except for the fact that she was so very tired.

But why had no one come for her? You didn't just *skip* things at Morning House. You would no more miss the day's activities than you would walk around the house naked. Why had no one knocked at her door?

Another question: *When* the hell had she fallen asleep? She remembered coming back to her room—the morning in flashes. Breakfast. The heat. Exercise being called off early. The glint of the water and the cast of the sky. Coming inside. After that . . . nothing. Her lack of control troubled her. Moreover, she didn't hear anything. No creaking of floors, opening of doors, voices from other rooms or outside. Morning House might not be loud, but it was never silent, never completely still.

She forced herself upright and swung her legs off the side of the bed. Her head was full of cotton. She heard . . .

Nothing. No sound aside from the ticking of the clock at the end of the hall. No voices. No sound of people moving, cleaning, chatting. She put a tentative foot to the floor and lifted her body heavily from the bed. Out in the hall, the doors to her siblings' bedrooms were closed. Victory moved toward the stairs, where someone was walking around.

Victory followed the noise and found Max's nurse in the hall, worry twisting her features.

"Miss Victory," she said. "Have you seen Max? I . . . fell asleep. I can't seem to find him. I've looked all over downstairs, upstairs . . ."

Victory's heart began to hammer in her chest, beating her into awareness.

"Maybe he crawled into bed with someone," she said. "I'll check our bedrooms."

She ran back to their hallway and began with Unity's room. She was asleep on her bed.

"Wake up! Wake the boys up. No one can find Max."

"What?"

Victory moved on to Clara, who was also asleep on her bed in her exercise whites. This was like a terrible dream, some fairy tale where a sleep takes over a castle. Victory shook Clara hard, and her eyes flew open.

"Max . . ."

Clara immediately sat upright. "What about Max?"

"He's missing."

Clara rubbed her eyes hard and swung herself out of her bed. She stood for a moment, visibly trying to rouse herself, to think, then she began moving. She ran with such raw purpose that Victory followed her—down the grand stairs, out the front door, into the hazy sunshine and pulsing heat, the green waters shining all around them. Clara kept running down the lawn, down the stairs, toward the lagoon. She pulled off her clothes at the water's edge, stripping down to her undergarments, and plunged in. Victory was steps behind her, still trying to wake up and put everything together. Clara was already cutting through the water in large archangel strokes. She dipped under the surface.

Victory stood, unsure, then jumped into the water fully clothed. The shock of it bolted her awake a bit more, and she began to look as well, taking a deep breath and sinking under. She swam along this shallower edge, where the water was only a few feet deep, surveying the rocks and vegetation, looking frantically. Her hair flowed around her, obscuring her view. She stood up to push it back.

This was when she saw Clara come up as well, carrying Max's body in her arms.

17

I woke in a sweat, late, blinking myself furiously back to consciousness. I'd dreamt all night of police coming in through the window of my playhouse room, holding up bits of ladder and looming over me. They were not there when I opened my eyes. Logically, I knew they wouldn't be, but guilty dreams bleed into reality for me. And I had been doing something questionable the night before.

I skipped the shower, panicked myself into my Morning House shirt, smoothed back my hair, and hurried to my position down by the house entrance. I almost ran into one of the black swans in the process. It made a noise like a demon woken from its unholy slumber and stretched out what looked to be about a twenty-foot wingspan and lunged at me. In my sleepless confusion it seemed like I was being chased by a black dragon and I scrambled up to the veranda from the side.

But there was no boatload of people coming up the path. Van was stretched out on one of the lawn chairs with a cup of coffee and his vape, scrolling on his phone.

"No rush," he said. "Cops have called off tours for the morning. Relax."

He gestured to the empty chair next to him. I dropped into it, my head thrumming.

"They're searching the water around the island. And everyone's extra nervous because of the storm."

Liani and Tom came across the lawn together, both in their bathing suits. We got a wave from them, and I held up a hand in return. They continued on, toward the lagoon.

"Did you see Riki this morning?" I asked.

"Nope."

"I just have to go talk to her for a second."

Van nodded and returned to his phone. I went back toward the door, avoiding the swans, and entered the hall I'd been in just a few hours before. There was a beautiful coolness in the morning. The magnificent glimmer of light from the thousands of glass pieces in the dome. The Ralstons were settled calmly in their frames, ready for tennis and boating and swimming. I jogged straight up the steps toward Riki's turret. I didn't know what I was going for, exactly. There was an impulse to see her, to confirm that last night had really happened. I got to the door at the top of the round staircase and knocked.

No answer.

We'd definitely done it. Climbed ladders and photographed research and sat on the floor together and . . .

And nothing. We sat on the floor and talked about soap and snacks and then she went to bed. I walked back down the steps, feeling a bit deflated. I was about to go all the way downstairs, but paused by the large room that led out to the high balcony where Dr. Henson did yoga. I went to the little storage closet where she kept her mat. I pressed the panel and opened it up. Inside was the broom, the mop, all the usual things. But no yoga mat.

Why had she taken it to her room instead of putting it back? Especially if it was wet?

Dr. Henson was gone. The paddleboard was drifting down the river on its own—but she had been up here with the yoga mat. I'd seen the dry mark on the ground. She'd told me she kept her mat up here, but it was back in her room.

I could just mention this to the cops. But then they would ask me when I had seen it in her closet. I could tell them I saw it when I was looking for her yesterday morning when the research student was waiting for her. That would be a lie.

What I couldn't tell them was that I saw it when we broke into her room at four in the morning on a flying trapeze to record all her work. And I *would* eventually say that—it would spill from my mouth.

I realized I was starting to hyperventilate. I took a moment to lean against the wall and take long breaths. This cleared my thinking. So the yoga mat was in her closet. So what? So she told me she normally kept it upstairs. But *normally* doesn't mean *always*. So she brought her mat back to her room. It meant nothing. And it had nothing to do with being lost in the river.

I repeated this to myself as I went back outside and rejoined Van.

"April was looking for you," he said. "She had a cinnamon roll for you."

I nodded blankly.

"You okay there?"

"Fine," I said, trying to shake it off. "Yeah, just . . ."

"I know. It's freaky. Do you want . . ."

He proffered the vape, and I shook my head no thanks.

"What's going on with you and Riki?" he asked.

"Nothing," I said.

"Listen," he said. "I get it. I went out with the bad boy too."

"Chris?" I asked.

"Chris. Mr. Christopher Nelson. Our Christopher."

He shifted around in his seat, tucking his knees up to his chest. "Do you know how much time he spent rescuing puppies? Genuinely. His family let him foster dogs all the time. He always had one or two, but sometimes he'd take care of a whole litter of abandoned puppies. This one—it was a newborn, so small, eyes closed . . ." Van squinched his eyes closed. ". . . it needed constant care and bottle feeding, so he got permission to carry it around all day. It only weighed a few ounces. It was tan, with these little floppy ears about the size of a thumbnail, and had a tiny pink belly. You could hold this puppy in your palm and she'd sleep. He made a sling so that it was up against his chest for warmth, up against his heart, and he would feed it from a little bottle between classes. Do you have any idea what it is like seeing the hottest person you know carrying around a tiny blind puppy in a sling and giving it milk?"

I took a moment to imagine Akilah doing this. I could even picture what outfit she would be wearing.

"Here was the other thing about Chris—he *knew* people. He didn't like bullshit either. He lied honestly."

"That's not a thing," I said.

"It sort of is? Everyone knew he hooked up with about half the tourists he took out on Jet Ski tours. He cheated on Liani. You knew Chris would do stuff like that. But if you needed him in the middle of the night? If you had to talk to someone? You could call him. He was probably up with a foster dog, anyway."

Van smiled, but there was an uncertainty at the corners of his mouth.

"He didn't cheat on me," he said. "We weren't *dating*-dating. I just asked him to tell me if he hooked up with someone. He didn't tell me. I had to hear about it from someone else. That was the problem. I found that out the night of the party and I was pissed. I argued with him and I walked away. I went back to get another drink and hang out and dance and yell at the moon. I just needed a few minutes. I was going to go back and we were going to make up. That's the best part, anyway. But when I walked away, he fell."

Van pursed his lips, and for the first time, I saw something cross his face that wasn't jovial.

"Some people even thought I pushed him. Argument, off he goes. I even had to talk to the police. We all did. We've done this already this year." He rubbed at the bit of stubble on his face. "When you think about it, and I have, a lot of us here would have wanted to push Chris off a cliff at one time or another. He was that kind of guy. But that was also what made him the best. He made no sense."

Van wiped the serious expression and went back to his regular half smile.

"So that's our baggage. We had a Chris-shaped hole in everything. Then you appeared. I think I know why Dr. Henson wanted you to come. We were all in a daze. Having someone new shook things up. All of this is to say that I get it. I liked the person who was trouble."

"Riki is trouble?" I asked. "What's the deal with that, anyway?"

"My advice? Honestly? Don't worry about all that. That story isn't sparking joy, if you know what I mean. No offense intended with the whole spark thing."

As we spoke, Riki appeared from below us, coming up the steep slope of the lawn from the direction of the boathouse. She was carrying a shopping bag and taking long, determined strides.

"Marlowe!" she said, noticing me. "I need to show you something."

She continued toward the front door. She was far enough away that she wouldn't hear anything we were saying, but Van leaned over to me anyway and spoke in a quiet voice.

"Don't let anyone give you shit about Riki. Go forth and multiply, I say. You have my blessing."

"We're not . . ."

"You will be," he said, tapping the side of his nose. "You don't live here. You won't have to deal with any fallout. If you're broken up, move on."

He flapped a hand at me, indicating that I should run off now. I got up, feeling a bit dazed as I followed Riki toward the house.

"By the way," Van said. "I had about forty milligrams of edible this morning and I'm not sure if it kicked in, so maybe don't take my advice."

"What the hell," Riki mumbled. "What's he talking about?"

She looked good this morning. She hadn't done anything different, really. Same smudged black liner and oversized black clothing. The sky suited her. The gray clouds made her eyes stand out like gems.

"Puppies," I replied.

I mean, it wasn't a lie.

July 27, 1932, around 4:00 p.m.

Someone was running inside Morning House. That wasn't something that often happened. Running. Knocking.

Benjamin opened his eyes to find his sister Unity standing over him, shaking him awake.

"No one can find Max," she said. "We have to go look for him."

It took Benjamin a moment to get his thoughts together. Why had he been sleeping? And for how long?

"Huh?"

"Max," she repeated. "Is gone. We need to help find him."

Benjamin had no desire to move. His body weighed so much. His limbs were bags of sand. But he was a Ralston, and he could force himself to move, to get to the business at hand, no matter how confused and tired he was.

"We should look in the playhouse," Unity said. "He's always curious about it."

Benjamin nodded, though he was still not quite processing what was going on. Something, something, Max. Max was always up to something. Benjamin would have been completely content to let him remain unfound all day.

They were coming down the stairs as Clara came through the front door, Max in her arms, wet and still. Victory was behind her, visibly shaking.

"I found him," Clara said simply. "In the water."

Reality shifted for Benjamin. He knew how to look at things, at poses, at people. He knew that the angle that Max was at was not one that living humans usually fell into. It was too straight, too still. And his color was a strange blue white. There was a shock of wet blond hair sticking to his head. He was not screaming, not having a tantrum. He made no noise, no movement.

Dead. He was looking at his dead brother. He shook his head, trying to stimulate the blood, thoughts. He had been asleep a few minutes ago and now Clara was holding a dead Max.

Faye tore along the third-floor landing. She looked down and saw what Clara was holding and let out a scream that could have caused the glass dome above them to shatter. She was a professional singer, after all. It looked for a moment like she might hurl herself over the rail to get downstairs faster, but her maid was behind her and guided her to the steps. They ran, feet pounding down. Father, meanwhile, emerged from the direction of his office and stood frozen for a moment. He and Clara locked glances. Father snapped out of his momentary shock and rushed forward, taking Max from Clara. He carried Max into the breakfast room, setting him gently on the table. He bent over Max, opening his little shirt, listening to his chest, feeling his skin. There was a dreamlike quality to everything.

Aunt Dagmar came from somewhere and pushed her body between them and the door, closing it.

"No," she said. "No. Turn around. All of you. Come with me, come with me now . . ."

She took Benjamin and Unity, each under one of her arms, and escorted them toward the front door.

The air was so thick it felt like if Benjamin tried to let himself fall, the humidity would hold him up. The butterflies on the flowers flapped their wings lazily. They were taken to the playhouse, where they were soon joined by William, Edward, and Victory. No one seemed to know where Clara had gone. She simply vanished after handing over Max.

Unity and Benjamin briefly conveyed to William and Edward what they had seen in the breakfast room. Victory said nothing. She sat in her favorite rocking chair, gaze set into the middle distance, and rocked back and forth relentlessly. Edward vanished. Benjamin began taking all the books down, shelf by shelf, and putting them all back again. A pointless exercise, but something that kept him moving. Upstairs, William began to play frenetic scales and arpeggios—the ideal music for the madness taking over the house.

Unity stepped outside and picked some flowers. She assembled these into a vase that sat on the windowsill. This seemed like something you should do when someone has died.

Elisa and some of the kitchen staff brought over trays

of food along with pitchers of milk and ginger water. There were blackberries and strawberries, piles of the grim nut cutlet sandwiches on hard grain bread that featured in so many of their lunches. There was what passed for comfort food or sweets—junket with stewed strawberries and plain graham bread. Due to the gravity of the situation, Elisa added some items she knew the children might want: sliced ham on buttered soft bread, cold fried chicken, lemon cake, oatmeal cookies, sweet lemonade, and fudge. The forbidden items that they usually craved and treasured. They sat untouched, attracting flies, until William came downstairs, sweating from the effort of playing and the close heat of the studio. Edward followed, holding an unmarked bottle. He held it out, but there were no takers.

"Well," he said, breaking the silence. "He tried to swim after all."

"He must have fallen in," Benjamin said.

"I wonder if Faye is all right," Unity added.

Victory stopped rocking.

"No," she said firmly. "He didn't fall. He was much too far out for that."

"He tried to swim," Edward said again. "Dad was always on him about that, making Clara teach him."

"No," Victory said again. Her fury seemed to calm her. "He didn't fall, and he wouldn't go swimming on his own. He'd never do that. You've all seen how he is with the water."

"Then what happened?" Benjamin said.

"I don't know." Victory got up and circled the room.

"None of this makes sense. I was sleeping. Were you sleeping? Any of you?"

"I was," Unity said.

Edward nodded. William did as well.

"Why were we all sleeping?" she said. "What is going on?"

No answer at first.

"The heat," Edward said. "We were asleep, and he was hot."

"We've been here loads of times when it's hot. We never all fell asleep for an entire afternoon. Never. Our falling asleep. Max going to the water by himself."

"What are you suggesting?" Benjamin asked.

"I don't know. I only know that this makes no sense."

"But you have to be suggesting something."

"I'm suggesting that two things that never, ever happen have both happened at the same time. *Everyone* was asleep. Why would that happen?"

Her voice had taken on a manic edge. Benjamin got up to put a hand on her shoulder, but she brushed it away.

"Clara went right to the water," Victory went on, almost to herself. "She knew right where to look."

"What?" William said.

"She went right to the lagoon."

"We were told to go look for him. Clara looked in the water."

"But right to the very place he was found. Not any other part of the shore. I followed her all the way out of the house. She ran right from the front door to the lagoon, never looked anywhere else. She dove in, went underwater. She found him within five or ten minutes. Out of all the shoreline, all the water around us."

"Victory . . . ," William said in a warning tone.

"That's where he knows to swim," Edward said, trying to get his theory back into the conversation. "He went to the place he knows. He tried to do it himself . . ."

He ran out of energy and slumped down on the floor in between the piles of books. Victory and William faced off, both their chests rising up.

"I'm going to find Clara," William said, storming out of the playhouse.

An uneasy quiet fell in his wake, broken only by Faye's screaming sobs that carried across the lawn and into the room.

"We'll have to be very good to them," Unity said. "To Father and Faye."

A lost butterfly floated in through the open door and flapped around for a moment. Benjamin watched it with fascination. None of this felt very real. Maybe Max had become a butterfly.

The boy who could not swim could fly.

18

"Smell this," Riki said.

We were sitting on the floor of her room in the turret. Riki had led me straight up here without a word, shut the door, and motioned for me to sit down. From the look of her eyes, and under her eyes, I don't think she'd slept. There was a can of energy drink next to her bed and a huge mug of coffee on the floor. She took a small green glass bottle full of dark liquid out of her bag and picked out the rotting cork with a nail file. The bottle looked old to me. Something about the shape, the thickness of the glass.

She leaned over and held it under my nose.

"What is it?"

"Smell it," she said again.

I didn't want to smell what was in this old, highly questionable bottle, but as you can see from what I've said so far, I'll apparently follow along with anything. I sniffed it. My nostrils warmed and flared from the sweet smell and a slight burning sensation. Then I let out a juicy sneeze.

"This is some powerful, old-ass booze," Riki said. "This

shit could probably strip paint."

"Why did you want me to smell it?"

"To prove something to you. To explain. The tales the locals who worked here always told about the Ralston kids—at least some of them—was that they drank a lot. It was illegal then—Prohibition—but it was also illegal from the family standpoint. Phillip Ralston didn't approve of alcohol. But because of all the bootleggers that traveled along the river back and forth from Canada—this was like the floating Costco of booze. You heard what Dr. Henson said about her grandfather and this island. The story was that the kids hid bottles all over. So this morning I went looking. I found these six . . ." She pulled five more bottles out of the shopping bag. ". . . in the boathouse. They were on beams, under loose floorboards. That's six I found just today."

"You went through the house looking for old bottles of garbage booze?"

"I'm looking for evidence that the rumors were true, and . . ." She waved at the bottles. "Proof. People said the kids drank a lot and hid it, and here are the bottles. So there was something to those stories. See . . . what I said last night was only kind of true. I did— I do want to preserve Dr. Henson's stuff for her sake. For her family. But also, for everyone. Because she did the most research on them that anyone's ever done. She's writing a book. Last night, I read it. Or a bunch of it. And I went through some of the stuff we found in her room."

She'd had a *lot* of coffee and whatever else. She was moving her fingers like she was playing an invisible saxophone.

"It's like *The Daughter of Time*," she said. "There's the famous story everyone's heard, but Grant wants to know if it really happened that way. What if Richard the Third didn't kill his nephews? What if the stories were all bullshit, made up by his enemies and then passed along through history? Because that's what history is—passed-down stories, documents. And people choose the story they like the best a lot of the time."

"What," I said, "are you talking about?"

Riki let out a frustrated grumble, but focused. "The official story is that Max Ralston snuck out when his nurse was napping and drowned, and then Clara died of grief. But there's been a local story as well. People around town wondered about what went down at Morning House. These two kids die, then the family immediately skips town and never comes back. Some people thought that another family member killed Max."

"A family member?"

"Think about it," she said. "There are six kids, all adopted, all born at the same time, all raised together and regimented. All in a house headed by a raging eugenicist. Then a new figure appears—Faye, the new wife—and they have a little boy. These accounts in here, in these notes Dr. Henson has, say that Max was a nightmare. The textbook spoiled brat. Had huge tantrums, destroyed things, kicked and clawed at people. They hated dealing with Max. Plus he's the biological child. What if that was going to mess with inheritances? What if he was just too much of a nightmare to live with? Those are two solid reasons to want to get rid of that kid."

"That doesn't mean . . ."

"Then there's the one thing everyone said about that day—everyone was sleepy. Everyone. The family, the staff. Everyone seemed to be having a nap when Max snuck out. People talk about it like the curse of the Ralstons, like some spell came over them all. It wasn't normal for everyone in the house to fall asleep in the middle of the day. I always assumed that part of the story wasn't real, an excuse later for no one noticing a little boy wandering around on his own. Not our fault. Curse. Mysterious. But no. There are statements here taken after the fact, statements by staff. They all said it, the staff—that day was *different*. They said they really were sleepy, and that includes the family. Phillip Ralston was precise. The family followed the same schedule every day, no exceptions. Breakfast, then exercising. But that morning, they didn't exercise. They all came back in."

"Because it was hot."

"I looked up the temperatures," Riki said. "That wasn't the hottest day they'd had that summer. Phillip wouldn't have canceled exercise because of that. He canceled it because they all felt weird. I think people are telling the truth. They really did all fall asleep at once. How would you get a whole house full of people to fall asleep?"

No one had ever asked me this before. I had no answer.

"Drugs," she said. "You *drug* them. They all seemed to

234

fall asleep after breakfast. They were dosed with something. That's what makes sense. And it's not like getting drugs would be hard. Phillip Ralston was a doctor—he had an office, cabinets full of drugs. Anyone could have accessed the supply."

"So you think someone . . . drugged everyone and . . ."

"Point two," she said. "Another thing people said was that Max hated the water. Hated it. It was a big deal. All the Ralstons were swimmers and Max was supposed to be too, but he would lose it if they made him go in the water. No one thought Max would go swimming on his own. Maybe he didn't go to the water on his own. Someone *took* him there. Possibly the same person who literally danced off the roof later that night. I don't think you dance off a roof out of sadness. I think you may do it if you've lost your mind because you just killed your little brother. I think this death at Morning House thing was a murder."

July 27, 1932, around 4:00 p.m.

Everything was shaking. Clara didn't like it. She swung out her arms, contacting something tangible. Not a dream. Victory was standing over her, her green eyes wide with panic.

"Max," she said.

Clara's body responded before her mind could issue the command. She spun her legs out of the bed.

"What about Max?"

"He's missing."

So the time had come. She knew what to do now. Clara hurried out of the room, not bothering to put on her shoes. Her movements were fluid. She glided down the steps barefoot, like she had done so many times before—dancing, doing movie routines. She went out the front door into the pressing humidity, the air too thick and sweet. It was like breathing honey.

Victory was right behind her. Clara had run so fast that her sister had picked up her wake, sensing purpose. She continued down the lawn, to the lagoon. At the stone lip, she pulled off the exercise clothes she had fallen asleep in. Everything looked so oddly colored. The sky was like a giant sleeping eye, the color of a milky pupil. The waters of the lagoon licked the shore contentedly. As she stood there in her underclothes, her skin exposed to air and sun, for one moment, she felt utterly in possession of herself, of her mind and body. Everything had come to a single point, and she was ready.

It was too shallow to dive, so she leapt into the cool water. This shocked her a bit more awake, but still, she suspected she might be dreaming. She dipped under and scanned around, looking at the rocks, the swaying vegetation. She kicked her feet and they touched the bottom, the slime licking her soles.

She pushed off, propelling herself along under the sun-rippled water. A curious fish watched her go, then darted away. If only she could stay here, in this moment.

No. She pushed on, swinging her gaze around. She saw what she knew she would see. Clara moved toward it. The thing she sought was at the deeper end, maybe six feet down. An easy enough dip for her. She was a mermaid. She was looking for a pearl at the bottom of the lagoon. That was what she would tell herself.

Then Clara tucked her dead little brother, Max, under her arm and swam into the light.

19

The next day, the police allowed the tours to resume. The income was too important to the tour operators, especially with a storm on the way. The day was beautiful in the morning, but apparently the storm was going to start rolling in in the early evening, and by nightfall we were going to be in some kind of swirling, biblical mess.

At this point, the search for Dr. Henson was all over the news. My parents called to check in, and I explained that she appeared to have had a paddleboard accident and that everything was, if not okay, then stable.

The cops stayed most of the day, coordinating rescue searches from the private dock. Divers swam all around the island in case she'd fallen along the shore. They swam under the docks of the boathouse. Every boat in the area was on the lookout for Dr. Henson. With every passing hour, though no one said it out loud, it was clear from their expressions that no one was looking for a living person.

We kept Morning House running as usual. Boats came

and went. The day staff came in to sell tickets and hot dogs. Tom managed the boats. Liani managed the shoreline and outside. Van, April, and I managed the tours until the boats cut off at four. When not leading a tour, I was left to meander the first floor and answer questions. I had just dropped a woman and a small child by the bathroom door, when a different woman in a gigantic straw hat approached me. (The hat was influencer big—no one would wear a hat this size otherwise; it was as wide as a satellite dish.)

"Can you just take some pics for me?" she said. "If I pose over here? By the fountain?"

This was also a major part of the job—holding the phone, taking the photo or video. I followed her and waited as she arranged her pool umbrella of a hat and found the right angle at which to stand, face sliced by sunbeams. I watched her on the screen as she adjusted the top of her dress.

The camera. Dr. Henson's giant camera. Had I seen that in her room? I rewound the footage in my brain. I couldn't see it on the record of our midnight adventure, or my visit to her room when she first went missing. I hadn't been looking for it, so it was possible I'd paid it no mind, but I feel like I *would* have noted it.

"Ready," the woman said. From her tone, I gathered she had already told me this and I'd been zoning. I took her pictures. As I handed back her phone, the woman with the child exited the bathroom and told me that the pipes were backing up and there was a terrible smell. I went in to check and got a whiff of the putrid sewage smell. I'd gotten a bit of it in the shower that morning, but it was worse now. Another glamorous job, and not one that I knew how to handle. I suppose I would have asked Dr. Henson, but she wasn't here, so I went to Liani, as she seemed like the most responsible person around.

"I'll call the plumber in town," she said when I approached her with the problem.

This is what I mean about Liani—she seemed adult in ways I didn't understand. I'd never called a plumber. My parents had. But if something went wrong in our house, I told them about it. There was something so dignified about being the kind of person who could call the plumber and then search a body of water.

Again, I drove a toy car and couldn't even be trusted with a candle.

As the afternoon went on, the sky began to darken. The tourists went home, the police boat tooted back to shore, the plumber left us, and we were alone. I walked to the gift shop, but Riki had already closed the door. I continued up to the turret. She had been reading Dr. Henson's book and materials almost without pause since we'd gotten them.

"Hey," I said. "Did you see Dr. Henson's camera when we were in her room?"

"Huh? No. I don't know. I don't think so. Look at this."

She handed me her tablet and I sat on the floor and read.

REPORT OF OFFICER KELLEY OF THE CLEMENT BAY POLICE

At 6:45 p.m. a call was received from Albert Ulridge, butler of Morning House, Ralston Island. He stated that there had been an accident on the island, that Max Ralston, four-year-old son of Phillip Ralston, had drowned.

At 7:00 p.m. I took the launch to Ralston Island along with Officer Bellard. We were met at the dock by Ulridge, who took us inside to a dining room, where the body of a young child was on the table, covered with a cloth. Dr. Ralston had already conducted an examination and had declared the boy dead at 4:37 p.m. He explained that the child's nurse had fallen asleep and the child had wandered away. The household was all a bit drowsy from the heat. Everyone was roused and searched the house. Clara Ralston, one of the six older Ralston children, swam around and looked for Max. She found him in the lagoon.

I informed Dr. Ralston that all appeared to be in order, and we did not want to add to the suffering he was clearly experiencing. We did, however, need to speak to Clara Ralston to get her account of events. A member of staff informed us that the older children were all in their playhouse, a separate structure

241

from Morning House. Someone was dispatched to bring Clara Ralston in. This person returned several minutes later and reported that no one could find Clara.

Dr. Ralston insisted that we should be given something to eat, as our dinner hour had been disturbed. Clara Ralston would be found and made available to us. We were taken back to the servants' area and served dinner along with the rest of the staff. After the meal, we continued to wait in the kitchen, as Clara Ralston had not yet been located. The cook, Mrs. Elisa North, said that Miss Ralston had an independent spirit and could be anywhere as she "swims like a fish." She suspected that in her grief, Miss Ralston had taken to the water to get out of the house and think.

One of the housemaids ran in and said that Clara Ralston had just returned to the house, wearing only a bathing suit and still wet. She had gone directly up the stairs, and she seemed "intent on something."

As we left the kitchen area, we heard screams coming from multiple directions, and we noted a commotion coming from somewhere outside the large sitting room. We went through this room and out a set of double doors, where we found the body of a girl on the flagstones. She was obviously dead.

William and Benjamin Ralston, two of the children, ran toward us. They had been coming back in the direction of the house at the time of the fall. Dr. Ralston ran to the body, checking for signs of life. There were none. The fall was not survivable.

We instructed some staff members to take Dr. Ralston back inside the house. I took William and Benjamin away from the area and asked them what they had seen. They stated that they were coming up the lawn, having heard that Clara had been found and was back in the house. As they approached, they saw Clara Ralston moving along the edge of the high balcony, some four stories above us. William noted that she appeared to be dancing. She then pressed herself against the balcony wall, before tipping herself over.

Along with the head gardener, Peter Morton, we wrapped Clara Ralston's body in bedsheets and carried her inside, while two under-gardeners dumped water on the patio to wash away the blood. Clara was placed next to her brother on the table. Both Officer Bellard and I could clearly smell alcohol coming from the deceased. It was a strong smell.

Between coming into the house in a wet bathing suit, her demeanor as witnessed by the maid, the dancing witnessed by William and Benjamin Ralston, and the strong smell of alcohol, it is reasonable to determine that Clara Ralston was grief-stricken and inebriated at the time of her death.

We left the island at 9:15 p.m.

I'm not a big true-crime person, but even I knew that this wasn't great police work. Or, as Riki put it a second later, "This is some real shit policing, huh? Let's just pick up this body and dump water all over the scene. And look at this note."

She flipped to another document and pointed to the top of one of the pages. Dr. Henson had written there: WHY ARE THERE NO PHOTOS OF THE SCENE?

"She's wondering what I'm wondering—why no one took photos of Clara's body."

"I guess because . . . it just happened? Everyone saw? And it was the past and no one did anything right?"

"Except that everything she has here in these files is like that. There were copies of the death certificates in her files, both signed by Dr. Ralston. They're each two lines long. Max's death was caused by drowning. Clara's from blunt force trauma from a fall. No blood tests. No photos. No other information. No questions. Yeah, the past is some bullshit, but they still took photos and made reports. In this case, they did weirdly little. And then . . ."

Riki ran her hand through her hair.

"Here's a copy of a telegram Phillip Ralston sent the

244

next day to the butler of his house in New York City saying that they were coming home and that he should get the place ready for them. *The next day*. And the only direction you send about Morning House is to have the patio where Clara landed destroyed."

"You're saying . . ."

"What I am saying is that it seems pretty clear that someone in the house drugged everyone else, and when the others were sleeping, they took Max to the water and drowned him. Who would want to do that? Well, there are six older siblings here, six siblings who do what they're told and are good at everything, and then . . ."

She pulled up an image of the *Life* magazine article.

"They do all this work, and who gets to be the star of the show? Max. Spoiled Max. Max, the biological son of Phillip and his amazing wife. Was Max going to get most of the estate? In all accounts, Clara is the boss of the six older kids. She was like the captain. If something needed to be done, Clara did it. Something needed to be done about Max, so Clara took care of it for the sake of everyone. She restored the family arrangement. She got rid of the problem. She didn't jump off the roof because she was sad. She jumped because she'd just killed her brother, and then maybe got drunk, and then freaked the hell out. Because murdering someone is kind of intense. It has to be. And I think everyone knew what she did. So no one looked too seriously. No one took photos. They accepted the family account and closed the case."

The wind was kicking up. It whistled around the stairwell

and shook the windows of Riki's room.

"Everyone in town thought something was up," she said. "It's like Dr. Henson said—the most evil stuff happens right out in the open."

"But what if that's all true?" I said. "What happens? What changes?"

"Nothing changes," she said. "It's . . . it's just the truth. We'll have the story. I mean, then there's this . . ." She showed me another image. "These are copies of pages from Phillip Ralston's diaries from 1914, from January and from April. Look at the corner of each one. Dr. Henson highlighted them."

In the corner of each entry there was a letter. A few *E*'s, a few *G*'s, *A*'s, *H*'s.

"It's a code for something. Who knows what the hell this is."

My walkie-talkie crackled to life.

"Marlowe?" It was Liani. "Can you come help get ready for the storm? Tom needs a hand with the chairs."

Riki was reading again. She waved me off, lost in the past.

When I stepped outside, I could see that the situation had changed. Before, it had been cloudy. Now the sky was green and the water rushed. A sharp burst of wind smacked me right in the face. April and Van were securing window shutters with rope. Tom was rolling a stack of chairs down to the basement on a dolly.

"Get all the cushions of the chairs on the side of the

house," he said. "Put them in the blue tarps and push them inside the living room. We're short a tarp. Let me know if you see it."

I nodded and set to work. My eyes watered from the force of the wind. I untied cushions from chairs near the water's edge. A blast of wind came from behind, picking up one of the loose cushions and sending it into the water. By the time I got to it, it was four or five feet out, beyond my grasp. I debated climbing in, but having my boss disappear into the water made me recoil. I imagined her under there, looking up at me, her gray-white hair swirling up above her head. So close, and yet in a different world. The world of the water. Of death.

I wondered if I should tell the police about the camera, but they were not here to tell, and presumably everyone in town had more immediate worries with the arrival of the storm. The officers had left their cards, though. Maybe I should message them. Or *had* I seen the camera? Maybe it was right there, in front of me, and I simply walked past it.

Meanwhile, the cushion drifted peacefully away, carried on the current. There was no getting it back. There was something hypnotic about watching it go to start a new life somewhere.

I moved closer to the house, to the chairs around the porch and the busted-up patio. Another wind snatched at me, causing the cushions I was still holding under my arms to flap. I moved my arm to readjust them, but this made it worse, and also caused me to knock my walkie-talkie off my shorts. It dropped to the rocks and a piece flew off it—a little black dial cap.

I had to set all the stuff down, pinning the cushions under the chairs. I got down on the ground to look for the missing piece. This lower patio had been made of larger, flat stones. When it was broken up, it had been unevenly smashed into tiles and shards. It was a warren of tiny cracks. I didn't want to crawl around this, but I'd already lost a cushion and I didn't want to mess up any more Morning House stuff. I was sensitive to messing up other people's stuff. I picked through the rocks, lifting and poking. I found a worm, a bottle cap, a piece of broken ceramic, a little piece of white shell.

I was there, ass in the air, finding everything but this cap. The rain picked up a bit. I rubbed it off my face and kept looking until I finally found it, where it had bounced into a patch of grass. I was about to get up when my brain spun everything I had just seen around one more time. I bent back down and pushed away a stone at that place where I had seen the bit of shell.

I picked it up. It was tiny. Something about the shape of it reminded me of something. I held it closer to my face. I stepped inside, out of the wind, and stared at it harder. I took a picture of it and enlarged it. I googled. I examined it again.

I wasn't holding a piece of shell. I was holding a tooth.

July 27, 2002

The small launch containing Benjamin Ralston approached the shore of Ralston Island. Benjamin looked up at the red rooflines of the house peeking above the trees. They had grown so tall. While he was a child, they barely came up to the second floor. Of course, they had been growing all these many years that he had come to visit the island, but he'd never taken stock of them. That's always the problem; you never see what's in front of you, growing slowly but steadily.

While no one was technically permitted on the island, he had told the caretaker to turn a blind eye to locals who tied their boats there to fish or swim. In return, people kept the dock in good condition and let the caretaker know if there was an issue. If kids got onto the island or into the house—and they did, regularly—they were simply asked to leave. No one was ever punished for coming to the island. It wasn't like Benjamin had wanted Ralston Island or Morning House. He'd inherited it because there was no one else left. It had seemed wrong to let the place fall apart. He paid for all the care. It was expensive, but Benjamin was a rich man.

Eric, Benjamin's live-in assistant, rode next to him. He helped Benjamin with his day-to-day affairs, which more and more meant helping Benjamin physically move around. He climbed off the boat first and assisted Benjamin as he stepped from one surface to the other.

"Wait for me here, won't you?" Benjamin said to his friend. "Have a swim. It's a lovely swim here. One of my favorite places to dive."

"Let me come with you while you look around, Ben. The ground's uneven. . . ."

Benjamin waved this off politely. "Eric, I'll be fine. I have something I have to do. Hand me that bag, would you?"

"What's in here?" Eric asked as he passed the bag over. "What are you doing?"

"Burying treasure," Benjamin replied with a half smile. "I'll tell you what—if I don't reappear by nightfall, you can come looking."

Getting up the steep path was a bit tricky. Though general maintenance was done, some parts of the grounds and path were overgrown or covered with fallen leaves or sticks. Tripping hazards, his physical therapist called them. He had to laugh, thinking back on the countless physical drills he had done on this precise bit of ground. The endless times he'd had to run the circumference of this island, then swim it. To think a stick might stop him was absurd. He still had some Ralston spirit in this sense. He kept going, up the path, up the steps, until he was at the base of the house, at the large frontage. Even though the grand flower urns were empty and no internal light illuminated the sunburst above the door, the house still held him in its thrall. It was a remarkable place.

Benjamin climbed the twelve steps leading up to the veranda, leaning hard into the stone rail. He was winded by the time he reached the door but was satisfied with his progress. He might need Eric to bring the chair to help him back down to the boat, but he had made this journey on his own. Benjamin was growing weaker all the time. He didn't want Eric to know how bad it was getting. He would only worry, but there was no reason for that. This was a natural progression and nothing to fear.

He had to find the energy to complete this task, though. It was important. It was private.

The place he needed to go was best accessed by going through the house. He opened the front door with his key and stood in the middle of the empty hall, which smelled of both neglect and floor polish, and looked up at the great glass dome above him. That had cost him a fortune to preserve, but he was glad that he had done it. It was a piece of art. Others would enjoy it. He continued through the living room—that long, sunny room along the side of the house that they used to read and play. He loved to sit here as a child with his sketchbook, drawing his siblings, the view.

Two large doors opened out of this room onto what had been a magnificent flagstone patio with a beautiful view of the water. They'd had a lovely table and chairs here, a red parasol over the table. There had been large stone urns of lavender and mint, pots of jasmine. Faye had been fond of geraniums and hydrangeas, and they had encircled the space. And that massive lilac that perfumed the breeze.

That was the better way to remember this place. The garden. The peace. Not the blood. Not the bone. Not the twisted limbs. Not the body that had been right here, a foot from where he was standing.

Not a body. Clara.

After leaving the island, his father had had only one change made—the patio was smashed to pieces. Benjamin was glad it was gone. He would have destroyed it himself had the job not been done already. The view was gone, obscured by trees and brush that had sprung along the edges of the ruins. A bit of honeysuckle still clung to the side of the house, the scent tickling his memory.

He closed his eyes. Sitting here, with the breeze hitting his face just so, the sweet scent of the honeysuckle . . . he was back in 1932. William pounding away on the piano. Clara moving across the floor, graceful and powerful. Edward off to the side, snickering about something. Unity with her books. Victory trying to fix everyone and everything. Benjamin remembered the smell of his paints blending with the summer air. All those hours spent trying to understand painting by copying the strokes of others until he had the courage to make his own picture.

Their voices called to him through the trees.

Had he known? Not the details, no. But it had been coming, all that summer, in a steady drumbeat. That night—as he and William ran toward the house and saw Clara fall. The

252

sound of the impact, so dull and strange . . .

Benjamin opened his eyes and returned to the present, away from that memory.

After Clara fell, they did not discuss it. Father's heart gave out. Faye's trauma never healed. Edward drank and crashed his car. Unity was lost in an accident along with Aunt Dagmar. The bomb did the rest, taking William and Victory. The Ralstons were wiped away, leaving Benjamin to hold the truth alone.

He bent down with care, lowering himself to a kneel, and felt the various bits of crushed rock until he found one small and light enough to lift aside. Reaching inside the bag, he produced a slender alabaster box. It was designed to hold cigarettes—a lovely little piece, perfect for the job. Besides, he had stopped smoking years ago.

Using the trowel, he dug a shallow hole and placed the box inside. After covering it with a light layer of dirt, Benjamin moved the stone back into place. It was hard for him to stand after kneeling so long, but he forced himself up.

"I've missed you all so much," he said out loud. "But I will see you soon. We will discuss it."

With that, Benjamin Ralston left Morning House for the last time.

20

My fifth-grade teacher, Ms. Bamber, used to offer extra credit occasionally where she would give us a brainteaser, and the first person to solve it got to skip a Friday ten-question quiz of their choice. They were always things like: Mr. Brown lives in a blue house and has a black cat, and Mr. White lives next to the pink house and has a brown dog . . . stuff like that, and you'd have to work out who lived in all the houses and had what pet from what you'd been given. I *love* these things. I won a lot of quiz passes. It got to be the thing people knew I could do. The strange thing was, I'd start by taking a few notes on who lived where and had what, and then I'd stare at it and I would figure it out. Ms. Bamber asked me how I did it, and I couldn't remember. I remembered the *experience* of working it out. I had glimpses of moving the parts around in my head, but the last steps were a blur, and then they were gone. I was left with a buzz and an answer and a free quiz pass.

It had never really come in handy before. But say you're in an old death house and you find yourself stuck in a storm and you're holding a human tooth. You start to think about life a little differently. My brain began to assemble the pieces. The floating cushion and the paddleboard, both on their own, cast off from this island. The dry spot under the yoga mat, which wasn't where it was supposed to be. The camera. Everything Riki had been telling me about the house falling asleep all at once, the boy who didn't like to swim found in the water, a girl going mad and dancing off the roof . . .

Which took me right back to that yoga mat.

People fell in this house, or they drowned.

People fell from other places. People like Chris.

I looked up the stone face of the building at the balcony far above. Clara had fallen a long way. It must have been brutal. If you fell from the top of this building and landed anywhere on your face, you were probably going to lose a tooth. Now that I thought about it, I imagined someone landing and raining teeth, like a terrible piñata.

No one wants a piñata full of teeth.

Best-case scenario here—I was holding an old Ralston tooth. I don't know what happens to human teeth if they're left out for almost a hundred years partially covered by a patio stone. Of course, I'd seen lots of shows where they found bones—like that old show *Bones*, which was just bones as far as the eye could see. (The main doctor on that, the one they called Bones because she knew about bones—she might have liked the piñata full of teeth. That lady really liked bones.) On shows, the bones always looked dirtier. Brown. This was not dirty or brown. It looked like a fresh tooth. Clean.

A creamy color. I flicked the pad of my index finger against the broken edge and found it was sharp. I looked up the mullioned balcony edge—it had that up-and-down pattern that you see on the tops of castles. Sort of like teeth.

Everything was teeth now.

Dr. Henson had been on that high balcony doing yoga the morning she'd vanished. Exactly the spot where Clara Ralston fell from. The idea that had been slowly assembling itself in the corner of my mind—this little being of lingering glances and small thoughts—now had a literal bone to chew on. It stood up. It spoke to me. It said the thing I did not want it to say.

Dr. Henson had been murdered.

Of course she wasn't murdered. I wouldn't be in a house where a murder had happened.

I'd been in a place where a fire had happened.

But fires happen. Fires are natural. Murder is unnatural. And why would anyone murder Dr. Henson?

The sky had gone a dark shade of green. The invading cloud army was getting closer. It burped up internal rumbles of electricity. It would be here soon, and it would be bad. Whatever was happening, I was now the keeper of the tooth because there was no way of getting it to anyone who could do something useful with it.

I dragged the cushions inside and dropped them on the sitting room floor. I just had to play it cool, hide the tooth, act like nothing was wrong. Once the storm cleared, I could hand the tooth to the police and get the hell off the island.

I hurried through the hall, down the back steps, and tried to get past the kitchen door without anyone spotting me. I continued straight on, to the tunnel, and to the playhouse. I didn't feel great passing through the tunnel, and I kept looking over my shoulder. I got to my room and shut the door. It had no lock.

Where do you hide a tooth? It was small enough that it could go anywhere. But it could get lost. And what if I had to let someone know where it was?

I took the lipstick Akilah had given me and dropped the tooth into the cap. It fit back on when I pressed down. I probably wasn't going to use it again, what with the murdered person's tooth in it. And a lipstick tube covered in my DNA may not have been the best place to keep evidence, but it made the most sense to me.

"Job!" Van said, appearing at the doorway and causing me to scream out loud. He'd opened the door without me even hearing. That's how loud the wind was.

"What?"

"Power's going to go out for sure. So we have a job. We gotta eat all the ice cream. It's our duty as Americans or something."

"Why do you think the power is going to go out?"

"Because it always goes out. Especially on the islands. And this storm is a big one. Don't worry. We have lamps and stuff. But first, ice cream! Kitchen! Now! Come with me, fellow gay."

He extended his hand. I hesitated. Was this the moment

257

to start following people to second locations? Still, I had to play it cool. No one knew what I'd just found.

I went with him.

"I love a storm," he said. "I love the drama. Storms are nature's reality shows. Are you scared of them?"

"No?"

"You seem a little jumpy."

"I'm fine," I said.

It never, ever means that. Ever.

We emerged in the basement. It was darker down here than normal because there was usually some ambient light. Now there was nothing but brown shadows and rattling sounds. I stayed away from the pool, with its twelve-foot drop. Van and I arrived safely in the kitchen, where the others, except for Riki, were sitting around.

"Ice cream?" Tom said. "We have salted caramel, birthday cake, mint chocolate chip, Moose Tracks, peanut butter cup, and butter pecan. You like the Moose Tracks, right?"

I gratefully accepted the half-full pint.

The lights hummed and faded a bit, going to a low orange. I dug into my ice cream like it was the only thing between me and oblivion.

"I know what we should do," Van said. "We should sleep in the big house tonight. We should have a storm party. Let's sleep in the real beds, in the fancy ones. Who's going to stop us?"

"No one was ever going to stop us," Liani said, scooping

the last mouthfuls of the salted caramel from the bottom of the container. "Why would we want to?"

"Because they're there."

"They smell," Liani pointed out. "They're musty."

"Where is your sense of adventure?"

I dug fretfully into my pint as they went back and forth on how we should spend our stormy night. This one was thankfully loaded with extra chocolate bits, which were delicious, but again, required chewing, and therefore reminded me of teeth. The rain began to hammer down, striking the low basement windows with such force that it sounded like rocks.

It occurred to me that there was one more step I needed to take. The one thing I had been holding off on—now was the time for it. And I had a message to convey. My phone signal was poor, but it would be good enough. It had to be.

"You know," I said, "I feel like I should call home, just to let my parents know I'm okay."

I crept back out into the dark of the basement and went up the steps and stood in the wide, grand hall of Morning House. The sunrise had been extinguished, and the lamps barely held back the gloom. I opened my contacts. There she was, her face a glow of pure human goodness.

I hit the button and called her. It rang, rang again, and again, and again. It was going to go to voice mail. . . .

"Marlowe?"

There was a lot of noise behind her. Clanking. People

talking. I felt like I was falling. The floor of my stomach dropped out and I had to press a hand against the wall for balance. Her voice. Akilah—live, connected to me through waves in the air, in space.

"Hey," I said, trying to sound casual.

"Are you okay?" Akilah said. "I heard something happened to the woman who hired you? It's been on the news. I . . ."

She had been keeping track of me. Or, at least, she had seen the thing that was all over the local news.

"Listen," I said. "I just want you to know that *Midnight Rose* is great."

Crashing noises behind her. I hated everyone in that Cheesecake Factory. Why didn't they all just shut up for a second and stop dropping all their shit?

"Wait, I can't hear you. What?"

This wasn't how it was supposed to be. My first conversation with her. It couldn't be plates and people talking about appetizers and yelling.

"The Midnight Rose," I said loudly.

"The lipstick?"

"It's great. I *love it*."

"Okay?"

"And . . ."

And what? And I think my boss got murdered. And I think someone here did it. And I'm trapped in a storm. And I hid a tooth in her lipstick and I loved her.

I should have made this call so much sooner.

"Marlowe, I have to go, but . . . are you . . ."

I could barely make out what she was saying. Then the call cut out. Then the power.

21

We decided to spend the next part of the night in the living room. By we, I mean someone. I was feeling hazy, out of my body. I nodded at whatever anyone said.

No one knew I had Dr. Henson's tooth, I reminded myself. This was secret knowledge. So yes, I was almost certainly trapped on this island with a possible murderer—but they didn't know what I knew. Plus, because of the blackout, we were sticking together. At least, that seemed to be what was happening.

So we trailed up the basement steps in a line, carrying our phones or holding battery-powered lamps. The house whistled from the winds. There was air coming in from somewhere, spinning around the vast hall, causing a frigid draft. The living room was maybe not the best room in this regard, but it had a big fireplace. Someone had the foresight to stack firewood in there. It seemed we were going to ignore the "no fires" rule tonight. Who was going to stop us, anyway?

Liani and Tom stacked the wood into a pyramid and got

it going, and soon we had some light and warmth.

"So how are we going to spend tonight?" Van asked. "What kind of storm party are we going to have? You want to drink? Are we smoking? Are we playing a game? Having a séance? Doing each other's hair? What's going on?"

No reply. The fire crackled.

"Hey. What are you doing?"

We all turned. Riki had emerged from her turret and stood in the doorway.

"It's not your house, Riki," Liani answered, not looking over.

"I didn't say it was my house. I just asked what you were doing."

"Having a storm party," Van said, extending his arm. "Join us."

"What part of this is a party? It just looks like you're sitting in front of the fire."

"A party is a state of mind."

"Don't do this to her," Liani said.

"Do what? I asked her if she wants to come."

"You know what."

"Not everything is about you, Liani," Riki said. "Anyway. I'm going. Enjoy whatever this is. I'm upstairs, Marlowe, if you want to come up."

I half listened to all of that. I had become all-absorbed in the fire. Fire is hypnotic. Look at it long enough, and that's all you'll see. Faces appear in the swirls of orange and red.

Images. I saw a star. A dragon. A man wearing two hats. A long, twisting face that reminded me of the picture of Phillip Ralston.

"I think I'm going to bring up some more wood from downstairs," Tom said. "We'll run through it tonight."

"I'll help," Liani added.

"We won't see them again for a while," Van said as they disappeared through the dark doorway. "Tonight's the magic night."

"About time," April added.

This brought me back to the situation at hand. The murder. The tooth. I'd forgotten it while looking at the fire, which was odd. I wasn't worried, though. If I remained here, still, quiet, nothing would happen. I was safe here by the fire while the rain pounded the windows.

I had to pee. I tried to get up, but my body weighed more than I realized. I stumbled a bit, and April steadied me.

"You okay?"

"Yep," I said. "Just going to the bathroom."

But was I? The shift from the mood of my friend the fire to the cold and dark of the hall was almost too much. It made life feel wild and unpredictable. I decided to lie down in the middle of the grand foyer in the dark and look up at the shadowy contours of the stained-glass ceiling. Of course, I could barely see it, and certainly not in detail, but I knew the ceiling women were there, looking down at me through their blue glass eyes. They had seen it all. They knew the truth of

Morning House—the truth about Max, about Dr. Henson—but they weren't talking. That struck me as funny and I burst out laughing.

Van came and lay down next to me.

"What are you laughing at?" he asked.

"The ceiling."

He accepted that and tucked his hands behind his head.

"Do you want to know something fucked up?" I asked him.

"Always."

"I think there was a murder here."

What? Did I just say that? Why had I said it? My mouth was dry and tacky, but the floor was so cool and relaxing. The dark soothed me, and I wanted to tell Van everything.

"You mean the Ralston kids?"

Say yes. Say yes to that.

But that wasn't what I meant. I couldn't bring myself to say anything.

"Are you high?" he asked. "No shade, I applaud you if you are. I've just never seen you high before."

"No. What's high like?"

"Well, it looks like you look right now—down on the floor, laughing at the ceiling. You were also staring into the fire saying nothing for almost an hour."

I wanted to explain that the reason I was laughing was because the glass women in the ceiling wouldn't tell me who committed the murders, but then I ran that statement through my mind once more before committing and realized that I did sound high.

"Could I get high without meaning to?" I asked.

"No? Well, yes, if you ate an edible without realizing it, but I didn't leave any out. You really do seem high, though. Not to worry. You're in good hands. Best thing to do, relax and enjoy. I'll go get you a pillow and a blanket."

That was nice of Van. A pillow and blanket sounded good. That way I could watch the ceiling in comfort.

Wait.

How did I get high? I rolled back my memory of the evening. We hadn't done much. I'd found a murder victim's tooth, we ate ice cream, I called Akilah, the lights went out. And I'd had a Coke at some point—a can of Coke. I was trying to reassemble the puzzle of my night like an archaeologist trying to explain the past with a handful of broken clay. Maybe there had been something in my drink, something that was making time stretch and constrict, making the fire as exciting as a Marvel movie and causing the ceiling to mock me. I knew I hadn't taken anything of my own accord, which meant that someone else had done this to me. Someone else in this dark house. Where I was sure a murder had occurred.

I had to move, except I could tell that someone was watching me. Not the women in the ceiling. They may have been up to something else, but I wasn't worried about that now. One of the people in this house was looking at me in the dark. I could feel their gaze on me as physically as I could feel the floor. I heard them looking.

"Hello?" I said.

Only the storm answered. The storm, the dark, the essence of Ralston that swirled around the space.

I had to get to Riki's room. I had to tell her what was happening. Riki would help me.

I attempted to lift my head, but it weighed too much. It felt like someone had put an invisible ten-pound hand weight on my forehead.

I could stay here. It would be fine.

No. I had the tooth. I had to get up. Get to Riki. Riki was the safety zone. She would know what to do.

Since lifting my head was hard, I decided to roll onto my stomach and push myself up. This worked. I got to my knees and then managed to get to a standing position. Once I was on my feet, I was much steadier. My shoes squeaked on the floor, though. Someone would hear me. I pulled them off by stepping down on the heels. Now that I wore only socks, I glided across the floor. My movements were effortless. I was the night itself. Why hadn't I always walked this floor in socks? I couldn't go up the main staircase. That was too out in the open and, frankly, looked too hard to climb. I would go toward the gym and use the back stairs.

I slid along. I was a creeper, creeping through the exercise room. The hairs on the back of my head were prickling. Someone was following me. I skidded into the music room and dropped to a slide along the floor, banging my knee hard in the process. I didn't care. I had a plan. I was going to climb under the piano. It was draped, so no one would see me under there. Who looks under pianos in the dark?

"Marlowe?" Van was calling for me. I remained where I was. My heart was beating heavily. Not fast, just percussive, shaking my bones. The wind wrapped its tail around the building. I listened to the floors creak. Was that the wind too? Were those footsteps? Was someone still calling my name?

I peeked out from under the fringed end of the piano skirt. I couldn't see anyone, but I felt their presence as distinctly as I felt the texture of the floorboards under my fingertips.

Creak. Creak.

A step. The sound was distinct, and it came from the doorway of the music room. I willed myself to stone. I would stay here, under this piano, all night if I had to.

Creak. One step into the room. *Creak.* A step out.

If I stood, they might see me. I would crawl to the back steps. That was the plan—stay low to the floor. By doing this, I got to the door to the back stairs. I reached up and turned the handle slowly. I was hyperaware of every movement of my wrist. I got the door open quietly and slithered through, then made my way up the steps by pressing my hands into the walls of the stairwell as I went.

It took me six hours to get to Riki's room. Being high seemed to take a lot of time. My logical brain told me it probably wasn't six hours, but what was time, anyway? My journey through the house tonight was evidence it wasn't real. I finally made it to the fourth floor and shuffled upright to the passage that led to Riki's turret. Just one more set of stairs to go. I managed these pretty well. Knocking was out of the question. I let myself into Riki's room. She was on her bean-bag, reading something on her laptop. The glow of the laptop and a single battery lamp provided the only light in the room.

"Hello," I said.

Riki stared at me, wobbling in the doorway.

"I came to talk to you," I explained.

"Okay."

"But someone is watching me."

"Okay?"

"I have something very important to tell you," I said. "You should know I might be high. I've never been high, but I think I'm high right now."

"You think you're high?"

"I think someone gave me something," I explained.

"Who would dose you?" she asked, ignoring all the non-sense that was coming out of my mouth. "Van would never dose anyone."

"It was Van who noticed I was high!" I said excitedly. We'd made a breakthrough.

Riki sighed loudly and pushed her laptop aside.

"Okay," she said. "Here's what we're going to do. I'm going to put you in this beanbag here . . ."

She started to get up, but I held up my hand, indicating that she shouldn't move. I kicked the door shut. Then the words came.

"I need to tell you about teeth. Tooth. I need to tell you about tooth. The tooth."

"Huh?"

"You don't understand—you were right. There was a murder here. But not the one you're talking about. Dr. Henson. She saw what happened to Chris Nelson that morning at sunrise. She was here, looking over at Mulligan Island. Probably doing her sunrise yoga and maybe looking through her camera, but she *saw something*. And she was hinting at it at dinner that first night. She was telling me all along. And just before we came in, I found a tooth in the rubble of the patio. Don't you get it?"

"You're sure it's a tooth?"

"*It's a tooth*. Don't worry. I hid it. It's safe."

"I don't care where you put it. Why do you think it's her tooth?"

"Who else's tooth could it be? And it's new. New tooth. People don't just leave their teeth around. Doesn't matter. They can prove it . . ." I waved my hand at the wall indicating the police, technology, the woman from *Bones*. "I just have to get the tooth to them. But we're stuck here tonight and *someone* here did this so you need to tell me what to do."

The effort of saying all that both exhausted and exhilarated me. From the look on her face, I could tell Riki had a *lot* of questions. Luckily, I had more words.

"When Dr. Henson showed me around my first morning, she told me she did yoga every day on that high balcony and that she kept the mat upstairs, in the storage closet by the window. When I went looking for her that morning, there was a dry spot on the balcony in the shape of a yoga mat. The mat was gone. I found it when we went looking for documents in her room. It was in her *closet*. Whoever killed her didn't know about that."

I sounded smug, and it was because I *felt* smug.

"I think the first thing the killer did that morning was take the paddleboard and paddle and throw them in the river. Make it seem like she drowned. She didn't drown. That's why I have her tooth. Oh my god, my mouth is so dry. Do you have any water? Anything?"

"Yeah . . ."

Riki got up and moved slowly toward her stash of energy drinks and waters. I wavered in place a bit and looked around at her room. So circular. So pleasing. And all the things she had in here enticed me. The wind chimes. I walked over to look at them. They swung ever so gently in the bit of swirling air that was getting in somewhere. And there was one of the suncatchers with the small, mirrored disks, the ones she'd first seen me through. That's how she caught knee creepers. I was a knee creeper!

"You need to sit down," she said, "and start from the beginning."

I began to turn back but I tripped over something. I looked down.

It was Dr. Henson's enormous camera.

JULY 27, 1932

The morning of the deaths at Morning House

On the morning Unity Ralston killed her brother Max, she woke early because of the heat. Her bedsheets were sticking to her legs in the humidity. She peeled them back and went to the window to watch the sun rise over Ralston Island. The sky was milky, full of clouds that refused to rain. It would be an unpleasant day, sweaty and sluggish.

This was the day she had been waiting for.

She rinsed her face in cold water and hurriedly pulled on her white exercise clothes and her canvas running shoes, then combed back her blond hair and fixed it in place with a headband. It was five minutes to six.

After checking to make sure her door was securely locked (not that anyone was going to come into her room; still, with something this important, safety measures had to be followed), she set to work. Her father had given her a marvelous desk for her eleventh birthday. All the Ralston children got desks, but this one was special.

"I'm proud of all my children," he said as he showed her the desk. "But you, Unity, you have always tried so hard to live up

272

to my standards. I feel you and I understand each other. We know that sometimes, to do important work, we must have privacy. This desk has sixteen hidden compartments. . . ."

He showed her those compartments, one by one, and the delicate triggers that opened them. There were large ones, like the false bottom of the flat drawer under the writing surface, that could be opened by reaching back and unhooking a small clasp. There were also exceedingly small and tricksy ones, ones that had two or three steps to access. Her favorite required pressure on a bit of scrollwork that ejected a small knob that needed to be turned and pushed back to pop out a tiny round compartment, big enough for rings or a necklace. It currently contained a collection of twisted paper packets, half the size of a cigarette each, made of torn glassine envelopes. On these were written numbers—5, 10, 15, 20. The Veronal they contained had been easy enough to get. It was a common pill for nerves and sleep. She bought it at the druggist rather than take it from her father's cabinet, in case he noticed such a large quantity was gone. She needed two bottles.

She had learned the dosages by reading his medical books. The common therapeutic dose was about fifteen grains. Around fifty was fatal. She had ground the pills using the back of a spoon she had smuggled to her room and made the dosed wraps. Unity was good at math and chemistry—she had worked out precisely how to distribute the drug.

She left her room and went down to the kitchen, where their cook, Elisa, was preparing their breakfast.

"Oh!" She put a hand to her chest. "You startled me. You're up early."

"Couldn't sleep," Unity said truthfully. "It was too hot."

"Oh yes, it's going to be horrid."

"I'm starving. Could I have a few graham crackers and milk?"

"Help yourself, dear."

Elisa was busy filling a bowl for the staff breakfast, which was served at seven.

"You can take that in," Unity said. "I'll do the nursery tray."

Unity had always taken an interest in cooking, which Phillip encouraged, and it wasn't unusual for her to give Elisa a hand.

"You're a blessing, Miss Unity. An absolute treasure."

Unity smiled modestly and went to the stove, where a large pot of porridge was emitting primordial burps, and the kettle rumbled, about to whistle.

As soon as Elisa was gone, Unity set to work.

Max and his nurse took breakfast in a morning room off the nursery. Though coffee and tea were forbidden for the family, Phillip Ralston didn't go so far as to deny the staff or his sister. His nurse had a pot of strong tea on her breakfast tray. This Unity prepared, scooping two heavy spoonfuls of black tea into a pot. Checking over her shoulder to make sure she was alone in the kitchen, she then reached into her pocket and pulled out the envelopes and poured a twenty-five-grain dose into her teapot, nowhere near the fatal dose, but certainly enough to keep her out of the way for the morning. Twenty grains went in Aunt Dagmar's coffeepot before the tray was swept up by one of the maids.

Fifty grains each went into the pitchers of fresh orange juice and apple cider that were chilling in the icebox, with an additional twenty going into the ginger-and-lemon water that was also served with every meal. (They were permitted a maximum of two glasses of juice each, but you could have as much ginger-and-lemon water as you liked.)

While everyone had different preferences for boiled eggs, granola, stewed vegetables, or graham bread, everyone ate the fresh yogurt with cooked black raspberries, and everyone had a dish waiting at their place when they entered the breakfast room. The little glass dishes were empty and waiting on a tray. Unity got out the bowl of fresh, sour yogurt and spooned some into each dish. To each yogurt but one she added ten grains more of Veronal. The untouched one she set aside and stuck a spoon in. She would tell the maid that was hers and that she had taken a bite so it would be set at her place. She added a little here and there into cups and onto a fruit pudding that was chilling for the staff lunch. Everyone in the house was covered in some fashion.

She looked about the kitchen, checking her work in her head, counting the doses and portions one last time.

Everyone was thirsty that morning. Unity drank plain water, but everyone else had some juice or ginger and lemon. She kept a watchful eye on the levels in the pitchers. By her estimate, there were about forty grains' worth in what remained in the pitchers at the end of the meal. Elisa and the staff would consume this throughout the morning. All the doses would be nicely balanced. It was eight in the morning, and the Veronal had entered the Morning House bloodstream.

22

Riki stared at the camera on her floor, then looked at me. I backstepped toward the door.

"Why do you have this?" I said.

"I don't *have* this," she said. She appeared genuinely confused as she started to move toward me. I looked for something to defend myself, but there were few options.

I grabbed a bottle of Thousand Island dressing.

"Don't come any closer," I said. "I told Akilah about the tooth. She knows. If anything happens to me, she knows where it is. It's hidden and no one will find it but Akilah."

"Marlowe," Riki said slowly. "I did not kill Dr. Henson. I didn't bring that camera up here. Someone put that in my room, and that is *concerning*. Sit down and tell me what is going on."

"*You* tell *me* what's going on," I shot back. "Because right now you have her camera, and you broke in to take her stuff. With me. You did it with me so I'd be involved . . ."

I felt a wave of panic coming on. My heart was beating

277

too fast. I was having trouble holding up my Thousand Island dressing.

"Listen," she said, holding up her hand, "if I did something to Dr. Henson, which I didn't, and if I took her camera, which I didn't, do you think I would just leave it there? I'd deep-six that thing so hard the fish couldn't find it. I'd rip up floorboards. I'd cement it into the wall somehow. I would not, under any circumstances, bring it here and leave it on the floor. And if you *think* I would do that—first, fuck off, and second, hit me with that dressing, I guess. But the fact that the camera is here, on my floor, should tell you I didn't do this. Someone is messing around."

I considered this all for a moment, in my merry-go-round of a brain. The intoxication changed states. I pinged from fascination to fear to a desire to crash into Riki's fuzzy beanbag and sleep and forget about the tooth and the camera. But there was just enough of a background hum of logic and awareness that told me that sleep was not an option. And it was true—if Riki had taken the camera, she likely would have been more slick about it. I slid down the wall and sat on the floor, legs flopped in front of me like a rag doll.

"Okay," I said. "I need to understand something. I need to know what the deal was with you and Chris, because Chris's death has to be connected to Dr. Henson's. Tell me what happened, why you've all been fighting."

Riki played with the makeup brushes in the cup on her sink, considering. Then she sat down on the ground.

"You really think someone here killed Dr. Henson?"

"I don't think she moved her yoga mat, hid a camera in your room, scattered her teeth, and then went on a paddleboarding adventure on the open water."

"Yeah," Riki said, picking at the floor, "when you put it like that . . ."

I folded my arms, waiting for her to talk. I tried not to become distracted by the way the mirror chimes rotated slowly, moved by an imperceptible air current. I had to steer my brain like I was driving the Smart Car on a rainy day.

"Chris," Riki began, "was one of my first friends, but I always knew that you couldn't turn your back on him completely, you know? He could be the most honest person you ever met. He'd help you whenever you needed him. But then you'd find that he did something like mark your arm with a pen, somewhere you couldn't see, and if it was there the next day, he'd tell everyone you didn't shower. He'd save your life. He'd save the world. But he would take your Doritos and say he didn't. Which is all very minor shit, but it landed different the older we got. That's when he started working his way through the school, through tourists. He wanted to hook up with everyone, and he didn't want anyone to care. I think he thought if he didn't mean to hurt people, then he couldn't have hurt them, because he was such a good guy. Does that make sense?"

I nodded. I understood enough.

"I always thought he wouldn't get involved with our friend group. We were all too close. But I was wrong. He tested the waters by hooking up with April last year. That was just the once, and I think they talked and decided it was a mistake. But then, last summer, he and Liani disappeared together one night, and by the next day, they were a thing. He and Liani were serious. Liani *loved* him. I mean, she was all in. But I was worried about her because I knew what Chris was like. We all did, but she wanted to believe he wouldn't cheat on her, because she was different.

"One day, when I was at the register at the bookstore, these two tourists came in talking about this guy who worked at the Jet Ski and boat rental place, and from their description, I knew they meant Chris. One of them hooked up with him a few weeks before. I was . . . so mad. He wasn't just hurting Liani. He was hurting *us*, as friends. I tried to tell Liani that he was up to stuff, but she didn't want to hear it. I talked to the others about it, and everyone kind of knew as well. But no one was *doing* anything. So I made a plan."

Having participated in one of Riki's plans, I understood the significance of this. Nothing good was coming.

"One night, when I knew he was working in the rental shop alone, I got dressed up. Skirt. Makeup. You may not believe it, but I clean up pretty good."

"Why would you even need to get dressed up?" I said, maybe with a little too much feeling. She cocked her head but continued with her story.

"When I walked into the shop, I put my phone on a shelf and hit record. And then I started flirting with him. I said I would never tell Liani. I just wanted to, you know, see what I was missing."

I felt myself warming a bit as Riki told this story. There

are times for those feelings, and this was not one of them. This was a No Bone Zone. But there's no talking to hormones. And I'd been given *drugs*.

"It was gross," she said, putting the lid on the steaming pot. "I didn't want to make out with Chris. He was like my brother. But I could see from his expression that it was working. I made sure never to make the first physical move. He stepped over to me, put his hands on my waist, leaned in to kiss me, and then . . ."

She paused as the house creaked in the wind.

"I backed up and started yelling at him, telling him he was a dirtbag, that I was telling Liani, that it was all over. He called me a stalker, a psycho, stuff like that. I was kind of riding high on emotion, so I turned around and yelled, 'Good luck with that. I got it all on video.' And I held up my phone. I'd gotten him. Except . . ." She sagged a bit. "As soon as I got home and watched it, I knew I had a problem. The place I'd set the phone down had some kind of—I don't know what the hell was there, a vent or something, something I'd never paid attention to but turns out is the loudest thing that has ever existed. There was a hum coming through the entire video, so you could only make out one or two words. And because of the weird angle, the video looked like me coming on to Chris, him rejecting me, and then me freaking out. It was a disaster."

I saw her retreat into herself a little as she remembered.

"But it was too late to stop the plan now. I'd done it, and I'd *told* him I had a video. So instead of my original plan, which was a lot slower and well thought out, now I had to get to

Liani before he did. But the video. Oh god, the video. I called April, told her what happened. She was, as you can imagine, completely freaked out. I looked at her face as she watched the video and I could see that things were even worse than I thought. She tried to calm me down. She said, don't show Liani this video, because it would not help my case at all. But since I'd told Chris there was one, it was unlikely he would say anything to Liani either. The best thing to do would be to drop it. Do nothing. Things might be weird with me and Chris now, but we would just have to deal with it. And that plan worked. For a day."

"What happened?" I asked.

"He called my bluff. He told her. It must have been a safe bet that the video was going to look pretty squirrelly—me coming to his work, me hitting on him. Even if he seemed to be receptive, he could explain it away by saying he was shocked or nervous or just trying to be polite and get me out of there or something. Liani confronted me. I tried to explain. I thought we were better friends than that. I thought she'd be mad but we'd talk it out. That is *not* what happened."

She picked at the ground.

"I stayed away a little, and then a little more. And then when I texted the others, I noticed there were long pauses before they texted me back. Everyone drifted away. Chris and Liani broke up at some point in October, I think. I don't know why for sure, but I think he did it. My guess was that he realized he liked guys more. He was bi, but I think he was really falling for more guys, just, percentage-wise. Van was a surprise, only because things had been complicated when he'd dated in our friend pool. I didn't think he'd go fishing there again. I thought those two were more like brothers, but it was a big romance, prom, all of that. And then he died. So that's the story of me trying to help my friends and being a creepy fuckup and ruining my life."

A quiet came over the room.

"It's not so bad," I said. "I *burned a house down*."

"Yeah," she said, taking a breath. "You're probably the only person who has ever fucked up more than I have."

"So you came here to the island anyway?"

"We made the plan for the bookstore to have a shop here last summer," she said, shrugging. "That was my other genius idea. Hang out with my friends and open this extra business here on the island, so we could make some actual money for the bookstore. We've got those Thousand Island dressing dollars coming in. That part worked. And I even thought that if Chris was here, we could fix things. We'd all talk it out. But Chris isn't here. It's easier for all of them to keep being mad at me than it is to deal with the fact that Chris is dead, and he died in a stupid, pointless accident. Except, you're telling me he didn't. And I'm starting to think you have a point. But none of them are murderers. Those are my *friends*. Or were. I guess part of me always wondered about what happened that night. But no one would *kill* him. That's not a thing that happens, is it?"

"You've been telling me for days about how Clara killed her brother," I replied.

"Fair point. But I don't know Clara."

"Tell me what happened that night at the party," I said. "Because if someone did what I am pretty sure they did, it started there."

Riki rubbed her hands over her face. I scooted closer so I could see her better, leaving behind my Thousand Island dressing, and also the support of the wall. I had to lie on the floor to listen.

"I skipped prom," she said. "For a lot of reasons. Mostly hating the idea of prom, but also because of everything that was going on. I stayed at the store and did inventory and listened to *Carrie* on audiobook. Seemed fitting. But I went to the party. Everyone went to the party. My best friends weren't talking to me, but I had other friends."

She said it as if I'd suggested otherwise.

"I got there early with a few others who gave prom a miss. We were happily wasted by the time everyone else arrived and had already eaten the good snacks. Once everyone else got there, things felt weird to me, so I went off on my own with a sleeping bag to keep listening to *Carrie* until I fell asleep. I woke up to people screaming. Liani pulled Chris out of the water. I saw that much. I think he'd been on the rocks, but he'd washed off and was floating. I went over to her, and she wasn't mad at me anymore. But then Tom and April came over, and I got pushed out."

"No one saw?"

"No one," she said. "We all assumed he fell. He didn't jump. There are rocks there, just under the surface of the water. We know where to jump, and that is not a jumping point."

"This happened at dawn?"

"The sun was up when I opened my eyes," Riki replied. "You're saying that Dr. Henson was out that morning, doing yoga. I mean, she was here at Morning House by then. She came to stay out here in March. She could have been on the balcony that morning."

"How did everyone else get along with Chris? Were there any other problems?"

"Tom tolerated him," she said. "Chris worked for River Rescue, and they were targeting Tom's dad's fishing business. Tom's a true believer when it comes to his dad, but his dad is full of shit. Everyone seems to know this but Tom. I think he knew what I knew—that Chris cheated. That Chris, wonderful Chris, was kind of gross. But not liking someone much and killing them are different."

"What about that argument Van had with Chris that night?"

"Van wouldn't kill someone," she said. "Liani was over it, and April loved the guy. I mean, the trouble is he did have good qualities. He did do good stuff. The guy *did* spend his weekends saving puppies and trying to keep the river clean. That's all true. But he also was a dirtbag. I hated him the most of anyone, and I didn't kill him."

"So maybe there's something you don't know," I said. "After all, you barely talked to everyone for a year, right?"

"I guess…" She sniffed the air. "Do you smell something?"

Now that she mentioned it, I did. I had been so focused on what she was saying that I had shut off my brain to anything else. But now I was tuned in, and I smelled it clearly.

Smoke.

I've read a lot about fire since my time with the candle. Here's an important thing I learned: if the door is hot, don't open it. I guess I never thought I would encounter a hot door, but when I put my hand against this one, it was like a heater. I opened it just a hairline crack anyway.

"Oh," I said.

My big orange friend was back. Fire. And it was filling the round stairwell.

23

Say you're in a tower in a mansion on an island and someone sets a fire on the stairs leading to your little tower and you are trapped, and you have a bad and altogether-too-recent history with fire. And you're already in a situation where you think you may be trapped with a murderer. What do you do?

"Call 911," I said.

"I have no signal."

Neither did I, as it happened. Riki ran to open the window. Some inner voice told me to grab her and hold her back, so I did that, tackling her around the waist.

"What?" she said, screaming at me, her eyes glazed in panic.

"Don't open the window," I yelled back.

"The smoke!"

"Fires love oxygen," I said. "If you open that window, you're going to feed it. Where's your fire ladder?"

She looked at me hopelessly, and I remembered that she had taken the ladder from her room for our escapade to Dr. Henson's. Riki had a walkie-talkie. I grabbed it.

"If anyone can hear us," I said, "we're in the turret and it is on fire. *The building is on fire.*"

Nothing.

I entered a new phase of my first experience being high—calm. The situation was so serious and insane that I felt fine. Not good, but clear.

"Okay," I said. "Here's what we're going to do. Soak a towel and stick it at the bottom of the door so we can keep the smoke out as long as possible."

Riki was crying and not moving.

"Riki," I said, taking her by the shoulders. "Soak. A. Towel."

She nodded and rushed around the room looking for a towel. Meanwhile, I tried to solve this puzzle. We weren't going out the way we came in because the fire would come through the door soon. The windows were the only way out, but we had no ladder.

I tried to recall the facade of the house. Where were we? I hurried to the piles of gift shop supplies and clawed into a stack of photo brochures and posters. I flattened out one of the latter and found a picture that showed the turret we were in. There was nothing below us—this part of the building was a straight drop. We could, however, maybe get to the roof by climbing over to the part where the turret attached to the house. It wasn't that far. Riki had gone about that distance in her stunt with the ladder. We could do this.

Riki was stuffing the door crack with a wet towel while still crying. She turned to me. "What now?"

"We need to go out the window and get to the roof," I said as if this was the most normal thing in the world.

"You said not to open the window."

"Well, we're going to open it, and we're going to leave."

Perfect clarity now. Hyperfocus. I had reached flow state.

As soon as I opened the window, I heard a rush of air sucking through the room. The smoke began to reach fingers under the door. I looked down to see if there was something we could walk along. There was a lip edging this bit of roof-top, but it was four inches wide, at most. You couldn't get your whole foot on it. This was a surface that would have been treacherous in the best of times, and we were in the worst of them. The rain came down sideways. About two feet above me, there was a small bit of decoration on top of the window—an ornamental point. I stared at it for a moment and got fascinated watching the rain coming down at my face.

"Marlowe!"

Riki grabbed at me. The room had started to fill with smoke. I slammed the window shut.

"We're going to need to go on our toes around the lip of the roof," I said. "We'll need something to hold. I think we could swing something over the point above the window so we have something to hold on to. Do you have rope?"

No rope.

I considered the wind chimes, but they wouldn't work. The curtains. The ones Riki had sewn. They were long enough.

"Get these down," I said, tugging at them.

We almost tore the curtain rod from the wall in our efforts to get the curtains down. There was no time to think this through anymore. The door was blackening, and it was getting hard to breathe.

"We have to go," I said. "You go first."

"Why?"

"Or me, just . . . we have to go."

"You go," she said.

There was terror in Riki's eyes. Pure, unadulterated terror.

"We can do this," I said to her. "We have to. Someone did this to us. Someone set a fire. Stay mad."

"Stay mad," she repeated.

I opened the window, and the storm rushed in again. The smoke billowed. I took my curtain and tried to swing it up over the point above the window, but this was not as easy as it had seemed. The wind kept whipping it around.

"I need something to stand on!" I yelled.

I heard a crash as she dumped all her books out of a wooden box she had been using as a bookcase and stuck it by my feet. I stepped up on this. It occurred to me that I would have to go through the top part of the window to get at the point.

"We need to break this!"

The smoke was burning my eyes. The top of the door was gone. Riki was coughing as she raced around the room. She pushed me aside and smashed the window with a chair, hitting several times to clear the shards that would have disemboweled me if I leaned over them.

This time, with the box and no window, I was able to hook the curtain over the point.

The fire had entered the room.

"Now," I said.

I grabbed both ends of the curtain and swung my leg out the window. Wind slammed me from all directions, throwing my hair in my eyes. The rain was filling the rest of the space. I reached my toe down, looking for that little lip. I couldn't find it. There was only air below me.

I was going to die. That much was obvious. I could not do this and live. And yet, I could not stay in the room and live either. There was a cheerful simplicity to it all.

I felt for the lip again. My toe landed on it this time. One leg in, one leg out. Time to commit. I gripped the windowsill as well as the curtain and lowered my second leg. This time, I found the lip more easily. I was standing four stories up in the storm. All I had to do now was shuffle along. . . .

I went to move my foot and missed. I started to fall backward into eternity. Riki grabbed my arm and pulled me back. I inched along just enough so she could join me. She took the other end of the curtain. Now we were counterweights for each other.

"Move!" she yelled against the window. "Marlowe, go!"

I had zoned. It was time to shuffle. Maybe it was easier that I couldn't see anything, hear anything above the roar of the storm. Also, whoever had done this to me probably hadn't factored in that high Marlowe was apparently chill-in-the-face-of-danger Marlowe. Cat-burglar Marlowe.

I took my first step. Riki moved, leaning into the building, clawing at it for dear life. We moved again, and again. Five feet of this, working our way around the curve. We ran out of length of curtain quickly, so we had to hold on to whatever we could on the building facade, which was nothing really, so we stretched our arms into wide hugs and leaned in. Then the roof was below us, maybe three feet down. It was a hard slant, running with water. How we could get to it wasn't clear.

I did the only thing I could think to do. I dropped to it. Maybe I thought I would land and stick, but I did not land and stick. I was on the world's worst slide. There was nothing to grab, so I cascaded down wet roof tiles until I slammed into the peaked top of a dormer window. Riki was still hugging the turret, her black hair snapping around her face. She looked down fearfully at the roof I was on.

"Jump!"

"I'll slide off!"

"I'll grab you!"

"You're high!"

"Do it anyway!"

Down she came, landing hard, rolling, clawing at the roof. She slid right past me and almost kept going, but I managed to catch her ankle. She was splayed on the roof like a starfish, her head facing the ground. She was attached to me, and I was attached to the top of a window. The rain slickened her leg and my hands kept losing their grip, slipping down to her socks. I clung with all my might, the top of the window digging into my abdomen.

"What do we do now?" she screamed.

"Can you turn to get to the window?"

She used some bad but highly inventive language to let me know she could not, and that I should not have asked. Through the rain, I could see Tom and Liani down below on the ground, dragging cushions and pillows into a pile. There, in the mud and driving rain, were the elegant furnishings of the downstairs rooms, all those pillows and bits of the sofas.

That seemed a bad option. Four stories down, and *maybe* we would hit a bunch of wet sofa. I was starting to think that maybe we'd spend our forever on the roof, as long as I could keep hold of her. Then Van's curly head appeared from the window I was stuck on top of.

"What the fuck?" he screamed.

He had a point, of course, but there was no time to address it. A fire ladder tumbled from the window, landing a few feet from Riki. She clawed for it, but it was too far. He pulled it back and threw it again, this time landing it on her head. She pushed it off and turned herself around. I saw her hands slip off the rungs once or twice, but she managed to climb up. I saw her body disappear through the window. Now it was my turn.

Van and April craned up to look at me.

"We've got you!" April said. "Drop toward us!"

"I'm fine!" I said.

"What?" Van asked.

I played it all out in my head. I could spend the night

jackknifed over this window. I'd probably make it. A helicopter would come for me. A claw would come down, pinch me, and carry me into the sky. All I had to do was wait. Being stuck on the top of the triangular dormer of a window during a storm isn't great, but falling four stories is worse. I'd gone this far. I didn't want to go any farther.

"The house is on fire," Van screamed. "You have to do this, now."

Oh yes. The fire. You can't stay on the roof if there is no roof to stay on. Everyone knows that. I could not stay here, but there was a 50 percent chance that someone below me was a murderer. Liani, April, Tom, Van. It was one of them. Not ideal conditions for a trust fall.

But Riki was in there too. She'd made it.

I wiggled myself so that my legs came up and my head slid down. The roof, while slick in the rain, was composed of many tiles, a dragon skin's worth of scales, nooks to dig my fingers into. Nothing gave me any purchase, though, and now only my feet were hooked over the crest of the window. Once I shifted, I was going down.

"Come on, Marlowe!" Riki called. "Come on . . ."

I straightened my ankles, and I began to slide, bumping down over the tiles, headed for the bottom of the roof and the edge, to the ground . . .

Something caught my foot. Someone. Then I was pulled up, up, up, my chin slamming against tile edges, my knees scraping. They pulled me by the shorts, my shirt, my hair, and then I was falling back into someone's grasp and collapsing on the floor of the upstairs hall, back in the house I had escaped minutes before. The smoke was snaking through, causing me to break into spasms of coughing and tearing my eyes.

"Go go go," Van said. "Gogogogogogo."

Riki hauled me to my feet and the four of us tore down the steps as smoke billowed from the upper floors into the main open hallway. A cloud of it drifted between us and the stained-glass dome, obscuring it. Down, down, down, through the main hall, under the sunrise transom, and out.

As the rain came down around us, we huddled on the lawn and watched the upper floors of Morning House light up. Left unchecked, the fire wandered like a ravenous guest, eating the furniture and carpets and drapes. It ate floors and stairs. It ate the desks and pianos, the cushions and the pictures. It drank the Thousand Island dressing in the gift shop.

Funny, with so much water outside—the countless gallons of the St. Lawrence and this storm—that nothing could stop it. The house was well insulated from the elements. It kept to itself, tight and snug, and burned. Then there was the strangest noise I've ever heard—a twisted music of whistles and screaming pops, followed by a tinkling like a thousand tiny, demented bells.

"There goes the dome," Riki said.

The women in the ceiling. They were leaving, their glass faces breaking from their lead prisons, dripping down, free at last.

July 27, 1932

The day of the deaths at Morning House

Unsurprisingly, Unity was the only one keeping up with that morning's calisthenics. Everyone else was yawning and slow, pausing after their jumping jacks.

"It's a miserable morning, isn't it?" her father said, wiping his brow.

"Let's forgo the running this morning," Faye said. Her eyelids were lowering and she sat down on one of the garden walls. "Why don't we take a morning break and have extra swimming later?"

Her father disliked changes in their routine, but the drug had gone to work on his willpower.

"All right," he said. "No run today, everyone. Go wash up."

Clara, who usually took the stairs with a graceful, bouncing gait, plodded up. Unity took the opportunity for this minor victory and sprinted ahead of the rest.

Back in her own quarters, Unity took a cool bath. About an hour—that's how long she had decided to wait. She rested on her bed, reading *The Wizard of Oz*. She liked the first chapter the best—the cyclone, the house in the air. She always wanted to be Dorothy at that moment: "It was very dark, and the wind howled horribly around her, but Dorothy found she was riding quite easily."

Unity listened. She had trained herself to hear the house. The outside was impervious stone, but the inner workings were organic—wooden floors and steps and doors, human movement. It had a heartbeat, a flow. It was slowing. People were falling asleep.

It was time.

Barefoot, she stepped out into the hall. All her siblings' doors were closed except for William's, who had kept his open a crack. She pushed it open and found him at his desk with his head on the book sitting in front of him. While this was the desired effect, she went over to him and made sure he was breathing normally. She had done her research and was sure everyone would be safe, but there had been a small part of her that worried.

He was fine. Snoring, in fact.

Everywhere she went, the house was quiet. Doors were closed. No one had gone to the gymnasium. Clara was not dancing in her studio. Peering into the kitchen, she found Elisa with her head on a table, fast asleep next to a pile of potatoes and a cutting board.

Unity felt an unexpected rush. She was the most alive person in Morning House.

She opened the door to Max's nursery. His was a wonderful room, one of the best in the house. It had large windows that opened up toward the American side. Miss Clarkson was stretched out on a daybed, fast asleep. Max was on the floor next to her, half dozing, his toy soldiers in his hands.

"Hello, Max," she whispered. "I came to play with you! I thought we could do something naughty. Would you like to throw rocks at the swans?"

Even though he was tired, Max picked up his head in interest. He loved throwing rocks at the swans, because the swans chased him when he got too close and tried to tease them. Unity had no intention of throwing a rock at a swan, but it was a good lure.

"Aren't they terrible?" she went on, holding his clammy little hand. "I hate them."

"I hate them too," Max said. "Hate them."

Max was a bit enthusiastic now, working against the Veronal.

"We'll have to be quiet. They'll try to stop us if they see us. We'll go the fun way."

She led her brother down the winding stone servants' steps. These did not creak and were used infrequently because they were so tight and awkward.

Morning House had several basement-level passageways all around the property to allow for the servants to bring in supplies and move around unseen. She was able to take him outside. Again, there was no one in sight. There were boats on the river, but they were a good distance away. No one was watching except the black swans circling on the lagoon.

"Oh, Max, look! This is the perfect rock. Come over and see."

Of course he came. He knelt next to her and looked into the water.

The actual act was not what she expected. It wasn't physically that difficult, though he did kick and flail. Unity was strong. This was just another exercise—a test of her resolve. A few blows landed on her face and arms, but she could cover any bruises and scrapes later with some story.

She pulled off her dress, revealing the swimsuit underneath, and waded out into the deeper parts of the lagoon, pulling Max with her. Not too deep. The middle, under the surface. Best that he not be found right away. His body was sinking. She dipped under the water with it, holding her breath. She pushed him into a tangle of vegetation and wedged his foot between some rocks. That would hold him long enough.

She slipped out of the lagoon, dried herself off as best she could, and redressed. She entered the house through the lower passages and the back stairs. She passed no one.

Back in her room, she removed the swimsuit and rubbed her bobbed hair hard with a towel. She sat in front of her fan for several minutes, leaning her face toward the cage that contained the whirling blades, until her hair was dry enough. There was a bit of a bruise blossoming on her arm and a thin scratch above her eye. The bruise could be covered with a sweater; the scratch got a light tapping of cosmetic powder. Then she climbed onto her bed, resting on top of the white coverlet.

Unity listened to the ticking noise of the fan and the birds outside. Morning House creaked gently, and downstairs, the clock chimed. She had done the thing that was hard. She had done it for her family—for her father. Her *father*. She had done the thing that she knew he wanted to do but could not do himself. She was the strongest Ralston. She squeezed her eyes shut and found that the rush from before slipped away. She'd had no Veronal, but a calm sleepiness took over. A natural one.

When she woke, it was Victory standing over her, gasping that Max was gone. She noted the time. Almost four in the afternoon. Longer than she'd anticipated. She prepared to join the search and started waking up her brothers. Clara was already gone.

Unity had barely gotten started when she heard the wailing coming from the hall. She got to the steps just in time to see Clara coming in, carrying Max's body. His color had changed, but otherwise he appeared to be asleep. Father came tearing out. Unity heard him make a noise—a terrible noise—one she had not expected. Of course, he must appear sad. He likely was sad. This noise was deeper. Faye's was positively primal. Two people had to grab her to keep her from going over the railing when she saw what was happening below.

They carried him to the breakfast room and put him on the table. Benjamin was by the door, his face glazed in horror. Unity had to look for herself, see that the work was done. She barely had a chance before Aunt Dagmar swept in, shutting the door, gathering them up and ushering them to the playhouse. She could hear Faye screaming. She felt bad for that. Faye would be upset—she'd known that going in. But it would pass.

The police came. Unity looked out the window of the playhouse and watched the two officers walking the lawn.

Elisa made them trays of forbidden foods—cookies and sandwiches with meat and sugary lemonade. It was improper, but Unity had to be patient today. There would be disruptions to the normal order of things at the start. It would be all right soon enough.

Edward got drunk. Victory was catatonic. Benjamin pulled all the books down and William banged on the piano upstairs.

Clara was nowhere to be found. She was hiding somewhere.

This was the first thing that caused Unity to worry that day. It had all gone well, perfectly to plan. But Clara finding the body so quickly and then vanishing, this disturbed her. Clara, perfect Clara. Clara, who Father thought should train for the Olympics. Clara, the first picked out of the six of them. Clara, with her little joke about coming to breakfast exactly on time. Clara drinking and speeding along in her boat. Whispering with William. Complaining about being here, about the rules, about Father's beliefs.

Clara knew just where to look for Max. How?

Once they were permitted back into the house, Unity rushed to her room. The compartments in her desk were open. How was this possible? No one knew about her desk. Only Father . . . and Father was downstairs. Father had not come up.

Clara. It had to be. She knew. She was going to *ruin* this

somehow, this important thing Unity had done. But where had she gone? What was she doing? Clara had hiding places.

She would come back to the house. Unity would have to wait for her. Confront her. She should understand. In fact, the more Unity thought about it, the more she knew that Clara would understand. After all, Max reserved some of his worst behavior for Clara. He'd just thrown a rock at her head only a week or so ago. Clara might be mad that Unity had done the job first. Perhaps she might congratulate her.

That was the most likely. She would be jealous. Clara jealous of her! It was so delicious to think about. Perfect Clara, Olympic Clara, dancer Clara—bested by bookish Unity. The one with the power and self-control.

It made her quite smug, really.

Unity sat on her bed and waited. The sun began to go down. Finally, she heard someone walking heavily up the steps. Those were Clara's steps—they had a rhythm. Unity got up and met her on the landing. Clara looked at her for a long moment.

"What did you give us?" Clara said. "Why were we sleeping?"

Unity considered lying, pretending she had no idea what Clara was talking about. But that would only work for so long, and what was the point in that?

"Veronal," she said. "It didn't do you any harm."

"And you killed him."

Unity did not reply. Though she was proud of her actions,

she also could not voice them. There were other people to be considered.

"So what now?" Unity asked.

Clara stalked out of the room. Unity followed her up the steps. Clara kept going, right to the top floor, to the open gallery with the balcony that towered over the trees and the river. She stood there, still dripping, looking at the moon.

"What now, Clara?" Unity asked again.

"I've been watching you," Clara said. "I saw how you were looking at him. For a while, I wasn't sure what you would do or when, but as soon as Victory said he was gone, I knew. The water. He can't swim. No one would question it. We all slept and you put him in the water."

"Someone had to do something," Unity replied. "Max had no self-control. He wasn't even *trying*. You know that better than anyone. He hit you. I know that's why you pushed him. You were trying to make him learn. You have to understand. . . ."

"Understand?"

"Father deserves better," Unity said. "You know that. He's always telling us we have to be strong, do the things that are hard. . . ."

Clara reached back and punched Unity in the face. Blood shot from the corner of Unity's mouth as she reeled backward.

"You . . . ," Clara said, coming toward her, "are a monster. A murdering—"

303

Unity scrabbled to her feet, reeling from the blow. Clara was far stronger than she was.

"Stop!" she yelled. "I'm your *sister*."

"Max was my *brother*."

"He wasn't as good as us. He didn't deserve what he had."

Clara was looming, preparing for something. Another blow? They'd never fought. And Clara was drunk. Father had said that alcohol was poison. It had poisoned Clara.

Unity was afraid. She was alone with Clara and the night sky.

"What are you going to do?" Unity said.

Clara rushed forward. Unity reached for one of the wrought iron chairs they had on the balcony. Though iron, they were easy enough to lift when you were full of adrenaline. She swung out, making contact with Clara's shoulder and head, causing her to stumble, to fall against the balcony wall. Clara caught herself at the last moment, grabbing at the crenellations, looking out at the dark water, the electric blue of the night sky, the white moon.

She did not see Unity lift the chair to strike her a second time.

24

We were too wet and cold to stay outside any longer, and our eyes were burned with patterns of dancing flame, so we returned to the playhouse. When we couldn't reach anyone off island to report the fire, we scattered to our rooms. Riki had no room, so I brought her with me.

"Here," I said, shoving an unused towel at her. I dried myself with a pair of dirty sweatpants sitting on a chair. My teeth were chattering from cold, from shock. I may or may not have still been under the influence. It was hard to tell. I dug into my drawers and found two pairs of pajama bottoms. I threw one to her, along with a shirt. I felt like we might never be warm again. I climbed into my bed and huddled. She stood, rubbing her arms.

"Get in," I said, holding up the blanket. This was not a romantic gesture—it was purely an instinctual one. Riki didn't hesitate. She slid in next to me. I'd never been in a bed, under a blanket, with a girl before, and these were not the circumstances I'd expected for my first time. I was startled when Riki threw her arms around me in a tight embrace. She was smaller than me, and I wrapped around her. Together, we pooled our warmth into the tiny space between our stomachs.

"We're alive," she said. Her breath was warm on my face.

"I think so."

"I thought we were going to die. I really, really thought we were going to die."

"We didn't."

We reeked of wet smoke and we were streaked with soot. She buried her face against my shoulder and held tighter. I pulled her closer, and we brought each other back, breath by breath.

"Someone tried to kill us. Someone killed Chris and Dr. Henson."

"I know."

"But no one is going to believe all that. They're going to think I caused the fire, because I'm the one with the fire, and that I'm making things up to get out of trouble."

I wondered how much I cared. I was holding Riki. We had this little space under the blanket, humid from our wet clothes and our breath. She pressed her fingertips into the palm of my hand, pulsing them gently.

"I have no fucking idea who did this," she said softly, "but when I find out, I'm going to kill them."

She touched my cheek. I closed my eyes, letting the world swirl away. Then I felt the spring of the bed and saw that she had slipped out and was pacing the floor next to it.

"They say if there's no body," she said, "there's no crime.

Up until this point, everyone thought Dr. Henson drowned. But now it looks like things didn't happen that way—just that someone wanted us to think that by putting the paddleboard in the water. Dr. Henson was up on that balcony on the morning she vanished. We know that from the yoga mat. You found her tooth under the balcony, which seems like a pretty strong clue that she landed there. Which means there is a body on the island. So we find the body."

"That body is gone," I said. "It's got to be in the river."

"Does it? When would whoever killed her be able to put her in the river? It was daylight when she was killed, probably. How could you risk rolling a dead body down the lawn in daylight? And it would have been found—they searched the shoreline."

"She's probably out farther."

"How? You'd need to get to the Jet Ski to do that. And think about this—falling from that balcony onto the rocks— that's going to be *messy*. There's going to be a lot of blood. The body is going to be in bad condition. But there was no blood on there that morning."

"It rained," I said.

"A *lot* of blood," she repeated. "Hard to clean off jagged rocks. And that wasn't rain like this. You'd need a hose, but you'd need to really be thorough. You'd need a way to contain the situation."

I mused on this for a moment. The answer became obvious.

"When we were gathering the cushions," I said. "There was a tarp missing."

Riki's head jerked up.

"One of those big blue ones? What if . . . you put that over the spot before she fell. You push her. She lands on the tarp. It's still a mess, but you could wrap her up pretty quickly and pull her out of sight. And say, in the process, a tooth rolls or flies off into the rocks, you wouldn't see it and you might not catch it if you went back and looked. So she's in a tarp."

"Like a burrito," I said. "A murder burrito."

(I was getting kind of hungry. I blame this on the edible.)

"Sure," Riki said. "She's a murder burrito. The body is heavy. It's big. Now what? Drag it all the way to the boathouse, throw this murder burrito on the back of the Jet Ski and go out on the open water and very publicly dump her? There was no time for any of that. The cops were around too much at the start for anyone to go out and dump her, then the storm came in. And again, it would be hard to do on a Jet Ski. No, the easiest and safest thing would be to keep her here until the coast was clear, until you could get the boat, go out far."

"We searched the house," I said. "We searched the grounds."

"It's a big house," she said.

"Yeah, but . . . she told us, my first night at dinner. Her grandfather was a bootlegger, and there's some crawlspace somewhere."

"Yeah, but where? I've probably read more about this house than anyone, and I have no idea where that is."

"It sounds like Dr. Henson heard it from her grandfather," I said. "It's just as possible other families talk about it.

It was concealed but not secret. She said it was dank. Somewhere the family didn't go. What is *dank*? Sounds . . . Swedish. German. Dank. Is that dark?"

"Dark, maybe gross?"

Dark. Gross. Someplace the family didn't go.

"That's the basement," I said.

"It's a big basement, and we searched it. And we can't look again because the house is on fire."

"It's a good idea to burn down a house if you'd hid a body in it. Especially if you have someone nearby who already set a fire once this summer who you can blame it on."

"Jesus." Riki went to the window and opened it a little, letting in a spray of rain and wind and a trail of smoke. I was overwhelmed by the smell of petrichor. The ground after the rain, mixed with fire.

The mix of petrichor and fire smoke lifted my senses again. A smell could completely hijack my brain, take me somewhere else.

"Oh my god," I said. "Oh no. Oh god."

"What?"

"Don't bodies smell?"

"I think so," she said.

I pushed back the blanket and got to my feet. I found I was a little dizzy, but not so much that I couldn't stand.

"That smell coming from near where the bathrooms are?" I said. "The smell that started right after she vanished?"

"Shit," she said.

"Or, not shit," I said. "That's not sewage. It's *her*. We're going to have to convince the police to dig through a million tons of rubble or climb under the unstable wreckage of a burned-up mansion to see why our bathroom smelled so bad. That's not going to happen."

I knew what I was going to do, and it wasn't the edible—it was the fact that if I didn't do this, I would be the one with the fire forever, and I would know there was a dead woman under a house in the Thousand Islands.

"I'm going," I said. "I'll be fast. You stay here in case I don't come back."

"There is no way in hell," she said, stepping toward me, "that I am letting you do this alone."

"We make bad plans," I said.

"Yeah, well, we live in weird times."

"We're doing this?" I asked.

"We have to."

I grabbed the tube of Midnight Rose. If I didn't come back, I was going out with Akilah's gift. And if I did come back, I needed to keep this safe. I opened the door, and we walked together to the passage that went back to Morning House.

The smoke had not gotten into the tunnel passage. We were far enough from the fire, and the fire door on the house end did its job. Once we opened it, though, the smell was strong. It wasn't here yet, but it was hot, the air thick. Above us, the house sang a strange song—creaking and shrieking as the fire consumed it.

"Fast," Riki said. "Fast, go . . . go."

We pointed our flashlight forward and ran to the bathrooms. I let my nose lead me, as it had led me into this mess to begin with. I closed my eyes and tried to push the approaching smell of smoke out of my mind.

There it was—that meaty, putrid odor.

"Somewhere around here," I said.

We tapped and smacked the walls around the bathrooms, trying to work out where there might be a walled-off area. There were several small open spaces where tools and supplies were kept. These were creepy, spidery places in the corner of the basement that I had never examined closely.

Inside one of these nooks, I realized the interior walls were shorter than the ones in the other compartments. This was the nook where the metal racks of cleaning supplies and toilet paper were kept. I shook the rack to test its weight. It moved easily. Riki and I grabbed opposite sides of the rack and pulled it away from the wall.

The wall behind was a different sort of brick. I put my face up to the corner where it should have, in theory, met the outside wall of the building. I felt it on my lips first—a slight movement of air. Then I got a noseful of the stench. I saw it last—a space, millimeters thick, between the two walls.

"Here," I said. "Right here . . ."

"Marlowe!"

Her voice had taken on a new tone. I turned to look at her, then to look behind us. Tom was standing at the opening of the nook, holding up a sledgehammer.

July 27, 1932

The night of the deaths at Morning House

Unity did not look down to see what she had created on the stones below. The fall would be fatal. She had killed two of her siblings. One had been intentional. The second, improvised. Necessary. That one she would have to explain.

Below, screaming.

She returned the chair to its proper position and went back to her room. Clara had bloodied her nose and cut her lip and the blood had dripped down the front of her dress. She washed off the blood, changed her clothes. She could tell other people she fell, tripped up the steps looking for Max. No one would care. The house was chaos now.

Unity waited for Father to come to her. He would come— he *had* to come. He would realize that she had done what was necessary, had been brave and strong.

But he did not.

He was busy, of course. The police, the bodies. He would have to do something official to mark their deaths. She would go to him. She rose and walked out of her room, down the hall, down the steps. She felt tall. Grand. Complete. Unity felt like she was gliding on ice as she walked up to his study door and knocked. She opened it to find her father sitting at his desk, head in his heads. He looked up at her.

"Unity," he said quietly. "Clara is dead."

"Yes," Unity said. "I know."

"Clara," he repeated. His voice was hoarse. Unity fought back the fingers of panic that were creeping around her neck. This should have been her moment of glory. Clara, ruining everything again, being the star of the show.

"I came to tell you something," she said, primly taking a seat on one of the plush green chairs.

He looked up at her, his face gray. "I wish you would not."

This was confusing.

"But I have to. You realize what I did, don't you?"

Unity did not believe in spooks and spirits, but it seemed like something left Phillip Ralston, some animating impulse that kept him upright. His eyes hollowed.

"The household was asleep all day," he said, his voice a rasp. "It was not natural."

"Veronal."

"Veronal," he repeated. "That does explain things."

"I'm sorry about that, but it was necessary. I was very careful about the dosages. I studied them from your books. I was extremely precise, as much as I could be. The dosage anyone took likely never exceeded twenty-five grains. . . ."

This was familiar ground—telling her father her work. The look on his face was much more familiar. He was listening, following her calculations. She expected him to correct

313

her on some of the methods she had used. Someone could have overdosed if they had had too much of something. But her plan had worked exactly as she anticipated.

Unity waited for the praise that was certainly coming—the speech of pride and gratitude.

"Did anyone else see you?" he finally replied.

A rush of relief spread through her. Her lungs expanded and she straightened up.

"I thought you were going to do it," she said. "So many times. Or I thought you were trying to get Clara to do it. I thought she might succeed as well. She threw him off the boat. Victory pulled him out, because she's sentimental, isn't she. . . ."

"Clara was trying to teach him to swim, Unity."

"It could have worked. It would have been easy—just to say he fell from the boat and we couldn't get to him in time. But it didn't happen, so I did it. It was very peaceful. And Clara, that was an accident. She came after me and punched me, Father. I hit her back. She fell. That's all that happened."

Her father—the great Phillip Ralston—appeared to shrink. He sank into his chair and put his hands around his head and sobbed.

It was the most terrible sight Unity had ever seen.

"We will say Max drowned by accident," he said, struggling to catch his breath. "And that Clara jumped from the roof. Do you understand? This must be the story. To everyone. To Faye, to your brothers and sisters, to your aunt. Everyone."

"But I did—"

"Tell me you understand, Unity," he said. The tears were rolling down his face and his voice was thick. It was repulsive.

"Yes," she said, turning away. "Yes."

"Go. Go to your room. Go, Unity."

Unity held her head high as she left the room and went up the stairs. She did not look behind her. Someone had been listening at the door. Of this, she was certain. She was glad. Someone knew of her triumph. Someone knew she was the brave one. If she didn't know who it was, it would be anyone. It would be everyone.

She was the true Ralston.

25

Tom, huh? Funny, I didn't know who had done all this, but my gut hadn't been with him. He was simply too . . . meaty. But there he was, about to pulverize us in a burning basement with a sledgehammer.

"No!" Riki, to my amazement, jumped, webbing her tiny body in front of mine. I was about to die, probably, but Riki was going to go down with me, defending me.

"Move!" Tom yelled.

Or not.

Riki grabbed my arm and we skittered out of the way. Tom swung back and landed the sledgehammer into the wall. It didn't precisely fall down, but it made a sound like a bowling ball hitting some pins. There was a dent where some of the bricks had been loosened. He struck again, then once more, and a portion gave way, making a gaping black hole.

The smell hit in earnest. Tom had to step back and cover his nose and mouth with his shirt. Riki reeled. I told myself to ignore it, and for some reason, my brain obliged. I turned my flashlight into the hole. I was staring into a space maybe six feet deep, with some broken bits of wooden crates and glass.

Off in the corner, there was a large bundle of blue tarp.

I had the presence of mind to take a few quick pictures on my phone, before jumping back to allow Tom to move in with the sledgehammer and knock a bigger opening into the wall.

"Oh my god," he said. "Oh shit . . ."

Riki had gotten one of the wheeled standing carts used to move stacks of chairs. It wasn't perfect, but it was good enough. Tom and I each took a side of the bundle and hauled it onto the cart. The stench was almost unbearable now, tearing at the lining of my nose. What was inside was heavy and felt far too fluid for my liking. We ran out into the driving rain with our lumpy bundle juddering on the cart. In the process of running down the lawn, the tarp package came off the cart and started to roll. It had opened slightly.

Out flopped a purple-green human hand.

"What the actual fuck is that?" Van said as we dragged the horrible bag, slick with rainwater and possible other liquids, into the entryway of the playhouse. He, Liani, and April came to the door to greet us, and all reeled from the stench.

Dr. Henson may have been a bit squishy and stomach-churning in odor, but that was not her fault. It's only right to address the body in the tarp properly. I tried to think of a delicate way to explain what was going on, but Riki simply said, "Dr. Henson. Mushy. Bad." She punctuated this by stepping

317

back into the rain to dry heave for a moment.

We put Dr. Henson in the common room in the playhouse and shut the door. Liani shoved a towel under the crack of the door, but that didn't help much.

We went to the second floor, to the large open studio where Liani and April slept, and opened all the windows. There was no escaping that odor, though. It was on our clothes, our hair. I could taste it. Luckily, we had an entire burning building to factor into the mix. It was a real feast for the senses.

The mood, to put it as mildly as possible, changed.

Now that Dr. Henson had been deposited, Tom's body gave up the effort of holding back the sickness. He threw up outside for five minutes, before staggering back inside and collapsing on Liani's bed.

"How did you know where we were?" I said to him. "What we were doing?"

"I didn't know what you were doing," he said, his voice raspy. "I heard some of what you were saying, something about knowing where the passage was. Then you came out and I saw you go down into the tunnel. I didn't know you were looking for . . ."

"So why did you follow us?" Riki said.

"The treasure," he said, rubbing his brow. "That first night Marlowe was here, Dr. Henson mentioned some secret place in the house—and it sounded like it was in the basement—I went looking for it."

"I heard someone," I said. "I called out. You didn't answer."

"I didn't want anyone else looking."

"You ran back into a burning building looking for a *treasure*?" Liani asked. "An imaginary treasure?"

"Well, they went back in. The fire is still on the higher floors . . ."

"Seriously?"

"Okay," Riki said. "Forget the treasure. No one gives a fuck about the treasure."

"Clearly, someone gives a lot of fucks about the treasure," Van pointed out. His voice utterly sober, not a hint of a joke.

"Are we safe in here?" April asked. "How long before the fire spreads to us? The fireboat can't come out during a storm like this."

Last Chance would be here long after our chances were gone.

"Forget that too," Liani said. "We'll stay here as long as we can, and the rain may hold off the spread. If not, we can go to the boathouse. We need to talk about what you just brought in."

"What we brought in," I said, "is Dr. Henson."

It would have sounded better if I didn't let out a loud belch to punctuate that statement. Liani had given me a can of sparkling peach water when we came in. My mouth was so dry and tacky and my throat so sore that I'd pounded it.

"So," Van said. "We have Dr. Henson's body in a tarp and the building is on fire."

"Correct."

"But why is the building on fire?" April cried.

319

"Because someone set it on fire," I said. "Not me. Most likely the person who put Dr. Henson in the tarp, and who decided to use the fact that I accidentally set a fire as a good way of covering her up. Literally. With an entire building. And taking Riki and me out with her. Also, the same person who dosed me."

"*Dosed* you?" Liani said.

"Someone gave me an edible," I said. "I have been out of it for most of the night. I think it helped me, though, because I stayed calm."

"I didn't give you anything," Van said, holding up his hands. "Anyone's welcome, but I never give anyone anything they didn't ask for."

"Well, it got in me. But the only thing I ate was . . ."

Of course. The Moose Tracks, the one with all the extra chocolate in it.

"Do you have weed chocolate?" I asked Van.

"Yeah?"

"Well, that's how they did it. In the ice cream."

"Yes, but why . . ."

"Because we found a *goddamn tooth*, is why," Riki snapped.

"I found it," I corrected her in a soft voice. I didn't want ownership of the tooth—I just like to be accurate.

I pulled the Midnight Rose lipstick from my pocket and twisted it up.

"Tooth," I said.

Five faces peered through the glow of a battery-powered lamp, looking at the grisly nub of lipsticky bone.

320

"I found it in the rubble under the patio when I was putting stuff away before the storm. But let's take this story in order. The prom party on Mulligan Island, somewhere around dawn, Chris Nelson falls off the cliff face into the water. No one sees it happen—or so everyone thought. Because someone did. Dr. Henson is here, on Ralston Island, doing morning yoga on the balcony that overlooks the river. She has a camera with a high-powered lens. She sees *something*, but she's not sure what. She hints at this a few times. She keeps mentioning things happening right out in the open, that she's seen things from that balcony. She talks about evil happening in the open. No one pays any attention to this except the person who killed Chris Nelson. But the night before she disappeared, when we were all swimming, I mentioned that she'd told me that she wanted me to spy on all of you, kind of. The next morning, she went over the edge of the balcony. So if we know who pushed Chris, we'll know who pushed her. The truth is somewhere in your drama. Let's start with you, Tom. Chris was in the River Rescue and targeting your family."

"I literally just helped you," he said.

"You helped us because you thought there was treasure, but you could have hit us instead. You helped us get the body out. I'm not sure why you would do that, since she's technically evidence, and for all we know there's DNA all over her that would have been burned up in the fire. But hey, who knows? So in my mind, it's Liani, or April, or Van."

"This isn't funny," April said.

"No," I replied. "It's really not. Chris cheated on you,

321

Liani. And you, Van. And April, he never cheated on you exactly, but I'm guessing he kind of let you down? He didn't break up with you, but he broke up all of you, as a friend group. So you're not out of the mix."

"I tried to save him," Liani said, her voice brittle.

"You got him out of the water," I countered. "Doesn't mean you didn't put him in there. But Van—you were really the closest to the action. You fought that night."

"We fought a lot of nights, because we liked making up," he said. I couldn't read his expression because he was leaning back.

"If you're right," Tom said, "and Dr. Henson saw someone kill Chris, she would have done something about it. She wouldn't keep it to herself."

"Not if she didn't know what she saw," I said. "She said it herself—she'd had eye surgery recently. She couldn't tell if the mirror in the dining room was crooked. And what must that be like? Thinking you saw someone push another person to their death? What if you really weren't sure? You'd think about it. Turn it over in your head. What if she just didn't know? I mean, if I saw something in the distance that might have looked like a murder, I'd doubt myself. I'd talk myself out of it."

"None of us knew where that hidden room was," April added.

"Clearly, someone did," I said, thinking out loud. "She gave us a hint my first night here, and it didn't take me too long to work out where it was. It was hidden but it wasn't secret. It wasn't impossible to find."

They were really trying to poke holes in my story, but I was not for poking, not that night. I am a patient person, but I have limits.

"The thing about this is that it was personal," I said. "Right? This had something to do with all of you, some grievance, some petty thing that got blown up. And maybe whoever it was did it by accident—lashed out and he fell. You didn't mean to do it. But once you did, you had to keep yourself safe. You killed Dr. Henson to stay safe and set the fire. But . . ."

My brain caught up with one outstanding fact.

". . . you also did something else—you put Dr. Henson's camera in Riki's room. That was weird of you if you were just going to set us on fire. That's petty. You've had that for days. I guess you found nothing on it, or you erased the pictures. It would have been enough to leave the camera. Riki would have gotten the blame. No. You had to go and set a fire because *I'm the one with the fire* and you thought it wasn't good enough until we *died*. Because all of this—all of it—has been about you."

Van leaned forward suddenly.

"Something occurs to me," he said. "That night, at the party, you know how I found out about Chris cheating on me that time?"

Remember a while back, I told you about how I could do brainteasers in my head? Check back. I said it. Well, my brain must have been working on this one—moving the camera and the fire and the tarp and the tooth and all of it—and so far I had no answer. But I had a feeling. A vibe. Because I knew what he was going to say next.

"April," he said. "You told me. Why?"

"What do you mean?" she said, her voice sharp.

"Why tell me?"

"Because—"

"Because why? Because you stir shit? I mean, I've always known that about you. It's what I like about you. Chris didn't like it, though. He knew you were in love with him. He used to joke about it. He said you needed to be at the center of everything, and that people always got into fights after talking to you. He called you an underminer. I mean, what he said was you were full of shit."

Liani sat up straighter.

"You told me about Riki and Chris," she said. "You showed me the video."

"Wait," Riki said. "What? You were the one who told me that she shouldn't see the video. You said the sound was bad and it came off like I was coming on to Chris, not trying to trap him."

"I didn't think it was true," Liani added. "All that shit you were saying Marlowe said."

She had turned on April, who was coiled in on herself, legs tucked up to her chest.

"What did she say I said?" I asked.

"Basically that you thought I was a bitch for being mean to Riki. That Van was burned out. Things like that. I didn't get that vibe from you, but she was repeating entire conversations."

324

"I never said any of those things."

"I told you," Van said. "This is why we like her. Seriously, was I the only one who knew this? Why did you guys hang out with her?"

A warm tingle of annoyance crawled over my skin. She had been saying things about me, making me seem untrustworthy, backbiting. The April I saw now was the same in all physical ways as the one I had known since I had gotten here—same long red hair, round, open face. But there was a lock in her jaw and a set focus in her eyes that was cold. Maybe it was the edible, or the storm, or the *dead body* downstairs—but this was a scary face. The face of someone who might lash out and push you to your death.

"That night," I said, "it was prom. It was almost the end of everything you'd ever known. You had one summer with everyone, and you were all going to be together here. Chris was going away after that. It was the last chance. You'd made sure Chris and Liani were broken up. And now Van and Chris were fighting. This was your moment. Van ran off, and then you appear, ready to help."

"You're listening to some drugged-out person who literally *burned a house down*," she said.

"Yeah," Tom said. "We are."

"Based on what? Nothing. This is insane. You are my *friends*. And this is based on nothing."

She had a point there. This was just a story I was telling about her. A story that made sense, considering the facts. None of it was proof. None of it would hold up.

I went back into my mind and ran the footage again. I replayed that whole morning, when Dr. Henson first disappeared, looking for anything at all that stood out. One thing did.

"The morning Dr. Henson vanished was hot," I said. "Sticky. Remember?"

"It's summer," she said.

"Hotter than usual. And you were wearing your fleece."

"So?"

"So what I'm thinking," I said, "is that knocking someone off a balcony is pretty direct, but what if that person lashes out. Someone strong, who does yoga every day. What if they reach for you, scratch you? What if they rip off your necklace."

"I lost my necklace looking for her," she snapped.

"No, you *said* you lost it looking for her. Riki and I saw you take off your fleece and jump in. Neither of us were looking too closely. You said you got stuck."

"You saw me bleeding when I came out," she said.

"That's not hard to do. You scrape yourself alongside a rock, flail around, say you got stuck. Nothing to it."

"What are you doing?" April said. "How high are you?"

"I have no idea," I replied. "You tell me."

April must have realized, just as I did, that it was over. She tried to protest, tried to explain, but her voice seemed more and more distant. The others let her talk, and I drifted away on my own thoughts. It was only when I burst out laughing that everyone else stopped talking and turned to me.

"It . . . doesn't . . . matter . . ."

"Marlowe?" Riki said. "You okay?"

I got myself under control enough to speak.

"It doesn't matter if Dr. Henson saw who killed Chris. Let's say she didn't. What matters is—*it sounded like she could have*. Think about it. Say you get here and you realize that Dr. Henson has a dead-on view of Mulligan Island and this camera with an amazing zoom. You find out she wakes up early and does yoga here. She says a bunch of stuff that sounds like she saw something, but maybe she didn't! Maybe she meant exactly what she said when she told me she wanted to keep an eye on everyone—she wanted someone from the outside to read the room because *you'd all just had a friend die*. Maybe she just wanted to know if you were all *okay*. When she said that stuff about evil things happening out in the open, she was talking about this house, about eugenics. In other words, maybe she meant exactly what it sounded like and what we all thought she meant in the first place. What if you killed her for *nothing*, you *paranoid freak*?"

"This is bullshit!" April screamed. "Why are you letting her do this? She's a *pyro*. You are my *friends*."

"We're not letting anyone do anything," Liani said, standing up. "If you didn't do this, fine. But if that necklace is out there somewhere, we're going to find it."

26

I mention smell a lot. Smells evoke emotion and memories. They linger. They perfume. And then there are smells like the one we had in the house with us now. Smells that speak of danger and decay. Some scents whisper. This one screamed. It kicked the smoke away like it was nothing.

There was a stash of N95s on a shelf. Liani and I put these on, shoving paper towels in the gap, and we could still barely stand to open the lounge door. She bent over, fighting back a retch. I thanked the power of whatever I had been given—the weed was at least keeping my nausea at bay. I went over to the tarp and kicked it open slightly, exposing the hand that had come out.

It was slightly clawed.

"See that?" I shouted to her.

That was enough. Liani nodded, clasping the N95 to her face. We backed out, slammed the door, and ran out into the rain, trying to wash that odor and the experience away.

"It looks like she was grabbing at something," Liani said, gasping. "Or holding something."

"If it was the necklace, it's either in there . . ." I tipped my head back toward the building. ". . . or it's out here."

"I'm never going back in there."

"And if it's out here, I don't know if we'll find it," I said.

"Of course we will," she said. "Come with me."

She ran through the driving rain in the direction of the lagoon, slipping and sliding over the muddy lawn. Once we got to the shed, I knew what she was doing.

She pulled the metal detector from the back.

"Should we use that in this weather?" I asked.

"Probably not," she replied. "We're going to anyway. I've got rubber boots around here. Maybe I can ground myself."

We were quickly joined by Riki, then by Tom, then by Van. Everyone mashed into the tiny space.

"Who's with April?" I asked.

"Well, they ran after you," Van said, "and there was no way I was staying with her."

"So is she back at the playhouse alone?"

"Forget about her," Liani said, pulling on the boots. "Where's she going to go?"

"She could take the Jet Ski," Riki said. "Or try to, even though it would be dangerous."

"I took the keys out when we were prepping," Tom said. "Safety precaution. So, where do we look first?"

"The patio," I said.

We pulled the cover off the fountain to use as an improvised group umbrella. We each took a corner, with Liani in the middle with the metal detector, and shuffled across the lawn, slipping and sliding as we went—a human amoeba, slithering toward the burning house.

"Record this," Liani said. Tom and Van both whipped out their phones and got the search from different angles.

Liani began sweeping the detector over the stones. I became the searcher on the ground while everyone else tried to keep the flopping tarp above us and flash their phones and cameras. She got several beeps for old beer bottle caps, which I picked from the mud. She got a solid one at the edge closest to the house. I pulled back a stone and dug my fingers into the mud. There was a little flash of smooth pink. The ground didn't want to give it up at first, but I clawed at it and fought the suction. It came loose.

It was a slender pink box, rectangular in shape. Though it was stone, it was almost translucent, like a salt lamp. There was a small silver clasp and hinges that had weathered a bit, but it looked solid. I opened it and saw a plastic bag with papers inside. At any other time this would have been the most exciting thing to ever happen, but it was not April's necklace. That was the only thing in the world that mattered at the moment. I thrust it over to Riki, who accepted it, wide-eyed, and tucked it inside her hoodie.

"The basement," Tom said. "It might be in there? We can't go back in there, can we?"

It was possible, but I hadn't seen anything glinting down there earlier. It wasn't worth the risk.

"The tarp with the body in it came open when we were running," I said. "On the lawn."

So we ran again, our strange little tarp creature with ten legs, through the rain. We worked from the public basement door that we'd just come out of and made a sweep of the area. The ground was so steep and slick that we were all slipping and falling, the tarp coming with us. Liani kept going, swinging the detector back and forth over the ground.

Of course we would not find it. Of course this was all a hallucination. This was what happened when you had an edible. Maybe this summer had not happened at all. Of course it never happened. I had never burned down Juan and Carlita's house, never gone out with Akilah, never come here. I was back at home, tooling around in the Smart Car, serving up hot bottoms.

Except the thing was beeping again. This time, Van went for it, because he had slipped and was already on the ground.

"Look what I found," he yelled up to us.

He was holding a gold necklace with a letter *A*.

We made a run back to the playhouse, but now that we had breathed the clean air, we couldn't stay. Clearly, April had decided the same because she was nowhere to be found. It was unlikely she had run back into Morning House, which meant she was in one of the outbuildings.

"The boathouse," Tom said. "Has to be."

The place with the only means of escape. And it was where we found her a few minutes later, standing near the Jet Ski. The lockbox was open.

"Now what?" Riki said. "You can't push us anywhere and

you can't burn the whole island down. What's the move?"

"*Why are you doing this to me?*" April screeched.

"Because you killed our friend," Liani said, her voice low and controlled. "Because you killed Dr. Henson."

"Your friend? He cheated on you *all the time* and you did *nothing*. He didn't want to be with you. I don't even know why he was. And you . . ."

This was to Van, who was the most sober I'd ever seen him, leaning against a rack of canoes.

". . . you didn't even care. You let him do anything."

"But he never did you, honey," he said. "Yeah, Chris was kind of a dick in some ways, but he always called it like he saw it. He said he made out with you once because he was trying to be nice. And this big fight with Riki—you made sure that happened. Why was that? Because Riki also knows bullshit when she sees it?"

"Sounds about right," Riki said.

"I'm leaving," April said, tears pouring down her face. "You're all crazy. I'll swim."

"You won't," Liani replied. "You've never made it on a clear day. You won't get ten feet tonight."

"I'll do it!"

"Okay." Liani shrugged. "Do it. I'm not getting you out. You go in, you get yourself out. Let's see it. Good luck."

April looked down at the water of the empty slip. It slapped the sides of the dock. Outside, the water was a gaping mouth that would eat her whole.

There was no road left for her.

It's hard for me to describe what April became next. Now that she was exposed, she seemed to twist. Her fury pulled at her features.

"It was an accident! He was wasted. He . . . We were talking. He was . . . yelling at me. He . . . I didn't even do anything. I just pushed him back a little."

"Let's say that's true," Liani said. "What about Dr. Henson?"

"It wasn't my fault. She . . ."

She dissolved into gasping tears and collapsed down onto the dock. She continued to scream about what we were doing to her, while we all watched. This went on for some time. Tom wandered out at some point, then returned.

"*Last Chance* is here," he said.

I walked to the doorway and looked out at the still-burning remains of Morning House and started laughing uncontrollably.

27

As the storm gasped its last, the fire and emergency crew stepped off *Last Chance* and began assessing the sheer chaos that was Ralston Island. While the fire crew figured out what to do, the EMTs examined us and found that we were alive and mostly undamaged, aside from some scrapes and cuts. The smoke hadn't done us any serious injury. We told the police about Dr. Henson's body in the playhouse and gave them the contours of what had taken place. They were, to put it mildly, surprised.

It was decided that we wouldn't cross back to shore until the storm had abated, so we were to stay in the boathouse. The police took April out, though. I'm not sure where they went.

Riki grabbed me by the sleeve. "Come on," she said.

By now, I was used to following Riki around. This time, though, I knew what we were doing.

The upstairs of the boathouse had previously been the quarters for the captain and the crew. These had been allowed to rot, unlike the lower part of the structure. The new tenants had already knocked the walls down and it was a blank, open space with a new wooden floor. It looked like a yoga studio, or a spot for tech bros to engage in some kind of free-flowing experience. Bad apps would be born here.

We sat down under a window. Riki produced the box from her hoodie and opened it. Inside was a plastic ziplock bag with letters inside.

"Plastic bag," she said, prying it out of the box. "No ziplock in the 1930s."

Inside, there were two old envelopes with handwritten addresses. The top one was to Benjamin Ralston and was postmarked May 3, 1995. The second one was visibly older, more delicate, the handwriting more formal. This was addressed to someone called Irene Wallenberg in Boston and was postmarked December 28, 1932.

"Oh shit," Riki said. "Oh my god. What is this?"

"The treasure," I said. "*This* is what Benjamin brought here and buried. He wasn't kidding."

She handed me the more recent letter while she examined the older one. I began to read it:

Dear Mr. Ralston,
This letter is coming to you a bit out of the blue. We've never met, so I apologize for the strange nature of our introduction. I was ill recently and laid up in bed and was looking for something to do and decided to go through a trove of letters I found in my aunt's house when she passed away. I came to the letter you will find enclosed with this one.

*I considered giving it to the police, but I don't know what
they would have done with it. I read up about you and the
work you've done, and I realized the only responsible thing
would be to send it to you. I worry that the contents might
upset you, but then I weighed that against your right to know
what happened to your family. Maybe you've always had
questions. . . .*

Riki was feverishly scanning the other letter.

"What is it?" I said.

She went back to the start and began to read aloud. . . .

Letter from Dagmar Ralston to Irene Wallenberg

December 28, 1932

My sweet friend, my love,

So many times we have said to each other that we have no secrets between us. I have said it with honesty—to a point. There is something I have not told you. Do not think I wanted to hold something back from you, who are so dear to me. The reasons for my silence are justified; there are some things that weigh so heavy that we cannot force the ones we love to carry them. Even as I write this now, the pen moves slowly. It does not want to tell the story. But the snow is falling and the day grows short, and I must move with some haste.

You are well aware that my brother is infected with that spiritual disease running rampant across the country called eugenics. You know that he admires the fascists in Europe, and that he holds the most abhorrent views on race. He first became interested in these things while in medical school. My brother has always been easily led. The blight quickly took hold of him. For this reason, I maintained distance from him. It was during this period that you and I were able to spend so much time together, something I look back on with such joy.

Our mother died when we were young, and with the passing of our father, the Ralston fortune went mainly to Phillip, with some provisions for me. However, all moneys passed through Phillip and were dispensed at his discretion. I was at the mercy of my younger brother. Unlike him, I had not been able to attend university. (This despite the fact that I was clearly more gifted in academics. I have never recovered from the unfairness of it, but I have no time to digress. You know about this.) Phillip went to England right before the Great War and remained there once it began. I approved of this, as it seemed that he was doing valuable work, helping the sick and wounded and setting up clinics. And as you also well know, he called for me in the spring of 1915. You and I were separated when I went to England. I am the sister—I have no control over my own fortune. I go when I am called.

He had let a house in the Cotswolds. I remember arriving and seeing this wonderful place on a warm day in early June, the gardens shaggy with flowers and herbs, with an overwhelming drone of bees. And there in this golden house of Cotswold stone, I heard the unmistakable wail of a baby from the top of the stairs. *Babies*, rather.

Six cradles. Six babies; three slightly larger, and three still quite new.

He had delivered them all and adopted them from their

mothers, who were unable to care for them. He had seen so much suffering, he said. He was compelled to help. And I would help as well. I would serve as mother to these children, wouldn't I?

It was not what I had planned to do, my dear. You know that. But when I held Clara, when I felt her tiny fist grabbing my finger, I knew—I knew I would do exactly as he asked. I was overwhelmed with such an unexpected joy. My life changed in that moment.

We sailed home from Southampton with six babies and four hired nannies supplementing our staff.

Over the years, I became quite a competent nurse, with six children to care for in various respects, while working at my brother's side. I took a strong interest, and soon I was helping dispense medications and could give basic treatments. My brother was an organized man who kept meticulous notes in dark blue leather-bound diaries. I sometimes helped with the administration of his office and his affairs. One day, while going through his notes from the year the children were born, I noticed short entries. I recorded them. They read as follows:

7 January 1915, Bristol, Elizabeth
15 February 1915, Stroud, Mildred
23 February 1915, Cheltenham, Pamela
6 April 1915, London, Georgina
19 April 1915, London, Mary
21 April 1915, London, Alice C.

These were obviously records of the birth of the children and the names of the mothers. I don't know what made me think of it—just one of those times that thoughts coalesce in your mind. A suspicion, some lingering idea. Maybe the fact that just the first names were given, except for an initial with the last one. Something I'd seen. Something I already knew . . .

I turned back to the notes, going back nine months from each of these dates. In April and May my brother had been doing work in a hospital in Bristol, England. Stroud and Cheltenham are easily reachable from Bristol. From June to September he was in London, doing work at St. Bartholomew's. All during that time, he was adding single letters to many of his daily entries. In Bristol: E, E, H, A, E, E, Mi, H, T, T, M, P, H, E, A, A, T, M, E, P . . . In London: G, G, Ma, S, S, GS, M, Ac, G, Ac, Ac, S, S, G . . .

There were ten in all. On a few occasions in the London entries there were two letters for each day, frequently G and S appearing together. On one spring day in London he noted: G, S, M.

A code, but not a particularly difficult one to crack. And quite proud of himself as well. My brother had been a very busy man. All these women had been his lovers. He had been trying to impregnate them. He tracked it, like a good scientist. Like a good eugenicist. I could envision him hurrying across town each night for his assignations. Or afternoon, perhaps, considering that sometimes he had several per day.

I can only assume that his contacts with A, S, H, and T produced no result.

I sat with this knowledge for several weeks. When the children came home from school for the holiday, I observed them more closely than usual. Once seen, it could not be unseen—the tip of the chin, the angle of the nose.

"It is strange," I said to him one night, "how the children take after you so. And each other, in some respects."

He did not look up from his book.

"I should imagine they do," he replied. "They eat the same good diet, live under the same roof, complete the same exercises."

"Please tell me," I said as nonchalantly as possible, "what exercise changes the shape of the nose?"

"Are you happy here, sister?" he asked.

"I am."

"I'm glad to hear it."

He didn't need to say any more. I had been warned.

Then, of course, Faye came. What a sight she was! The first time I saw her she was wearing a gold lamé gown that clung to her figure. I'd never seen a woman so tall. Though she was glamorous, she was also unaffected. I gathered that her time on the stage and screen had not always been pleasant, and she was happy to leave it behind.

Once she arrived, Phillip and the children didn't need me in *quite* the same way—but I got along well with Faye, and she truly did love the children like her own. I credit her for this. I did not like sharing them, but I came to terms with it. She is a good mother to all the children. And we all came to an unspoken but solid understanding—while she would support the children in any way she could, I had been their mother figure, and I should remain in the role. Phillip and Faye both allowed me my place and respected my presence. I was extremely grateful.

Then came Max. This was when everything changed completely. I tried to explain it to you at the time, my love, the shift in the tone of the household, this new air. The world spun around Max. Faye was besotted, as is to be expected. Phillip loved his son as well, but he also regarded him with a fascination that unnerved me. Like he had done with the other children, Phillip was always measuring Max. His height. His limbs. How fast he learned to walk, to speak. Everything was charted. He was a regular little boy, prone to outbursts and tantrums. Phillip was determined he must be something more. Faye attempted to counterbalance this in her own way, blanketing him with affection.

It was then I realized what effect I must have had on the other children. I had always encouraged them to play along with their father's games. And there were six of them, which helped defuse their father's influence. The chemistry did not work as well with Max. He was alone with two strong-willed adults, spoiled, with no other children or outside influence to set him to rights. He needed to socialize with other children, to be allowed to play but curbed when necessary. Completely ordinary things you would do with any child. But Max was not ordinary in Phillip's eyes. Nothing could be wrong with Max, so Max's weaknesses were treated as strengths. His tempers were considered healthy bursts of energy. His destructive nature was a desire to make his own way. Max began harming the staff. I found out about this in whispers, though noticing how they all avoided Max, the bandages on their hands. He bit. He threw things. He pinched and cut them. Nurses never stayed very long. I would have offered help, but this would have broken our understanding—the older children were mine, and I was not to interfere with Max.

Then Edna Danforth fell down the stairs. I do not think this was malicious on Max's part. I think he had a tantrum and struck out. I do not think he was trying to make her fall. The situation was serious indeed. She suffered a broken skull and bleeding of the brain and was in a hospital for months. Phillip paid for her care and Faye visited regularly, but neither wanted to speak of the incident. I did something I normally would not—I confronted both Phillip and Faye. Something had to be done. Max needed rules, and he needed to be with other children, to learn how to behave and respect others. Faye agreed with me to a point and spoke of bringing in other doctors to examine him. Phillip would not consider it. He would treat the boy himself through diet and exercise.

I was thankful the other children were away at school much of the time. I missed them terribly, but it was better for them to be away from the house. During the summer, I kept a close eye on all of them. I watched. I knew something was going to happen in Morning House.

343

Clara knew this as well. Such a strong, perceptive girl, my Clara. Nothing escaped her attention. One night, I saw her steal a knife from the table. She did it quickly, knocking it into her lap and secreting it away. I followed her and kept watch. It happened that this night, Max's new nurse was ill (I had suspicions) and he was sleeping alone. I watched her door. Just after eleven, she emerged, carrying a bundle under her arm. The knife was certainly inside. I followed her silently to Max's room. I was about to spring out as she got to the door, but she stopped there. She was not there to hurt Max. She stood in front of his door for hours, guarding it like a sentry. That night, I knew my fears were founded. Whatever I was afraid of, Clara was afraid of it as well.

Soon after that, the three girls took Max out for a boat ride. Clara pushed him into the water, trying to make him swim. I understood what she was doing—the obsession with swimming—she was trying to force him into learning, into surviving. My fears grew, and my uncertainties. What was it we were both so frightened of?

We would know it soon enough.

The day it happened it was extraordinarily hot. This is my predominant memory. I had breakfast on a tray in bed. I could just about stand the food served at breakfast downstairs and I could not abide the lack of tea and coffee. Phillip forbade it, so I was happy enough to have my meal in private, with a pot of tea and some scrambled eggs and bacon. After that, I would normally bathe and go downstairs. When I got into the tub, I found that I had trouble staying awake. I came close to falling asleep and slipping into the water, so I got out and rested on the bed for a moment. At least, I meant to be there for a moment.

I woke hours later. Morning House was still—and that set me on edge. Something felt off. By the time I was out of my room, it had already happened. Clara came through the front door carrying Max's body. I had failed. The boy was dead.

I had to get the children out of the house.

Their playhouse was their haven. Safe and small and entirely theirs.

Phillip shut the breakfast room door while he examined his son. Faye's screams echoed throughout the grand hall, bouncing from the marble of the floor where I stood up to the glass dome above us. I know now why screams are described as "piercing." I could feel them, plosive, cutting into my skin. The police arrived—two officers from town. They went into the breakfast room to see the body and speak to Phillip. One came out and asked for Clara. I sent someone to fetch her, but she was not in the playhouse. Clara was missing. And through this time, I kept hearing people mentioning that they had been sleeping. The children, sleeping. The servants, sleeping.

I realized I needed a moment to sit and process what was happening. I went to my room and splashed water on my face, forced myself to think. I realized that the unnatural quietness of the house was probably not an accident.

Clara was missing. It had been Clara I'd been watching, and Clara had told me with her eyes, with her long, sideways glances. Her eye always turned in the same, strange direction at the table. To Unity. Good, sweet Unity, dutifully eating her mushy peas and nut loaf, conjugating her German verbs, putting in extra practice on the piano, on her swimming, on her needlework. Unity, slavishly devoted to her father and her father's vision of the world. It was to Unity's room I went. I looked around, opening drawers, pushing books aside from the shelves, lifting cushions.

Phillip had gifted Unity an ornate writing desk for her last birthday. He'd had it made in Vienna by a firm that made furniture for the Hapsburgs. He'd been so pleased with it that he had shown it off to me before presenting it to her, and I had liked it enough to write to the makers and have one made for myself, with compartments in different locations. (I wanted a place to keep our correspondence, something less conspicuous than the small, locked box I had always used.) Because of this, I knew how to spring the various small drawers and holes, though it took me a moment to remember all the various hidden buttons. I pushed on a bit of scrollwork and out popped a tall and narrow drawer. Inside, there was a small piece of paper with Unity's writing on it. It was full of calculations, specifically ones that measured things in grains. A few more attempts with the desk revealed another tiny drawer. This one contained a glass Veronal bottle, almost entirely empty, just a few tablets rattling at the bottom. I examined the small page of calculations again.

Everything became clear in a terrible instant.

Veronal is a powerful and common sleeping drug. It is

easy to acquire. Any druggist would have it, and I knew that Faye kept some for her personal use. Phillip certainly had it in his cabinet. If I understood the numbers I was looking at, we had all been dosed to a high degree, one that danced around, but did not cross, a lethal level. Certainly, it was enough to keep everyone fast asleep for hours and dazed for hours more. I could still feel its effects on my mind, though the adrenaline cut through.

She had put us all to sleep while she killed Max.

I picked up the house phone and called down to the kitchen, where the cook—her voice thick from crying—answered. I told her to make me a pot of strong coffee and bring it to my room, and that she should also prepare some food for the children. Good food. Things they were not allowed. Fill a tray and take it to the playhouse. They needed sustenance and comfort. I needed to wake up and to figure out what to do next, how to counteract the evil that had taken over the house.

Once I had consumed the coffee, I felt some of my faculties returning. My telephone rang. It was a message from Phillip, asking me to gather the children and arrange for their dinner. He wanted it served in the dining room and for things to be kept as normal as possible. I directed Unity, Victory, and Benjamin back to the house, to their rooms to wash up. William declined. He barely acknowledged my presence as he sat at the piano. I did not push him. It was Unity I was watching. She carried herself with quiet dignity. I saw it so clearly now. The lift of her chin. The stride in her step. She had killed Max a few hours before, and she was calm. Proud.

We were not free of danger. I set about looking for Clara. She had always been good at secreting herself away. The staff were looking for her, the police, everyone. She was nowhere to be found. I became feverish with fear, calling her name. I waded into the water. It was almost nine in the evening now and growing dark. Where *was* she?

I heard William and Benjamin saying her name and something about her being at the house. I don't exercise every day like the children do—I do not run. That night, however, I moved with shocking speed across the lawn, catching up to Benjamin and William. We all saw her, moving so strangely against the parapet. She leaned against the edge, as if she was about to call down to us so far below, and then . . .

I cannot describe it except to say I saw her clutching at air as she came down, as if there was an invisible rope she might catch. A gardener—his name was Anthony—held the children back. I was given something to drink from a flask.

Someone took me inside, I think. Perhaps I went myself. I do not know. Annie, the downstairs maid, ran to me and walked me to one of the low sofas on the side of the great hall. She helped me lie down, putting my head flat and pillows under my feet. She covered me with a blanket. Victory came down the stairs screaming and ran outside to her brothers. I didn't have the energy to move. There was a buzzing in my ears. I was in my cocoon of Veronal and shock, trying to find my way out, but the world was shrinking around me.

Annie tried to nurse me, but I told her to go to the children. I would be all right. I would regain my strength in a moment.

I don't know how long I was there. Fifteen minutes? An hour? I am Aunt Dagmar. I am invisible at the best of times, and these were the worst. I was off to the side under my blanket, staring into the starry depths of the glass dome and listening to my heartbeat. Aside from the occasional examination by Annie, I was left alone and blended into the woodwork.

This is where I was when Unity came down the stairs— those magnificent stairs, with the great glass dome overhead. Morning House felt like it was quaking, like the thousand tiny pieces of glass that made up that dome would fall on us like snow and delicately slice us to ribbons.

She moved a bit more slowly than usual, but with that same youthful spring, taking the steps in two-step beats, her canvas tennis shoes silent on the treads. The look on her face was eternal. It was not a smile, not precisely. It was a look of utter conviction, of a terrible peace. If she noticed me, she did not acknowledge it. I don't think she did. I watched her go to Phillip's office and shut the door. I pushed the blanket back and forced myself to my feet, taking slow steps across the cavernous hall to the office door. I turned the knob gingerly and pushed my finger through the opening to crack it just wide enough so that I could hear what was being said.

It was everything I feared, everything I described, with one addition. Clara had gone to the roof when she came inside, perhaps for air, perhaps to make the world make sense and realign herself by navigating the stars. Unity met her there.

It was, in Unity's words, an accident. A fight. She had sent her sister off the roof.

Max. Clara.

Unity.

The thunderous bleakness that followed—I have described this to you many times.

We left the house within days. The only things taken from the house were my brother's personal papers, the jewelry, and some clothing. Everything else was left behind—all the children's projects, our books, and all personal items. We went to New York first, back to the house on Fifth Avenue. Faye could not leave her room and had to be nursed constantly. Her crisis was almost a welcome distraction from the pain. She was someone we could try to help.

I watched Unity there for the next few weeks. She behaved in all the ways that were appropriate—she looked somber. She was entirely helpful to her father, supporting him as Faye began to break apart. Unity sat with her and brushed her hair, read to her, painted her nails with varnish.

Every once in a while, I would catch her looking at me. Was that a challenge in her eyes?

The children were sent back to school in September. Though I worried for them emotionally, I was glad they were no longer under a Ralston roof together. I think I had been holding my breath for their safety. School seemed safer to me, a place with rules and many watchful eyes. School would hold Unity while I worked out what to do next.

The night they left, the house was quiet. Faye had been put to bed for the night and her nurse was sitting with her. Phillip and I sat in his study with the radio playing.

"Faye is not improving," he finally said. "I have spoken to some of my colleagues about her case. They recommend treatment beyond what I can provide. There is a private hospital in Beacon, just north of here, run by a very good man named Slocum. It's the most modern facility with views over the Hudson—there's swimming and golf, all sorts of healthy things. A few months . . ."

"That seems a sensible course of action," I replied.

A window was open between the two of us that had not been for a long time. Phillip needed me once again. I could talk to him.

"I know," I said to him. "About Unity."

When Phillip looked up at me, I saw many feelings on his face at once. Relief. Pain.

Fear.

"How?" was his only question.

"Does it matter?"

"No," he replied. "I suppose not. Do any of the children know?"

"I don't believe so."

He nodded once while continuing to look at the fire.

"You need to do something about Unity," I said.

"There is nothing that can be done."

"You refused to do anything about Max, and now Max is dead. Unity needs help. She killed two of her siblings, Phillip. She needs to be kept away from others . . . treated in some way. This facility you're sending Faye to . . ."

He shook his head.

"She thought what she was doing was the right thing to do," he said quietly. "Sending her there would reveal the truth. We have to say it was an accident. They were accidents. Accidents . . ."

I listened to the fade in his voice, his attempts to convince himself of a lie, despite the fact that he had just spoken the truth. His house had spawned a monster. My younger brother, so much of his hair gone suddenly white, was a weak man. Tyrants and those who ascribe to tyrannical beliefs are always weak at heart because they build their world on fear.

I knew then what I had to do. I had failed Max and Clara. I would not fail again. I didn't know how or when, but the opportunity has presented itself today.

He has gotten a house here in Beacon where we all have spent Christmas as close to Faye as we can be. It's snowing—a lovely, fluffy snow. It's been cold, and the pond in the woods behind the house is frozen, but the ice is not very thick. I went out after breakfast and tested it with a rock. It will crack.

After lunch I will invite Unity to take a walk with me. I have used her own technique. I have prepared a thermos of hot cider and morphine—plenty for both of us. She will be sleepy, my child, and I will lead her. I cannot abide a monster to live, and a mother cannot kill her child and survive. I am her mother, after all. I love her, despite what she has done. I should have protected her. We must go together. She will not be alone. I will take her there.

I will leave this now to be posted. By the time you receive it, the act will be done. I am at peace, my dear friend. Know that I love you.

Yours eternally,
Dagmar

28

I was in a cocoon. It was fuzzy and dark. I had absolutely no idea where the hell I was. In the tall grass of a magical land?

I blinked and rearranged the world. I was in a bedroom, sleeping on two fuzzy green beanbags. All the lights were off, but there was a glow over to the side. Riki was sitting up in bed, her face lit by a tablet screen. She looked ethereal.

"Hey," I said. My voice was croaky. Maybe I'd inhaled more smoke than I realized.

"You're awake."

"What time is it?"

"Eleven."

"Which eleven? Morning eleven or night eleven?"

"Night," she said.

"Is it still today?"

"Yeah."

This helped make sense of things. We'd been taken off the island in the midmorning, I remembered. We'd all been checked again at the hospital, then we were questioned. We never saw April again. My parents were called. I would go home at some point, but for now I was staying with Riki's family. I had come here, the beanbags were lumped together, and I got in them and fell asleep.

"Where did you get that?" I asked. Her stuff, of course, was gone. Burned up.

"It's Juhi's."

There was a sound outside the door, then it opened, pouring light inside. I lurched back. Juhi poked her head in, then opened the door a little more.

"What?" Riki snapped.

Juhi held out two compostable clamshell trays.

"Crab cakes, god," she said. "I heard you talking so I brought up the food we got. It's crab cakes and fries. Do you eat crab cakes? We also got shrimp, and we have other stuff."

I couldn't remember if I ate crab cakes. I couldn't remember anything about myself. It took effort for my mind to assemble the mental image of a crab cake—a roundish thing, covered in breading. Maybe I ate those. I nodded blankly, and Juhi handed me the containers and left the room, eyeing us both.

The aroma of deep-fried food pushed away the smoke. Things began to focus again.

"What," Riki said, "the actual fuck do we do now?"

She had a good point. We had *it*. The treasure of Ralston Island. The answer to the mystery of the Ralstons. Lacking a

355

better idea, I pushed a container toward her.

"I guess we eat these crab cakes," I said.

As soon as I opened mine and the steamy goodness of the fried food hit my nostrils, I was ravenous. The portion was huge, but I could have eaten two more full containers like it. The food revitalized us.

"I feel like I have to apologize to Clara," she finally said. "I really thought she did it. Everyone kind of thought she did it. But why did Benjamin bury the truth? Literally? Not just bury it, but wrap it in plastic?"

"What could he even do? They were all dead."

"He still could have told the world what happened," Riki replied. "Or he could have burned the letter. But he buried it. He even *told* people what he'd done. He said he was burying treasure. It was like he wanted someone to go looking for it."

"That sounds like the answer," I said. "He didn't know what to do. Unity was his sister too. Maybe he thought it was for someone else to tell."

"So leave it with your papers. Put it in a safe deposit box. Tell your lawyer to release it after your death. . . ."

"You sound mad," I said.

"I'm not . . . I'm . . ." She struggled to find the words. "I couldn't have gotten this letter and put it in the ground."

"You didn't live his life. All his siblings died. Maybe he just couldn't."

I poked my finger around the bottom of the container,

searching for any remaining fried crumbs. Maybe it was the grease from the food. Or the smoke still in our lungs. Just the general feeling of being alive after all this. Or the simple fact that Riki Rajpac was sitting next to me on the floor in a dimly lit room, and we'd solved a crime together. Two crimes. Maybe six crimes. It was getting hard to count. Whatever the case, the stillness came over us again, like it had that morning after we broke into Dr. Henson's room. This time, though, I felt myself lean in and I saw her do the same. This time, I knew what was about to happen. Our faces tilted toward each other and . . .

"Wait," she said.

I waited.

"Call her."

"What?"

"Call her. Call Akilah."

I leaned back to look at her. Her face was so beautiful, and so serious.

"The whole time you've been here," she said, "you've had a look on your face like a lost puppy. I wanted to get your attention. I was trying to . . . interest you. But your head was somewhere else."

"She broke up with me after the fire."

"Did she? You said she got another job. That's not the same thing."

"She quit because I set a fire."

"No," she replied, the sharp edges of her patience

chipping the smooth edges off the end of the word. "What were her actual words?"

"She said she was going to work at the Cheesecake Factory because the tips would be higher, but . . ."

"And why was she going to do that?"

"To get a new keyboard, but . . ."

"Did it ever occur to you," Riki said, "that she was telling the truth? That she got another job to make more money and get a keyboard? That it had nothing to do with you or the fire and she was just trying to tell you?"

"Then why was she so quiet?" I said. "Why didn't she say anything afterward?"

"Why don't you ask her?" Riki replied. "I really want to make out with you. I've been wanting to all this time. But you are thinking about her because you are in love with her, and you should be sure about what's going on. Because . . . I just . . . *call her.*"

I was stunned speechless. It had all been a lot. I took my phone and got up. My body was sore. I walked out of the room, down the steps, and crept out of the house by the front door. Outside, it was still raining. It would rain for days more, but not like it had. This rain felt fresh, and the world smelled of, yes, petrichor. The smell of a flying dinosaur.

Akilah picked up immediately. This time, there was no clanking. Our connection was solid.

"Marlowe! Are you okay? Was there a *fire?*"

"It wasn't me," I said.

358

"It was on the news? Your boss died? Something about a body?"

I had to reassure her a few times that I really was okay, and that the story was long.

"I need to ask you something," I said. "When you left Guffy's, you were, not breaking up with me, because we weren't . . ."

"Oh my god."

I couldn't make out what that meant.

"Marlowe," she said, "did you think . . . I wasn't breaking up with you. I just applied for that job because it paid more and I need to save for a new keyboard to take to college next year."

"But we never talked after that. Or, barely."

"I thought you were upset! I didn't want to bring up that night because you seemed really sad and scared and I wanted to give you space."

"But I was so bad with the fire," I went on as the wall tumbled before me. "I thought you were mad because I just stood there."

"You were in shock. I've been waiting for you to talk to me for *weeks*, and then you called last night talking about lipstick. . . ."

"Oh, that," I said. "I found a tooth. That was in case I died. I didn't. It's fine."

"What?"

"It's fine," I said again, knowing full well that April had

done this to me too. Except, it was fine. I wasn't lying. I am Marlowe and I was fine.

"So are we . . ." I didn't know what to ask. "I mean, I guess I'm coming home. My job burned down. That's not going to look good."

"When will you be here?"

"I don't know? When they let me go? Soon?"

There was a pause.

"I get an employee discount," she said. "At the Cheesecake Factory. Do you want to split some wings?"

As we got off the phone, which took a while—we were going back and forth and having a conversation that I'm embarrassed to repeat—I saw that Riki had come out of the house and was watching from the front step, just under the awning. I'd never let anyone down before. I came and sat next to her.

"Yeah," she said. "That's what I thought."

"I'm sorry," I said.

She shrugged. "You know what? We're not dead. That's tonight's win."

"It's a good win."

We sat and listened to the rain for a bit, breathed deep.

"Listen," I said. "Have you ever had a hot bottom?"

"What?"

"Life-changing," I said. "Tomorrow. I'll show you."

"What the hell are you talking about?"

"Trust me."

"Trust you?" she said.

She playfully whacked at the ends of my hair.

It would be all right. We had done it, after all. We had escaped Morning House. We knew things that had been unknown, and we would figure the rest of it out in time.

FOUR MONTHS LATER . . .

We were doing almost sixty going up I-81. It turns out, when you give the little Smart Car a chance, it will shine. I think that's true of people too. (The giving a chance thing, not the doing sixty up I-81.) Dr. Henson took a big chance on me, creepy firebug Marlowe Wexler, and I tried to show up for her. I'd found her yoga mat, her tooth, and eventually, her.

October was still warm. It felt more like summer than a week until Halloween. I was wearing a tank top and shorts, and Akilah was in a red cotton dress covered in a pattern of daisies. It was my favorite thing she owned. I was driving my girlfriend, Akilah Jones, in my Smart Car at sixty miles an hour. I wanted to go back and tell the Marlowe Wexler of early June to get up and take a shower because it was all going to work out so much better than she thought, but then, it was because she was hiding in bed and not showering that this all came to pass.

"I've been thinking," she said. I could tell from the way she said it that she wished she could lean back and put her feet up on the dashboard, but you can't do that in the Smart

Car. She contented herself with tucking in her knees. "Unity. Why do you think she did it?"

In the intervening weeks and months since I'd been at Morning House, we'd discussed the entire thing many times. Mostly, we talked about April, and the sequence of events that had caused her to kill Chris, then Dr. Henson, and almost me and Riki. Had she *meant* to kill Chris? I thought probably not; that it was an accident that started a chain of events. Akilah tended to believe she knew exactly what she was doing, that she'd been angry and struck out. Perhaps one day she would tell her story. But Unity was not here to tell hers. I didn't think about her as often since she had never tried to set me on fire.

"It could have been that Max was a scary little kid," she went on, "or that she was jealous. Or both, I know, but I feel like some kind of big emotion has to drive you to drown your little brother."

"I think maybe it was that Max wasn't good enough to be a Ralston in her eyes. If Max wasn't perfect, her dad was wrong, and her dad couldn't be wrong."

"Do you think if it all hadn't happened the way it did, that the other kids would ever have gotten away from what their father taught?"

It was a good question, and I had no answer.

We had gotten other answers in the time since my departure. The fire investigation was the first thing to wrap up. My old friends the fire investigators always get the job done. They were able to trace the source of the fire to the stairwell of the turret, as we had described. Had the fireboat been able to get there sooner, more of the house could have been saved, but the fire kept going, the windows blew out, and the storm winds blew in, feeding it.

We also got Dr. Henson's cause of death. It was, no surprise, blunt force trauma, almost certainly caused by a fall. She had thirty-six broken bones, including the tooth I found, which was matched neatly to a broken nub that was still in her jaw.

The story of the mysterious death of Dr. Belinda Henson at Morning House was a lead story for a day but was quickly swept away. I went back to work at Guffy's, handing out hot bottoms for another month or so until school started.

Akilah and I talked on the day I got back. We haven't been apart since. I wake up glowing. My hair seems shinier. I honestly think I've grown half an inch.

Now it was time to go back to Clement Bay. I'd been in touch with the others since I left town. Today I had been summoned because they had something to show me, and I thought if I had to go, I would take Akilah.

We had arranged to meet the others at the Blue Anchor, the small restaurant along the river's edge that had provided us with our butternut mac and cheese and chicken casseroles. I'd come to appreciate the place during the days I'd had to spend in Clement Bay after everything went down—it had free refills on regular coffee and was riddled with power outlets. It wasn't photogenic, but you could charge the shit out of your stuff while getting strung out on all the coffee you could drink. I'd spent hours on video calls with Akilah from here.

"I know this place," Akilah said, pointing at a table in the corner, next to the unstable-looking water refill and dirty dish station.

"That's my favorite power outlet," I explained.

"Get yourself a girl who has a favorite power outlet. Oh wait. I already have." She gave me a little kiss on the cheek.

"Girls!" someone said. "Making out in public? In this economy?"

Van looped his arms around my shoulders from behind.

"How's my favorite fire starter?" he asked. "And this **must** be the famous Akilah!"

"The famous Van," Akilah replied with a smile.

Van put his hand to his heart.

"They're outside, on the deck. Come on."

"I'll get us drinks," Akilah said. "Be right there."

I didn't need to tell her what I wanted. We drank hot chai lattes. We had a drink. I know. Gross. Shut up.

Outside, around a partially rusted wrought iron table in the corner of the deck, were Liani and Tom. Her hand was on the table, and he was touching the back of it in a soppy, romantic way. Happy endings all around. For most of us, anyway.

Liani and Tom had noticed us and stood to greet me. Liani, to my surprise, wrapped me in a hug and held me close. Tom extended his hand and gave me one of his crushing shakes.

In the distance, I could just see the outline of Morning House. From here, from far away, it looked completely normal. Maybe this was what Dr. Henson was talking about with distance and time, how things appear absolutely fine. You'd have to get closer to see the fire damage, and you'd have to know that there had been so many murders there. That there had been dead, broken bodies.

"What's going to happen to it?" I asked.

"Well, the bros who bought it are sad," Van said. "Camp Incel won't be happening."

"There was talk about letting it rot naturally so that wildlife can take over," Tom said, "but it's such a dangerous structure, they're afraid people will go in and get hurt. So it may get knocked down."

Akilah returned with our drinks. Introductions were made. Chairs were adjusted to make room for two more people.

"You said you had something to show me?"

"Not until she gets here," Van said.

"She's here."

Riki was behind us, headphones on, drinking from a heavily stickered bottle of water. She was wearing her I Like Spooky Shit socks, which I appreciated, and had a bulging black backpack with a sewn-on patch that said TRYING. We'd sent a lot of messages and talked a few times, but seeing her was strange, especially with Akilah next to me. I didn't have to introduce Akilah and Riki. Each knew who the other was, and they nodded to acknowledge the fact.

"How's it been?" I asked.

"Well, I don't have to sell any more fucking Thousand Island dressing."

"Or wind chimes?"

"Oh no. We still have those."

"I like wind chimes," Akilah said.

Riki threw me a look that said that out of the goodness of her heart she would not hold this against Akilah. She immediately set her huge bag down and crawled under the table, looking for the outdoor power outlet. I told you—this place was full of them.

"Now can you show me?" I asked.

"It's Tom's thing," Liani said.

"I'm allowed to tell you, but don't say anything, okay?" Tom said. "My dad knows the police chief, and they showed me this. They got it about a week ago . . ."

He reached into his pocket for his phone.

"There's a *fishluencer*," Van cut in.

"Van," Liani said. "Shut up!"

"A what?"

"A guy from California who makes videos about good fishing spots," Tom said. "He was doing a piece on the St. Lawrence the morning that Chris died. He went out at sunrise to shoot. People who fish go out early. He had lots of video from that day. He saw an article about what happened, noticed a mention of the day, and looked at the backup of the extra footage he took. Look . . ."

He held up his phone and played a ten-second video.

In the foreground, there was a man steering his boat along and talking about his fishing rod. Behind him was the sharp rocky point and two human figures. Tom paused the video, expanded the frame.

A girl. Redheaded. Blue dress. Talking to a guy with black hair.

I was too stunned to know what to say.

"They got her," Liani said. "On video."

"Well," Riki said, pushing herself up, "they have something, and her lawyer will try to get it left out or say she was just looking, or whatever, but . . ."

"They got her," I repeated.

"Kind of," Riki said. "They kind of got her."

She held my gaze for a moment, but in a friendly way. In a way you do when you've almost died in a fire together and the person who set the fire is going to probably face consequences.

Akilah wrapped me in a hug and gave me a kiss. Riki turned her head.

"Gimme a second?" I said to Akilah.

She nodded.

"Riki," I said. I jerked my head toward the restaurant, indicating we should step inside. She followed along. We went all the way through, back out to the sidewalk. She dug her hands deep into her hoodie pockets.

"So are you going to make this weird?" she asked.

"Well, yeah. Have you met me?"

"Good point." She gave a little smile and nodded, looking down. "She's very hot. I really want to hate her, but she seems nice. Did you tell her about me? How I'm the reason you two are together? At the very least, I want all the credit."

"I said it was entirely you," I replied, nodding. "I said I didn't even like her, but you were making me do this."

"Good."

This was hard. I took a deep breath. I tried to come up with something else, but the emotion of it all formed a clump in my throat.

"Listen," she said. "I'm making this podcast. When I get rich and famous from it, you'll be sorry."

Of course she was making a podcast about it. It only made sense, given her interest, her knowledge, and her direct experience. There were already networks interested, but she had refused to sign anything yet. Part of the reason I was here was to record.

"Deal. And do you want to . . . talk more?"

"Yeah," she said after a moment. "I think I do. You still never finished *The Daughter of Time*. Now, I'm going back in, because neither of us is good at this."

We returned to the patio. Riki clipped a microphone on me.

"Why are we doing this here?" Liani asked as Riki clipped microphones on the rest of them. "Why don't we do it at one of our houses?"

"I want to do some with ambient noise," Riki said,

peering over the edge of the table. "All serious podcasts have those interviews with noise in the background, like crunching leaves."

"ASMR," Van said. "I hate it."

"Everyone ready?"

"How will this work?" I asked.

"My idea is that I'm going to spread the story of what happened in the present over what happened in the past."

"What do I do?"

"I'll record you a few times, but for now, just say what happened, in your own words. You start and everyone can join in. We just . . . tell the story. Okay?"

We nodded. She hit record. I looked over at the distant remains of Morning House.

"Okay," I said, turning back to Akilah. "There was this girl, and she told me she loved the smell of petrichor. . . ."

ACKNOWLEDGMENTS

Nothing happens without my agent, friend, and coconspirator, Kate Schafer Testerman of KT Literary. She is a force of nature. I love you, pal. Endless thanks to my incredible publicists Megan Beatie and Nina Douglas, and my outstanding film agent, Mary Pender of UTA. Look at these amazing women I get to work with!

It takes a lot of people to get a book done. So many thanks to my editors, Erica Sussman and the incredible Sara Schonfeld, who must have six arms to get done all the things she manages to do. (And never once swore at me when I just needed "one day, two at the max, let's call it a week." Her self-control is amazing.) Thank you to Katherine Tegen, who brought me into the Harper fold. So many thanks to the HarperCollins gang who worked on this book so tirelessly and dealt with those *one day, two days, let's call it a week* notes: Taylan Salvati, Michael D'Angelo, Audrey Diestelkamp, Shannon McCain, Alexandra Rakaczki, Jessie Gang, Alison Donalty, Vanessa Nuttry, Sasha Vinogradova—and Simran Khurana and Kate Harvie at Harper UK.

Morgan Hodge of Clayton Island Tours has been an invaluable resource in learning the ins and outs of life in the Thousand Islands (including that fireboat, which really is called *Last Chance*).

My much-loved writer friends, who are the backbone of my day-to-day work and life and got me through the last edits of this book: Holly Black, Cassandra Clare, Kelly Link, Marie Rutloski, and Leigh Bardugo. A big, special thanks to Robin Wasserman for grabbing me by the arm and walking me through a dynamite edit.

More thanks. My pal Dan Sinker kept telling me I could do it when I did not, in fact, think I could do it. Kirsten Rambo, my hero, was there when I needed her. Shout-out to Dr. Will Flanary (aka Dr. Glaucomflecken), for his sage advice when my eye did a Bad Thing while I was finishing the final draft. (You guys, I blew up my eye with caffeine on the final draft. I BLEW UP MY EYE!) I'm so lucky to have these and all my friends.

Lastly, to my beloved pup, Dexy, for being a relentless weirdo when I was working. And to my beloved husband, whose name I withhold for my own strange reasons. He knows who he is and what he has done. He is my big everything; the one I'd get a scented candle for.

Watch out for those candles.